PRAISE FOR BILL RIVERS

"Bill Rivers's debut novel is a rambunctious ballad to boyhood, duty, and family and a heartfelt salute to those who became the patriots of the Vietnam War. The warmth of these irrepressible characters amid 1968's cultural storms gives heart to anyone wondering how to make sense of our own highly charged times. It reminds us there's nothing new under the sun and stubbornly insists we, too, can listen to our better angels."

—General James Mattis, USMC (Ret.), 26th Secretary of Defense

"Those seeking a reprieve from our confused and callous culture will find something much more important here: a heartwarming, authentically human call to hold to truth, family, and our common dignity—no matter the cost. In witnessing one brother's struggle to save another, we remember how, in every age, love renews our wounded world."

—Charles J. Chaput, O.F.M. Cap., 9th Archbishop of Philadelphia

"This unforgettable debut novel [is] sure to capture your heart."

—Lesley Kagen, *New York Times* bestselling author of *Every Now and Then* and *Whistling in the Dark*

"Part coming-of-age tale, part adventure narrative, this heartwarming and uplifting debut is perfect for fans of William Kent Krueger's *This Tender Land* or the beloved film *Stand by Me* (adapted from Stephen King's *The Body*)."

—Robert Dugoni, *New York Times* bestselling author of *The Extraordinary Life of Sam Hell* and *The World Played Chess*

LAST
SUMMER
BOYS

LAST SUMMER BOYS

A NOVEL

BILL RIVERS

LAKE UNION
PUBLISHING

Text copyright © 2022 by William J. Rivers III
All rights reserved.

Published by Lake Union Publishing, Seattle

www.apub.com

Amazon, the Amazon logo, and Lake Union Publishing are trademarks of Amazon.com, Inc., or its affiliates.

ISBN-13: 9781662500312
ISBN-10: 1662500319

Cover design by Kimberly Glyder

Printed in the United States of America

For Elizabeth and the boys . . .

The bravest are the tenderest,—
The loving are the daring.
—Bayard Taylor, "Song of the Camp"

Chapter 1

City Boy

Cousin Francis said come nighttime he could smell the fires in his city.

Not like that sweet woodsmoke scent me and my brothers love so much, but an awful, eye-watering sting in the air of burning brick and rubber and roofing tar. Wind blew that terrible smell all the way to his bedroom window from the West Lake housing projects where the fires burned and had been burning since sundown the day Reverend King was killed. Seven straight days the riots lasted, and on the morning of the seventh day the soldiers came, came and stayed. It went on like that for weeks, until the day Francis's father came up to his room to tell him he'd be coming to stay with us for that summer of 1968.

Francis did not like that one bit.

No boy wants to leave his father to face the world alone, police officer or not. Francis put up a fuss, but Uncle Leone was never one to fool with. Slim and dark and quiet, he had a fire all his own. Most times it burned low, like coals glowing on a hearth late at night, but it could blaze to life if the right breeze was blowing. And it was.

Truth be told, Uncle Leone didn't want Francis to leave their city either: he was only doing it because his wife—Ma's sister, our Aunt Effie—asked him in a way he couldn't tell her no. She believed boys don't belong in places where they can get killed. Uncle Leone thought leaving was running away and it was better to change the city so no boys, black or white, had to worry about getting killed.

Aunt Effie allowed that would be best, but Aunt Effie also had no hope of it happening this side of heaven.

So soon as school let out, Cousin Francis, all of thirteen years old and alone, slim and tanned like his father, took a train out to stay with us: my two older brothers, Pete and Will, and me; Dad and Ma; and our big dog, Butch, together in the stone house that sat alongside Apple Creek at the beginning of that awful summer.

"There he is, Pete," I tell my brother, over the hiss of the train.

At the platform's far end stands a boy who looks to be made of sticks: flannel shirt hangs off him like a flag on a pole. Beside him is a mud-colored suitcase that stands half as high as him.

My brothers and me have never met our cousin before, but I recognize him from a newspaper photograph Ma taped to our fridge. He'd won a contest for story writing and got his picture taken. Aunt Effie sent us the clipping, and Ma put it up, hoping that'd make my brothers and me want to work harder at school. It didn't.

Crowd's thinning out on the platform and the train's still hissing like an angry copperhead, but Francis ain't seen us yet. He stays blinking in the late-May sun, and that gives us time to size him up some. He's my age but even shorter than me, with hair black as boot polish and chestnut-tan skin. Hard to tell the color of his eyes because he wears glasses.

"What'd I tell you, Pete?" my other brother, Will, says. "A city boy. Useless." He spits.

Much as I hate to admit it, Will's right: Frankie looks like a stiff breeze would send him right off the platform.

Pete just grins around the stalk of onion grass in his teeth. Then, as Will's spit fries up on the tracks below, he walks over to Francis and sticks out a hand.

"Hiya, Frankie."

Frankie. Just like that, Pete changes his name. Our cousin is Frankie now. Frankie forever.

"I'm your cousin, Pete. This here's Will. And that's Jack." My brother tilts his shaggy head my way. "Stick close by Jack. He'll look after you."

"I sure will," I say, trying to sound more excited about it than I am.

Will snorts. He don't like it one bit Frankie's come to stay with us, what with school only being out a few precious months. My brothers been planning an expedition to find a wrecked fighter jet that crashed years ago the next county over. We ain't supposed to go, on account of the Air Force men never being truthful enough for Ma's liking as to whether they found all the bombs and missiles that were on it.

The wreck is far and it's rough country to get there, even for us. Will worries babysitting a city boy will ruin it.

That's how my brothers want to spend the summer. But I got a secret summertime plan of my own. And if, or how, our city-boy cousin can help, I can't say.

We simmer a bit on the platform, while above us white sky bruises slowly toward blue. Away to the west, storm clouds stack themselves one atop the other. Frankie still ain't spoken. Behind his glasses I spy a pair of soft, dark eyes that move from Pete to Will to me.

"Let's not stand here like a pack of fools!" Will seizes Frankie's suitcase as the train lets loose a final hiss, then a whistle as the whole metal monster groans to life and goes rolling away along tracks that gleam like spilled quicksilver through the fields of butterfly weed.

Pete leads us off the platform, down to the gravel drive where our pickup bakes in afternoon sun. He and Will climb into the cab while I heave Frankie's suitcase into the bed and hop up with him for the ride back to Stairways.

The train is far out in the fields by the time Pete brings the Ford's engine to life. With its tracks hidden in the high grass, the train looks like it's floating over Pennsylvania farmland. A ghost train.

Frankie watches it go, and I know by the look on his face he wishes he was still on that train, heading back home to his city.

But I don't know why he'd want to, with the whole place burning as it is.

Leaving the station, Pete decides to cut through the town of New Shiloh rather than go around. He drives us down Main Street past the redbrick storefronts with their stenciled letters, and old iron streetlamps and little metal benches that ain't comfortable at all to sit on. I figure it's mostly so he and Will can see if there are any kids around they know from school. Beside me in the truck bed, Frankie watches the town go by with a sad kind of look on his face, and I know he's comparing it to his city.

"Old Sam Williamson says once upon a time this was a wagon trail," I tell him.

Frankie looks at me, surprised at my sudden talk.

"Yes sir, this road carried pioneers in Conestoga wagons all the way from Philadelphia right on through to them mountains," I go on. "Nowadays, people still come from Philadelphia, only they stay here, mostly in the new houses going up the far side of town."

The new developments that Dad hates.

Frankie looks back to the streets and catches a faceful of sunlight blazing off the windows of the National Five and Ten.

Up in the cab, Will finds Bob Dylan on the radio. Dad never likes us listening to him, but Will does it anyway.

Pete sings as he drives with a voice that's got more to it in the way of strength than tune but still sounds nice somehow. Pete's seventeen. Sun-fired and glorious, with freckles on his nose and hair like straw. But it's 1968. The Vietnam draft is going on and it's a dangerous time for him to be so close to eighteen. He don't care.

But I sure do.

Will drums his fingers on the dash, annoyed at Pete's singing. I catch sight of my brothers' faces in the rearview mirror and it's like seeing double. Pete and Will look so alike most people think they're twins: green-gray eyes, pointy noses, moppy blond hair. But Will is sixteen. Not so close to the draft as Pete. When we get to the stoplight in the middle of town and the corner with the crowd of kids, he stops his drumming and sits up.

I say crowd, but really it's only a half dozen or so kids about Pete and Will's age, maybe older. Black and white. Some have long hair, and there's a red-haired girl in sunglasses wearing not enough clothes, so we can see more of her than we should through her knitted shirt. They're waving hand-painted signs at the few cars moving slowly down Main Street:

END THE WAR BEFORE IT ENDS YOU

INJUSTICE ANYWHERE IS A THREAT TO JUSTICE EVERYWHERE

LBJ GO AWAY!

RESIST!

The light changes and Pete gives the Ford some gas. "Hippies," he says, as we roll past.

At that, Will slides forward in his seat, and leaning himself far out the window, he lifts a fist in a kind of salute. The girl in the sunglasses sees him and gives a whoop. Will flops back into his seat and shoots a look at Pete.

"They're fighting to keep your ignorant hide here and alive, not to send you off to Vietnam to kill and get killed like that idiot Johnson wants."

"Better let me decide where my ignorant hide goes," Pete replies, glancing a last time at the girl in the rearview mirror. "And if you're worried about killing in Vietnam, you might talk to the communists who started the shooting."

Will snorts. "Pete, I swear if you ever grow an idea of your own, it'll die of loneliness. That's Dad talking."

Pete reminds him Dad's the only one of us ever gone to war with communists, but Will tells him Korea ain't Vietnam and anyhow civil rights here is more important, and they get to arguing from there. From my spot in the truck bed, I don't pay them any more attention.

Other than the hippies, there ain't any more kids out, and anyway we've come to the far side of town now. On our left, I spy the new development of square houses surrounded by the wood skeletons of still more houses being built. But Pete feeds the Ford more gas, and we're rolling away from town now toward blue hills.

That Dylan song is still tumbling out the window as we go, the sound falling like rain on cornstalks that'll grow twice as tall as me. Sometimes my dog, Butch, and I will crawl among those cornstalks. I pretend we're in a swamp and that the stalks are really mangroves. After harvest in the fall, we walk these fields and look for arrowheads turned up in the earth among kernels of cracked feed corn.

Beside me in the truck bed, Frankie doesn't see the corn. His eyes are shut tight against the wind, his fingers gripping the edge of the pickup bone white.

"Don't worry, Frankie," I say over the wind. "There's all sorts of fun things we can do while you're here. Hey, you know how to shoot?"

One eye opens. He shakes his head.

"We do, and I can teach you, if you like. We shoot all the time. Mostly old beer bottles." Thinking for a minute, I add, "One time a man came into our house at night when we were all asleep, and Dad had to shoot him."

Both his ink-black eyes open then.

"The man didn't die," I add quickly.

He seems about to say something when our Ford rumbles over a pothole in the road. The bed drops beneath us and Frankie and me are weightless for an instant, floating over the truck like boy-shaped clouds on a hot wind. I land on my tailbone with a thump. That ends my story, and it's just as well.

Around us, the day blazes to its hottest time. Sky's grown darker in the west. Up in the cab, the Bob Dylan song has fizzled out. We've lost the station. Will twists the dial trying to find another, but all he gets is static.

The Ford follows the curve of the road, and Frankie's suitcase slides over the bed. *Rip-rip-rip.*

I decide to try again to make conversation.

"We're awful excited you're here, Frankie. Ma's made a blueberry cobbler for dessert tonight, and Dad said he'll drive us into town to the movie theater, if we want."

Us Elliot boys love the movies. First one I ever saw was *Moby Dick* at a Saturday matinee. Dad piled us into the Ford and drove us down to the State Theatre on Main Street. That white whale scared the life out of me, but Will insisted it was Captain Ahab who was the most frightening. That made no sense to me, though Will's smarter than I'll ever be so I figure he's right.

The cornfields have dropped below and behind us, a swaying green ocean of their own now that Pete's driven us into those blue

Pennsylvania hills that looked so far away before. More often than not, you'll find streams curling around their rocky toes, passing between gray sycamore trunks. There's panfish in the shallows, sunlight glinting off their flat bodies, and in the deeper, greener holes, the trout sit fat and lazy.

Pennsylvania's rocky ribs close in around us as we wind through miles and miles of narrow mountain passes, dark in the shade of sycamores, poplars, and pines, until all of a sudden we bust into a sweep of honey-colored meadow. The smell of honeysuckle comes to us on warm wind.

"Almost home now, Frankie."

Frankie isn't looking at me. Instead, he's staring at the sparkling ribbon of water rolling deep and wide before us: Apple Creek. The road bends toward it, drawn as if by magic, and now we're following the creek upstream.

Beside us the creek twists like a fat black snake in a patch of Bermuda grass, past Jungle Junction, where drifters sit by glowing campfires waiting to trade ghost stories for fresh-caught trout (the bigger your trout, the better your story); past Blood Root Mountain, where Crash Callahan and his riders race motorcycle bikes down impossible cliffs of black earth; right up to the Hopkins Bridge, a rusty pile of metal that shakes and rattles every time our truck dares across its brittle bones.

At the top of the next hill is Stairways.

At the top of the next hill is home.

My dog waits at the end of the dirt road.

You might remember I mentioned Butch already. I guess he really belongs to all of us—Dad and Ma, Pete, Will, and me—but since he and I spend the most time together, I think it's all right to just say he's mine.

Old Butch waits for Pete to park us beside the barn, then trots over, tail swishing back and forth. Frankie sees him, and his eyes grow wide.

"Don't you worry about Butch," I say. "He's as gentle a soul as can be."

Butch showed up on our porch one day, a lean, dusty-coated German shepherd. He was starving. Dad took him a piece of meat and smoked a cigar while he ate it. When Butch was done eating, he laid down and put his chin on the toe of Dad's boot. He's been our dog ever since. Ma says God puts people in your life at different times for different reasons. I know it's true for dogs too. Butch has been my best friend long as I can remember.

I grab Frankie's suitcase and lead him for the house. Butch comes with us, sniffing Frankie's pant leg. Dragging Frankie's suitcase up the porch steps, I tell him Butch ain't ever hurt anybody, which is mostly true.

Our house is two hundred years old. Made from stone, it didn't have electricity when Ma and Dad first moved in. Electrical company man was too afraid to run cables through the attic because of the snakes, so Ma took his ladder, hitched up her skirts, and did it herself.

People throughout the county call our house Stairways because of the steep spiral staircase that rises up from the parlor, up through three floors, all the way to the room where my brothers and I sleep under the attic. *Other* things sleep in the attic, above the rafters. Snakes shed their papery skins on hot summer nights (sometimes I can hear them if I lie still and hold my breath), and come wintertime, the screech owls keep me awake all night.

My brothers and me like the room just fine anyway. Our bedroom window lets us look down on our yard and the lane, and Apple Creek beyond that. The window is convenient for sneaking out late at night, too, by way of the gutter down to the porch roof.

"This is where we sleep," I tell Frankie as we puff up the last of those steep steps. "Those bunk beds are Pete and Will's. That bed right there is mine. You'll sleep on the mattress by the window."

He looks at the mattress, then at me.

"You can look at any of Pete's records, but don't touch any of Will's newspaper clippings about Bobby Kennedy or he'll get awful sore."

Will positively loves Bobby Kennedy, one of the men running for president, and reads anything he can find about him—books, newspapers, magazines. He's got campaign posters on the wall, with pictures of the senator in a suit and tie waving, and he even has a blue-and-white campaign pin on his bookshelf. **ALL THE WAY WITH RFK** it reads. Dad likes Bobby Kennedy about as much as he likes Bob Dylan. He says he's a runt whose family is ruining the country. Dad wants Nixon to win the election.

A breath of wind comes through the window, and a few stray drops of rain pitter-patter the windowsill.

"Well, I'll let you get unpacked, but be downstairs for dinner in a few. Ma will want to see you. Dad, too, I guess." I try to think if there's anything else. "Don't take too long. Remember there's cobbler."

I close the door and start back down the twisting stairs. As I go, a sound from inside the room comes to me. Could be it's a cough from all that road dust. Or maybe it's the sound you make when you've been trying real hard to hold back crying and all at once you can't hold it any longer and it just comes out.

I think back to Ma's saying, and I wonder what reason God could possibly have for sending Frankie our way now.

Maybe it's to help me save Pete's life.

Chapter 2

Ma

"Why is Frankie's city burning up?" I ask Ma as we set the picnic table on our porch for dinner.

"Because some people lit fires," Ma says. "And fires burn." She brushes away a daddy longlegs spider and sets down a pitcher of iced tea. "Knives face the other way, John Thomas."

Only Ma calls me by my full name, *John Thomas*. I hate it.

I go around the table switching the knives while the storm purrs to itself, like a giant cat. It's hiding behind the pines on the other side of our hill, waiting.

"How does lighting fires do anybody any good?"

I can smell the storm's electricity in the air, can feel it along my arms and the back of my neck. Out in our yard, the trees look silvery, their thirsty leaves curling skyward. Ma stands and watches the world surrender to the green dark. When she puts her hands on her hips, I know one thing for sure: Ma will never surrender.

"When a person feels trampled under, sooner or later, something bad happens." Ma turns and her eyes find mine, and it seems my shoes are nailed to the floorboards then. "If you go long enough thinking you don't have a say in your life, you reach a point where you'll do anything to show others that you do. And when that time comes, you don't care what it is. If it's lighting fires, you light fires."

Behind her, the trees are swaying. A warm breeze is blowing, growing stronger. Her dark hair moves in it as her green eyes steal some of the storm's strength for herself. I don't feel funny saying that my mother is the most beautiful woman I've ever seen.

"Don't you go askin' Francis about this," she warns.

"No ma'am."

"And don't go baiting him, hoping he'll bring it up on his own."

I say, "No ma'am" again and sigh.

"Finish setting the table and go wash up," Ma says. "We'll eat soon."

I'm just about through the screen door when Ma stops me again, this time with her voice. It's sharp, like one of those knives.

"John Thomas."

I turn around. "Yes ma'am?" Her skirt whips around her knees and she's still got her hands on her hips.

"Don't you ever do anything to make somebody feel like their life is no account to you, hear?"

"Yes ma'am . . ."

"It's the worst thing you can do to a person."

"Worse than killing them?"

"It's a kind of killing," Ma says. "A killing of the soul. Don't you do it."

"I won't."

I leave her on the porch and go inside to wash up. I'm still thinking about the fires by the time I finish. All my life I've been told there's nothing more dangerous than fire, *nothing*.

You learn that when your home is surrounded by trees for miles and miles.

Mr. Kemper comes just before the storm. From our bedroom window, Pete spies his black sedan slithering up our hill.

"It's the worm," he says.

Will beats me to the window, wedging his way in beside Pete, and I have to peek over their shaggy heads to see down into the drive. Dad is already there, but Mr. Kemper honks his horn anyway. Dad tosses his work gloves in the wheelbarrow and walks over to the driver's side of the fancy car.

They talk a while, Mr. Kemper in the car, Dad standing outside it. Dad doesn't invite him up to the porch, and Kemper doesn't ask.

Kemper works for the county. He's scarecrow-skinny, with an Adam's apple like a tangerine and a voice that sounds like a windshield wiper dragging over dry glass. We can't hear what he says from our window. No need.

He's come to try to get Dad to sell our house and land. The county wants it so they can build their dam and flood the valley. Lot of the other families in the valley have sold already. Ours and just a few others are holding out.

"He's persistent," Pete says.

"Didn't think we'd see him again after last time," says Will. "Notice he ain't got out of his car?"

"And he ain't turned off his engine neither," Pete agrees.

The last time Mr. Kemper came, he got out of his car and announced to Dad that he was going to stay as long as it took until Dad agreed to sign over our home. Dad answered with a quick, low whistle. Kemper got to his car just in time, but old Butch got a piece of his pant leg.

I'm aware of a quiet presence at my side: Frankie's joined us at the window. He watches the meeting below in his silent, dark way.

"Tell him off, Dad," Will mutters.

In the drive below, Dad lights a cigar. A tiny orange flower blossoms in his hands as wispy clouds of blue smoke rise into the still air. From behind the pines, the storm growls again.

Soon. Very soon now.

Kemper is leaning out of his window, stabbing at the earth with one bony finger. His head bobbles at the end of his long neck.

"He really does look like a worm, don't he?" I ask.

Dad's shoulders bounce beneath his overalls: he's laughing at something Kemper said. Then he turns away, waving Kemper off as he walks for our porch.

Kemper thumps the dash and shakes his head. The rain has started by the time he backs his big, shiny automobile carefully down our dirt drive. Pete and Will move for the bedroom door, but I stay, stay and watch those yellow headlights through the trees and the rain until I'm sure the man who works for the county is across the Hopkins Bridge at the bottom of our hill. If it collapsed while he was on it, I wouldn't complain.

I'm surprised to find Frankie is still beside me when I turn from the window.

"Come on, Frankie," I say then. "Dinnertime."

As we start down the stairs I add, "Don't worry none about the worm. He won't bother us no more."

I don't really believe that, and I get the idea Frankie knows it.

Chapter 3

STAIRWAYS

The storm breaks at dinner, slapping Stairways with fat raindrops and pitching pieces of jagged lightning across black sky. We eat on the porch, listening to it howl out all the fury it's gathered up from the long, hot day. Soon, water pours down the eaves in a shimmering curtain that wraps around us and gurgles in thin streams between tree roots in the front yard on its way down to make muddy lakes in the lane.

When he finishes dinner, Dad slides his plate to one side and strikes a match. The scent of another Primo del Rey cigar mingles with the perfume of soaked earth and wet tree bark. He leans back in his chair and folds his hands on the table, holding the cigar between his teeth.

My father's hands are scarred, sunburned. Dirt under every nail. Bandages on two thick fingers, probably from repairing the barbed-wire fence at old Mr. Halleck's estate, where he works.

Mr. Halleck is a rich old man, with hair like downy fluff and breath that smells like sour mash whiskey whenever he bends down to talk to you. He keeps strange animals on his estate: peacocks, flamingos—even an ostrich. There's also a pair of antelope all the way from Africa. He has special people care for them, but Dad does just about everything else.

I want to ask Dad how he cut the fingers, but I don't.

Ma asks instead, in her roundabout way.

"Did it take long with those pines on the north slope?"

Dad puffs on the cigar. Smiles. "My fingers are fine."

Beyond our porch, lightning chases black treetops.

"Jack," says my father to me, "if you do not finish that meat loaf, you will get no blueberry cobbler." He taps the cigar and a bit of ash drops over the railing, sizzles in the rain, and is gone. "And that would be a shame."

I've spread my meat loaf pretty good across my plate, one of the fancy porcelain ones Ma set out in honor of Frankie. But it's plain to see I haven't had more than a mouthful since we sat down. It'd be easier if Butch was under the table where he belongs, instead of hiding in the barn like a big baby. Dang dog is terrified of thunder.

"Dad, can I have the paper?" Will asks. The *Evening News*, folded and damp, sits at Dad's left elbow. Will's been eyeing it all dinner long, hungry for news about his hero, Senator Robert F. Kennedy.

Dad gives the paper a toss. Even in green storm light I catch sight of the photograph on the front page as it wheels by: boys in the jungle, in uniform. Soldiers.

"You've brought cooler weather with you, son," Dad says to Frankie—as if he didn't see the photograph, as if he don't know his oldest son is only a few weeks away from a letter saying he's got to go to war in some jungle far away where nobody can look after him.

Ma joins Dad in talking to Frankie about the weather. "It's been miserable hot lately," she says.

"It's been hot at home too," Frankie tells her. "The thermometer read a hundred and one degrees when I left."

"Is that because of all them fires?"

Ma's fork makes a tiny clink as she sets it down and glares at me.

Dad frowns.

The one thing Ma told me *not* to talk about was the fires in the city, and I went and did it. Suddenly the smooshed-up meat loaf on my plate is the most interesting thing I have ever seen, and I stare at it, wondering who on earth came up with a name like "meat loaf" in the first place and knowing all the while that I'm a fool—and what's more, that I'm a *dead* fool.

I feel Ma's eyes drilling holes in my head. She wants me to look at her, but I don't. I keep staring at my meat loaf and no place else. I force down a fork-load and chew and chew and chew. Meanwhile nobody's said nothing, and I hear the blood pounding in my ears, and it sounds like the rain that's still coming down around us and—

"Aunt Addie, can I have some more meat loaf?"

Frankie's voice is so soft I can hardly hear him over the rain. At his question, Ma's mouth opens. I hold my breath for a whole minute while Ma ladles more of the loaf onto his plate. Next thing I know, Frankie's telling her how good it is and asking for more carrots. By the time Ma's done telling him they come from her garden, and how the rabbits have been after them all spring, she's forgotten me and my question.

I throw a sideways glance at Frankie, but he keeps on talking. I never heard him talk so much. Didn't know he could.

"It's beautiful here," Frankie says, again in his small, quiet voice. "I've never been anyplace like it. And it's so . . . *far* from anybody else."

That ain't true. Old Sam Williamson's trailer is a mile down Hopkins Road, and the Glattfelders own a farm five miles beyond it. And there's one more family, across Apple Creek on the other side of Knee-Deep Meadow: the Madliners. We don't see too much of them. That's fine by me because Mr. Madliner is as sour-faced a man as you'll find. His wife, Elmira, is awful sick, so that she can't hardly walk. And their son, Caleb . . . well, there's some people you just steer clear of.

Dad's cigar glows orange and bright. "Get the boys to show you around."

"Sure, we'll show him around." Pete grins.

Across the table, Will looks up from his paper and frowns.

"We'll introduce Frankie to the bears," Pete goes on. "And the cougars. Maybe a snapping turtle or two."

Ma gives him a swat.

"Don't you pay any attention, Frankie," she says. "Pete, you and Will clear the table."

Around us, the rain begins to slacken. The storm is wearing itself out, the nasty howling now a softer rumbling; the lightning a flicker on the far side of the valley.

After Pete and Will clear the table, Ma brings the cobbler and a pitcher of cold milk. Even Frankie brightens up when he gets a taste.

"It's delicious," he says.

"Got the blueberries fresh this morning." The pride in Ma's voice is plain to hear.

Over cobbler, Ma asks Frankie about her sister, Aunt Effie, and how she and Uncle Leone are. My brothers and me listen close then for any news about the fires and the riots, but Frankie don't spill anything good. When they finish their talk, Pete tells Dad about the joke he and his friend Davy Porter tried to play on Herb Mooney, the mailman. Pete had the idea they would wait in the trees for poor Herb to drive up our lane, and then swing out on a pair of monkey vines right before he reached them, screaming like Tarzan. Dumb old Davy Porter jumped too late on his vine and smacked right into the side of the mail truck. Dad laughs. It's a deep, rumbling sound. A thunder all its own.

Butch melts out of the wet night, his fur sprinkled with rain, pink tongue lolling out. He lumbers up the porch steps and finds his way over to me, his wet nose doing a dance.

"You're too late," I tell him, scrubbing the enormous head with my knuckles. "You missed it."

We sit, feeling full and fuzzy, smelling Dad's cigar and the clean freshness of the rain around us. Behind Stairways, the cicadas make their music, answering each other from dripping pine branches. In the meadow beyond Apple Creek, the frogs are singing: *knee-deep, knee-deep.*

I wonder how much the creek's risen from the rain. The thought of all that dark water moving so fast just a few hundred feet from our porch makes me think of Mr. Kemper and his dam. I shudder.

It's 1968, and the town of New Shiloh is growing. New streets and new houses all laid out in neat squares. All the same. White fences and tiny young trees, not like the giants that stand tall all around our hill. The county wants a reservoir to make sure there's enough water for all them people.

Could they really flood our valley, and Stairways with it? Dad would never let them. I look over at him and Ma, together at the end of the picnic table. Night has fallen and our porch is so dark it's not two separate shapes I see, but one. Neither of my parents speaks, but I know they're sharing thoughts just the same.

About Mr. Kemper and the dam.

About Pete and the war. Pete and the draft.

There is no thought in anyone's mind about Pete taking a deferment. Even if my brother wanted to go to college, he would never do it. My father would pretend he did not hear you even say such a thing. Ma would not speak of it. In our family, serving is one of the last great things you can do.

Grandpa Elliot made sergeant in the US Marine Corps for shooting a German sniper out of a tree in France in World War I. Same as shooting squirrels, he told me once. As for Dad, he spent his time in the Marines in Korea and saved a man's life at a place called the Chosin Reservoir. He don't ever talk about it—not ever—except when he and his friend Dickie Howell get together, and then only because Dickie was also a Marine. Dickie, who only has one leg.

For us Elliots, if the country calls, you answer. Simple as that. Maybe you lose a leg. Maybe you lose much more. But you go. Which is why I hate myself for feeling how I do. Because I don't want Pete going to Vietnam. I don't want my brother to die.

Rain's stopped. Dad's cigar burns hotly one last time in the blue dark, then fades. At almost that same moment, a tiny glow answers it from the grass beyond our porch. I wait and when it comes again, I spot two others floating near it. Tiny lights winking on and off, bobbing in the dark.

"What are those?" Frankie asks.

I'd almost forgotten my cousin, him sitting so quiet, so still beside me.

"Ain't you ever seen fireflies before?"

He stares out into what's now a sea of glowing lights and shakes his head.

"Does that mean you ain't ever *chased* fireflies?"

Another head shake.

"Well, goodness gracious, what kind of place do you come from, anyhow? You wait right here and don't go anywhere." I run and fetch a jar from the kitchen.

"Come on, Frankie. You and me are going firefly hunting. You follow my lead and do just like I do. We'll catch a bunch and put them in this jar. Don't worry, they don't bite or sting, and they got nothing to do with *real* fire at all."

I kick off my shoes and lead my cousin out into our yard. Butch joins us, his tail swishing a mile a minute, and we chase fireflies over cool, wet grass, following the little lights deeper into a night that smells sweet and clean. When Frankie finally catches one, you'd think he caught a pop fly in the World Series. He crouches on his knees, peering into his hands.

"I've got one. I've got one!"

"So stick him in the jar and go find another one!"

By the end of it our little jelly jar is glowing like a dragon's egg. And as we walk back to the house, our feet soaking wet, I've eased my worrying over Pete and the draft. And I've also decided that my cousin Frankie is all right for a city boy.

At first I think it must be Apple Creek I see rolling before me. The water is brown; the storm's churned up the bottom. But the trees on the far bank are shorter than the white oaks along our creek. And darker. Their arms reach out over the water, so low that their vines, like fingers, trace lines in the current. Pieces of red sky blaze between the trunks, like a poker left too long in the fire.

I am in the jungle.

I suck in a breath of hot air, heavy with the stink of rotten leaves, because I know what I'm about to see. Already the shapes are coming, moving under the trees just across the water from me: dark, green shapes sliding so quiet you'd think they were the shadows of birds passing overhead. But they are not birds. They are boys.

Boys in uniform.

Pete is with them. I don't see him. I *feel* him. But whether in the front of that line or still back in the deep shadows I do not know.

Stay in the trees.

The boys ignore me. One by one, they step out into a dangerous open space along the river, a tiny pocket of land that's opened up in the tangled mesh of jungle.

I shout at them to go back. Run into the trees. Hide. My lips drag around silent words. Like every time before, the boys on the bank cannot hear me.

The shots start downriver this time. I want to look, but someone's holding my head in a vise so the only place I can see is straight ahead. From the corner of my eye, I catch sight of yellow lights popping angrily in the green dark. On the far bank, the first boy pitches forward into the dirty river. He doesn't crumple up. He stays straight. He falls like a tree. He slips headfirst below the surface and is gone.

The next boy steps up. The others behind him don't run for cover, don't throw themselves into the dirt like they're supposed to. They simply stand in line. Boys like trees, standing, waiting to be cut down.

I squeeze hot jungle air from my lungs and my throat burns as I try again to shout. Not a whisper comes out.

The second boy slips under the water too, smiling as he goes.

A third boy steps out of the trees, a boy taller than the rest, with broad shoulders and a thatch of straw-colored hair. I don't look at his face. I already know who it is. Instead, I jump. That dirty river water is warm and I fight it, punching and kicking to get myself to that far bank in time. Can't shout, so I have to swim. And if I can just get to that bank, I can save him.

I have only a few seconds more. I kick harder, but now I'm sinking.

The air rushes out of me again, hissing past my lips into the river of death. I can't hear the shots when they come. But I hear the splash. I *feel* it somewhere above me.

A shape slides down in front of me in the dark water, feet first, the body ramrod straight. Pete grins as he goes by, his hair waving on end around his cheerful face. He sinks out of my vision, down deep into the black mud.

The water floods my mouth and nose then as I scream, and suddenly everything is dark and warm and dead.

It's a fat, cream-colored moon climbing over my windowsill as I lie listening to Pete's snores and the crickets out in Knee-Deep Meadow. My oldest brother is fast asleep in his top bunk, his arm hanging over the edge. In the pale moonlight, it's ghostly white. Will's still as stone in his bed. On his mattress on the floor, Frankie is a shapeless lump, his chest rising and sinking with all the noise of a falling star.

It's only me and my somersaulting mind awake now.

I sit up and the bedsheets come with me, sticking to my bare back and arms. I feel the night breeze through the open window, and I suck it in. A little while later, I cry.

My dream is the same every time. Those boys in the jungle line up and wait to get shot. Pete somewhere among them, and I can't do a thing to save him. So many other boys' brothers have gone to Vietnam. Signed up or drafted. It ain't fair of me to want to keep mine here all safe and sound, but I don't care.

I climb down from my bed and creep past my sleeping cousin to the windowsill. The moon spills its milky light over our yard and Dad's truck in the drive. Valley beyond is all wrapped up in mist.

I kneel down and pray.

My knees are numb by the time the words come:

God, help me save my brother. Help me save my family.

I repeat it over and over and over. My own river of words to fight that dark, deadly river in my dream.

When I lift my head from the window, the moon is smaller, higher in the sky. My feet have fallen asleep under me. I climb back into bed on tiny, stabbing needles. I am on my way out of the world again when Frankie turns in his sleep. From his mattress, he gives a long, slow sigh.

I know it then. It's the last thought through my mind before I switch off the burning hot bulb in my brain: Frankie is the answer to my prayer. After all my talking to him, God's said something back.

Chapter 4

New Shiloh

Sunday morning our family piles into the Ford and Dad drives us into town for church.

New Shiloh Lutheran sits at the town's edge, white wooden boards blazing in morning sun under a steeple that tilts like a scarecrow's hat toward the ocean of corn that surrounds it. Wind moves among the stalks as we pull up, making waves that lap the walls of the church like water against the hull of a ship. And it reminds me how Pastor Fenton said one time the church *was* a ship: seas could swell and rise against it, but it could never sink, and neither would you so long as you kept inside it.

We pass under the steeple's shadow, through the double doors, and into a creaky wooden pew. All around us, people fan themselves with paper song sheets so that the whole church seems full of giant white butterflies furiously flapping their wings.

Pastor Fenton reads a bit from the Bible and I try hard to listen close, but my button-down shirt clings to me like a second skin. Ma's eyes flash *John Thomas, stop your fidgeting or else*, and that settles me long enough to catch some of Pastor Fenton's sermon on redemption. With a voice that's surprisingly powerful for how small a man he is, he tells us nobody is beyond God's love, no matter what they've done, and thinking otherwise is a dangerous kind of pride.

After the last song, my brothers and me bolt for the doors before Ma's church-lady friends can find us and make a fuss. Dad is already walking down Main Street with a few of the other men, making for Mr. Hudspeth's barbershop. I'm about to run after him when Pete grabs hold of my collar.

"You ain't leaving him like that," he says, pointing me back to our pew, and I see what he means: Ma's church ladies have got hold of Frankie.

I do like Pete wants and go back to rescue my cousin. Their talk as I come up is about Aunt Effie, who most of them grew up with—and the fires in the city. One of them asks how Uncle Leone is faring, being a police officer and in the line of danger and all. Frankie answers that he doesn't know how his dad is doing, and I can tell he's worried.

The talk changes once the ladies see me, and I give my fair share of the "Yes ma'am" and "No ma'am" answers to all the same questions I got asked last week and the week before. Didn't I think Pastor Fenton's sermon was wonderful? And was I thinking of being a pastor myself someday?

Ma's dream. She's given up on Pete and Will, but she ain't given up on me yet and neither have her friends.

By the time I pry Frankie away, Dad is gone. Pete and Will are talking with some of the other kids out front, and the girls, and one girl in particular.

Anna May Fenton's blonde hair is held up with a purple headband that matches her skirt and the socks that come up to her calves on her long, creamy white legs. She laughs at something, and it seems the cornfields behind her laugh too, flashing smiles of gold and green that ripple out for miles.

Frankie slows down when he sees her. "Who's that?"

"That's just Anna May. Pastor Fenton's daughter." I hesitate a bit, then decide to say it: "Will's sweet on her."

Next to Anna May, Will stands with both hands in his pockets, head down, like he's seeing his shoes for the first time. Pete is telling a story.

"Will and Anna May are in the same class," I tell Frankie. "He don't see her much over the summer because she lives in town."

In one of those new developments that Kemper says need more water. Which is why the county wants the dam.

"Come on," I say, grabbing hold of Frankie's arm. "Maybe Dad will buy us gumballs at the barbershop. You like gumballs, dontcha?"

"Sure . . ."

"Well, Mr. Hudspeth's got a *giant* gumball machine in his shop. For a nickel you can get a gumball that'll last you hours, if you're careful with it." Slowly, Frankie lets me pull him away.

We start after Dad with a little help from a breeze coming off the cornfields that blows us down Main Street like two tumbleweeds. Our reflections stare back as we roll by empty storefront windows: Wistar's Hardware, which smells like grass seed and rubber; Geary's Shoe Repair, with rows of polished brown and black leather shoes winking in the sunlight; Ernie's Luncheonette & Homemade Ice Cream Parlor, with the soda machine behind the counter and all its shining silver levers standing at attention but nobody there to work them on account of it being Sunday.

Mr. Hudspeth's barbershop ain't open for business neither, strictly speaking, though his door is propped open with a brick, and if you really needed a haircut, I guess he wouldn't mind giving you one. We go in and catch a whiff of aftershave and newsprint and listen to a ceiling fan hum somewhere above us while we wait for our eyes to get used to the dark. When they do, we see empty barber chairs in front of empty mirrors, and Dad and all the men gathered along the back counter.

Sundays after services, they come here to read baseball scores and trade talk. Behind his counter, Mr. Hudspeth watches them with a pleased sort of look. A wiry man whose vest and white shirts are always stained brown with tobacco juice, Mr. Hudspeth is bald except for a horseshoe of curly red hair that starts above one ear and ends above the other. He wears a mustache to match.

Dad fishes two nickels out of his pocket for us when we come in. I lead Frankie straight to the gumball machine, drop in the nickels, and give the lever a couple pulls. I let him have the cherry one, and then we climb into the barber seats to chew gum and eavesdrop.

"See you got an extra one with you today, Gene," says Mr. Hudspeth, nodding toward Frankie.

"Seems I do."

"Your nephew?"

"Effie's boy. In from the city for a time."

Hearing this, several of the men turn to Frankie, watching, curious.

"Effie married the policeman, didn't she? I bet he has his hands full with all that bad business happening there." Mr. Hudspeth leans forward and lifts his red eyebrows. "I heard it's a war zone. People shooting each other on the streets. The kid ever say anything about it?"

"We don't ask," Dad answers, in a way that lets everybody know they shouldn't ask either. Mr. Hudspeth lifts his hands and retreats across his counter as another man chuckles.

"Now why'd the boy know anything about a war zone when he's sitting in your barber chair?"

"Unless he was getting his hair cut," says another man, and even Dad laughs some at that.

The men carry on with their usual talk about the town, the weather, and the crops, but I see Dad cast a quick glance to us. To Frankie.

Next to me, my cousin is calmly chewing his gum.

"So I hear Crash Callahan and his boys stopped by to visit Sam Williamson last night," says another man at the counter.

"Crash and his whole motorcycle gang," says Hank Wistar, who owns the hardware store. Mr. Wistar's stomach is a bowling ball behind his checkered shirt. Will says it's because he drinks too much. "Them boys looped chains through the door to Sam's chicken coop and rode off with it. Sam called up early this morning, asking if I'd open the store and get him some wire to keep his chickens in."

"Where'd he put the chickens in the meantime?" one of the men asks.

"His trailer. I heard them clucking over the phone."

More laughs.

"That Crash oughta have his ass kicked," Mr. Hudspeth says, spitting a line of brown juice into a paper cup behind his counter. "Him and his whole gang."

"That Crash is lucky he didn't get killed," Dad says. "Sam may be old, but he's a deadeye."

Dad's words start somebody else on a story about Sam's Fourth of July celebrations, how he lines up all his rifles against the porch railing, then, at the stroke of midnight, tears down the line firing each one lickety-split.

"Well now, what have we here, fellas, what have we here," Mr. Hudspeth suddenly says, bending over the newspaper spread out on the counter. "Look at this."

He sets his paper cup down and straightens up, bringing the paper close to his nose as he reads the headline: "'Boston students stage hunger strike to protest draft.'"

Somebody swears then. Someone else hushes him, and the men go quiet while Mr. Hudspeth reads more.

"'In protest of what they called America's atrocities in Vietnam, students from Harvard and Boston University staged a public hunger strike in Cambridge on Saturday.'"

Dad pulls a cigar from his pocket and strikes a match as Mr. Hudspeth goes on.

"'At a demonstration in which students spoke for several hours on topics ranging from colonialism to capitalism to segregation to feminism, student leaders declared their conscientious objection to the war in Vietnam and announced a hunger strike. Students then began burning draft cards.'"

The same man as before swears again, only nobody hushes him now. The men are quiet. All we hear is the ceiling fan's chain clinking above.

The gum's soft and chewy enough now, and I start blowing a balloon.

Mr. Wistar shakes his head. "Rich college boys," he mutters, "refusing to fight their own war. Almost can't believe it."

"Almost," says my father around his glowing cigar.

"It ain't just rich college boys," Mr. Hudspeth says. "It's Hollywood actors too. It's politicians, like that Kennedy boy, egging them on."

I start blowing another balloon, knowing their talk will be boring and about politics now.

Mr. Hudspeth goes on, "When we graduated high school, the boys lined up outside recruiting stations. Actors and auto mechanics. Made no difference."

Mr. Wistar splays his fingers and starts counting. "Clark Gable. Jimmy Stewart. Tyrone Power."

Mr. Hudspeth says, "Now, it's different. Now, if you're famous, you don't have to go to war."

My yellow balloon pops. With gum hanging across my chin, I go suddenly very still.

At the counter, the men murmur agreement. There are sighs. Some headshakes.

Mr. Hudspeth picks up his paper cup and leaks more brown juice into it.

Dad makes blue clouds of smoke with his Primo del Rey.

The men keep talking, but their conversation drifts back to where it began: the town, the weather, the crops. Though they are only a few feet away, I barely hear them. An idea is near. Hidden. Close. I don't know what it is yet, but I *feel* it.

Beside me, Frankie chews his gum and blows bubbles. Eventually, he hops down and walks from chair to chair, chewing as he goes, stopping to look at some of the magazines stacked on the windowsill.

But I stay absolutely still. My idea is floating beneath my waking mind, like a granddaddy trout easing along under the water's surface. I close my eyes, try to concentrate. The voices of the men fade, and I hear other sounds in the barbershop: the hum of the ceiling fan and the jingling of the metal cord hanging down as its end traces circles in the air over my head. I start chewing again, slowly, hoping maybe that will lure the idea up from the dark, up into the sun.

I come back to the voice of a man: my father, calling my name. "Jack." My father is already at the door, dark cigar trailing smoke. "Come on, son."

I sigh to no one but myself as I clamber down from my seat. Mr. Hudspeth leans over the counter, over the newspaper with the pictures of students burning their draft cards, and takes my hand and gives it a good shake.

I hold on to his hand for just a moment, hold and hope that maybe that will bring the idea. Nothing.

"You all right, boy?" Mr. Hudspeth asks.

I blink. "I just wanted to thank you for the gumball, sir."

He smiles. Yellow teeth below a bristly, red mustache. "Good, aren't they?"

I nod. He spits again into his cup. I let go of his hand.

Frankie and I follow my father out into a hotter, emptier Main Street. The breeze is gone now, and the sun beats down as we walk back to church.

We find Pete, Will, and Ma waiting for us on the steps. I look for Anna May, but she and the other kids have gone. It's only my family standing against the emerald cornfields.

I'm still chasing that idea in my mind when we climb into the Ford for the ride home, but like so many other fish, it's gone deep.

Evening comes, soft and velvety. After dinner, Will argues with Dad about politics and Senator Kennedy in the back room. On the television, Walter Cronkite tells them both, though they ain't listening, "That's the way it is."

Ma sends Frankie and me upstairs to wash. I let Frankie go first in the old white tub with the claw feet. I lie on my bed and wait and watch for the first stars in the purple dark outside my window.

Star light, star bright, first star I see tonight.

What's my wish? To keep Pete from dying in Vietnam.

Below, the screen door wheezes open, slaps against the frame. I hear footsteps pound the porch boards, crunch gravel: Will. Leaving, walking off again, furious from his fight with Dad about Bobby Kennedy and the Democrats, Richard Nixon and the Republicans. And the war.

One of these days, he'll go for good.

No, don't say that. Not Will too.

Frankie appears, smelling like soap with his dark hair sticking every which way, and it's my turn to wash in the white tub. As I pour warm water over my head, my mind goes back to the barbershop, to Mr. Hudspeth's voice playing like a tape recorder over and over and over again:

Now, if you're famous, you don't have to go to war.

Chapter 5

The Plan

I wake to find my idea bobbing on the line in the shallow end of my brain, like an embarrassed trout that ought to know better.

I lie still, barely breathing and almost crying with relief because I know now how to save my brother—and it all depends on my cousin.

"Frankie!" I whisper. "Come on and get dressed! Come on now!"

I give him a shake and reach for a shoe. My fingers are trembling so badly from the excitement, I can barely get the knot tied.

Frankie comes up from his mattress blinking, one hand feeling for his glasses.

"They're on the windowsill," I tell him.

"What time is it?"

"Shh!" I jerk my head toward the bunk, to Pete's and Will's sleeping shapes. They can't know. Can't have any part of it. Not Ma or Dad neither. Nobody can know—until the right time, and then *everyone* will know.

"About seven o'clock. Now hurry *up*."

"Where we going?"

"Apple Creek."

"What for?"

The truth: because I can't have Pete and Will hearing what I have to tell you.

"Just because," I say instead.

"At seven o'clock in the morning?"

"Best time of day—as good as any other. Now get dressed while I grab us some breakfast."

I leave him on the mattress and take the spiral stairs two at a time to the kitchen, where I spread some butter on a pair of yesterday's biscuits and stuff both in my overalls before screwing the lid onto a jar of orange juice. Frankie is at the bottom of the stairs by the time I finish. His shirttail hangs out of his pants. His hair dives off his head at odd angles.

"You're slower than molasses in January," I tell him as we push through the screen door so hard it slaps the back of the porch and wheezes back, nearly catching Frankie's elbow. Heavy perfume of summer washes over us: lilac and honeysuckle. Grass is still wet from the last of the dew, and the hems of our pants are damp by the time we pass the barn.

Butch finds us then, lumbering over to say good morning and sniff at the biscuits in my pocket. I watch Frankie make the decision to drop a hand on my dog's head and give him a quick scratch behind the ear. Butch plops down at once on his behind and points his nose at the sky, which is his way of telling Frankie to keep on with the ear scratching.

Any other day, I'd stop and accommodate Butch, but this morning I'm impatient.

"I think he likes me," Frankie says, yawning. "Does he live in the barn?"

"He only sleeps there," I tell him. "Come on, I'll show you. But real quick."

Cooler inside the barn. Dark. Motes swirl in a pair of light beams that slant through cobwebby windows and splash on Dad's gray Ferguson tractor, still asleep under its blue tarp. Enormous wheels make creases like mountain ridges beneath waterproofed plastic. The trailer hangs out the back of the tarp, filled with the tools Dad uses on old Mr. Halleck's estate: axes, shovels, chainsaws, hedge clippers, work gloves, a posthole digger, a jug of gasoline, and a paint-splattered pail.

Frankie spots our toboggan, tucked across the rafters.

"That's the best place for hide-and-seek," I tell him. "One time I stretched out on it to hide, and it was so comfy I fell asleep. I was up there hours and Pete and Will couldn't find me, and Ma was fixing to call the sheriff when I finally woke up. Good thing I never rolled nowhere. Only bad thing about it was the spiders."

I lead him back outside, where Butch is nipping at gnats in the yard, and down the worn flagstones to the lane. When he sees we mean business about leaving the yard, Butch gets up and trots along after us.

Above us, the sun is a soft ball of yellow egg yolk. Not one cloud in sight, which means it will be hot, and I'm glad when we cross the road and slip beneath the gray sycamores and pass into Pennsylvania's endless forests. Will told me once that you can walk from one end of Pennsylvania to the other and never once come out from under trees, if you don't want to. I believe him. There's a musty smell on the air of rotting leaves and fresh mud. Roots, like old fingers, reach across the deer trail we're following, which begins to dip down.

"Is it safe to be here?" Frankie asks, eyeing the timber.

"You bet."

"But no one knows we're out here, do they?"

"Me and Butch know exactly where we are!"

Ahead, Butch finds a hole. He puts his face in and digs.

Our path bends between a pair of giant white oaks, and that scent on the air grows stronger. I go faster now, wanting to put distance between us and the house. Last thing I want is Pete or even worse, Will, deciding to catch us up. I don't want to be found out. Not yet.

We follow the scent through a patch of rubbery jewelweed until at last we break onto a sandy bank and find Apple Creek rolling easy and bright, glittering like a green diamond in morning sun. Smooth river stones of pink and orange and pale blue lie scattered along the edge. Above the far bank, the meadow grasses blaze buttery gold in morning sun.

Inside every boy's head is a magnet that will lead him straight to water. Ours pull us right up to the water's edge, and we begin following the creek downstream.

"Don't get too close," I warn. "You can't see it, but the bank curves away underneath. If you're not careful, it'll crumble and take you with it."

"Has that ever happened to you?" Frankie asks.

I wonder how he guessed.

"Once," I say. But I don't tell him any more.

It was a few years back, after a heavy rain. Creek was high, and I pestered Will into taking me down to see it because I wasn't allowed to go alone. When the bank collapsed under me, I went in—and under. Will jumped in after me, got hold of me, and kept us both above water, letting the force carry us downstream until he could grab a mesh of tree roots and pull us out. We lay on the bank gasping for air a good long while until he had strength enough to walk again. When we got home, I was sent to bed without any supper, but poor Will got the belt from Dad for taking me to the creek in the first place.

I still feel guilty about that.

Hopkins Bridge slides into view, a rusty skeleton stretching over slow water and banks that sparkle with brown and green beer bottles people have pitched out of their cars as they drove past.

Butch ambles to the shade under the bridge. We follow him. Apple Creek is glassy smooth here and the sand is coarse, like brown sugar. We drop down to eat our biscuits and trade sips of warm orange juice from the jar as the day steams hotter around us. I find it hard to eat mine on account of the butterflies in my stomach, so I give the whole thing to Butch, take a breath, and say the thing I been waiting all morning to say:

"Tell me about them stories you write."

He looks at me.

"What stories?"

"The ones you got published in the paper. The one Ma taped to our fridge."

Frankie frowns and takes a bite of biscuit. "What do you want to know?"

"How long's it take you to write them?"

"Depends. Sometimes a day. Sometimes longer."

"Could you write stories here?"

"You can write stories anywhere."

On the far bank, the insects are buzzing. I drain the last of the juice from the jar, screw the lid back on, and stick it in the sand.

"I want you to write stories about Pete. I want to get his name in the newspapers and make him famous so he won't have to go to war when he turns eighteen."

I've said it. My idea is out in the world now.

Frankie's face is smooth as the creek.

"Pete turns eighteen in a month," I go on. "If he gets drafted, the Army will send him to Vietnam. I know serving is the most special thing a person can do. Only, I don't want him going. I don't want anything to happen to him. Yesterday at the barbershop, Mr. Hudspeth said something that got me thinking. He said, 'If you're famous, you don't have to go to war.' I remember those words exact. They been burning in my brain ever since. I mean to save my brother's life, Frankie. Your stories can do it. I know you can write stories about Pete that'll make him so famous the Army won't be able to send him to Vietnam, even if they wanted to."

Frankie's kept quiet the whole while. Now I wait for him to speak, but all he does is watch with those dark eyes.

From the poplars on the far bank, a jay calls. For a long time, neither one of us speaks and there's the jay making his sweet sound again and a stray breath of wind blows, carrying the smell of creek mud with it, and all that time Frankie ain't spoke a word.

"Well, what do you think?" I ask. "Will you do it?"

"You really think my stories can save your brother's life?"

"Yes, I do."

Frankie stands up slowly, walks to the water's edge, where he stoops and picks up one of the smooth river stones. He holds it in city-boy hands, feeling the smoothness of it. When he turns back to me, his eyes have a sudden hardness, like he's borrowed some from that stone.

"Writing takes time, Jack. I'll need time to think."

My heart thumps.

"Pete don't turn eighteen for a whole month. Ain't that plenty of time to think?"

He turns out his lower lip and frowns. "And I can't make anything up. Pete has to be *doing* things worth writing about."

"Pete does the most amazing things you've ever seen!" I stand up, because Frankie ain't said no yet and now there's excitement rising within me, blowing like a hot air balloon. "He runs. He swims. He fights with the boys in town. Hell, he and Will are planning an expedition to find a wrecked fighter jet! Ain't that exciting enough?"

"Running, swimming, and fighting, no, it isn't," Frankie says, shaking his head. "But a wrecked fighter jet, now *that's* different. That's exciting. Tell me more."

"It crashed on a snowy winter night ages ago," I say, aware that I'm talking fast now. "This was before I was born, mind you, so I don't remember it. Will barely remembers it. But *Pete* remembers, and Pete wants to find it."

Frankie slowly begins to nod. "An expedition. An *adventure*. That could work." He begins pacing beside the creek, shoes snuffing up clumps of creek sand. He passes the stone from hand to hand, and I know what he's really doing is tossing my idea, turning, feeling, testing. All at once, he stops. The stone falls with a *plunk*.

"Okay."

I'm trembling.

"I'll need a few things," Frankie says, brushing the sand from his hands.

"Anything," I say. My eyes are getting watery.

"I need a typewriter."

"I'll find one," I say. "If I have to steal it. What else?"

"A quiet place to write where nobody will bother me."

"The barn."

"The *barn*?"

"It's perfect! It's quiet, and you can use Grandma Elliot's old sewing desk." The blood is rushing in my ears. I can hardly believe it.

Frankie frowns.

"And I need one more thing, Jack: I need to be there when they find it. I *have* to be there. The story won't work if I'm not. You understand?"

I tell him I understand. I begin to sob. Next thing I know, I've got both arms around my cousin, thanking him over and over. Frankie don't know what to say. It's a while before I quit my blubbering, and by then, the softness has come back to his face.

"Don't thank me yet, Jack . . . Not until we get a story and get it published."

"We will. I *know* we will. You're the best writer I've ever seen!"

"Maybe, maybe," Frankie says. "But I need those things: a type-writer, a quiet place, and I go with you all when it happens."

I stand up straight and stick out my hand. "A typewriter, a quiet place, and you come with us."

We shake.

From his place in the sand, Butch looks up and barks.

It's another second or two before we hear what he hears, a deep rumbling from up Hopkins Road. Faint, like thunder. Only there ain't a cloud in the sky.

Butch barks again and stands up. And that's when I know.

"Better help me get hold of Butch," I say, grinning, wiping snot from my face. "Here they come."

"Who?"

"Crash Callahan and his motorcycle riders, that's who! Come on, now!"

We grab Butch by the collar and duck under the bridge just as the first rider comes ripping overhead. Something drops from above, a flash of sunlight on green glass, and an empty beer bottle smacks into brown creek sand a few feet from us. The rider lets out a whoop, a leathery voice that knocks back and forth off the water and the bridge. Next thing we know, Crash's whole horde is tearing across the bridge, flinging empty bottles that come down like a glassy green rain. Frankie and me hunker down beneath them, our fingers looped through Butch's collar, holding him close as he barks and bits of old birds' nests and flakes of rusty metal shake loose from the rafters and drift down around us.

We stay a while that way, my cousin, my dog, and me, hearing the growling above and feeling the earth shake under us.

I don't mind it. Not one bit.

Frankie and me are going to make Pete famous.

Frankie and me are going to save Pete's life.

Chapter 6

Old Sam

When the last of Crash's riders has gone up the road like crap through a goose, Frankie, Butch, and me scramble up the bank and watch the cloud of settling dust. Frankie and me are giggling like girls that none of them knew we were hiding under the bridge the whole time, but Butch is mad that he missed them and it's a good long while before he quits his barking.

"I bet I know where they been," I tell Frankie. "Up to Sam's place."

Soon as the words leave my mouth, I remember what Mr. Hudspeth said in his store, how Crash Callahan and his boys tore Sam's chicken coop apart, and that I shouldn't be laughing at all.

My feet are moving before I even know it, down the road, the opposite way the riders have gone.

"Come on, Frankie. We better go check on him."

"Few things you should know about Sam," I tell Frankie as we walk. It's about a mile and the day is hot now, with insects buzzing in the hedges and Butch trotting dutifully alongside. "He's hard of hearing, so talk loud if you talk at all, which you shouldn't because he don't much like talking. Second, he's got a smell to him. Pretend like you don't smell it. Lastly, now that I think on it, he might also have a typewriter for us."

"How so?"

"Because old Sam's a pack rat. He never throws *anything* away if he can help it, and Lord above, he helps it." Fact of the matter is, in Sam's musty trailer he keeps everything from empty milk bottles to spent cartridges to *LIFE* magazines. Ma says it's on account of the Depression; Will says it's on account of Sam being crazy. But crazy or not, Sam is famous in our valley for killing a whole mess of Germans in World War I in a place called the Argonne Forest in France.

Samuel Williamson was born with a rifle in his hands.

It's close to noon when we spy Sam's silver trailer shining at us from under the trees. He's lived by himself here ever since his wife, Myrtle, passed. You can tell it's Sam's place because of the mailbox Myrtle made for him: a box of tin hand-painted red, white, and blue atop a four-by-four post at the edge of the road.

When we come up, we find Sam wrapping a line of barbed wire around it.

He's wearing a wide straw hat and long underwear with the sleeves rolled up over his thick, muscular forearms. Sam's got a body like a bull, and the beard around his chin is like steel wool. He straightens up when I call out his name, watery eyes squinting at us from under the deep shade of the hat. The rifle comes up with him: a lever-action .22.

"Who's that?" The words come out like a breeze through marsh reeds. Old. Strong.

A real breeze blows then, and we smell something awful.

"It's Jack Elliot and his cousin," I shout.

The rifle dips. Sam's beard twitches in what might pass for a smile.

"Better than I was expecting. And what's Jack Elliot and his cousin want?"

Truth be told, we only come out this way to check on him after the riders. But I don't want to say that. I don't want to tell this old man I was worried for him.

"We're looking for a typewriter," Frankie says suddenly, loudly, at my side. "Thought you might be a good person to ask."

Sam turns the watery eyes on Frankie, looks him up and down.

"You're Effie's boy what lives in the city."

"Yes, I am," Frankie answers.

"You look it." Plucking a dirty handkerchief from his pocket, Sam snatches the hat from his head and dabs at his forehead. He returns the hat and goes back to staring at Frankie.

Insects buzz.

I look at the barbed wire.

"Trouble with the hogs?" I ask, though I know it ain't.

Sam's red face gets redder. "Not hogs, not hogs," he growls. "That's the *Hoodlums* did that."

Sam gives a mighty sneeze, and his body shakes with the force of it.

"Daggumit!" He whips the handkerchief to his nose and blows, a car horn blasting along the roadside. "Hay fever," he wheezes through the rag. Then he goes on: "The Hoodlums was out of range by the time I made the porch. But I shoulda knowed. They been coming once a week now, hollerin' like the devil's own in the middle of night and sometimes in the middle of day. Them fellers is getting bold."

Sam sighs and leans against Myrtle's red, white, and blue mailbox. He looks at us.

"So you boys are looking for a typewriter? Myrtle mighta had one. Let's see."

Sam's trailer is a jungle of junk inside. On a leaning pinewood table, I spy a pair of old fishing reels and spools of thread, cans of turpentine, empty boxes of Cracker Jack, and a roll of duct tape. Towers of dusty *LIFE* magazines from 1957 teeter in a corner; a machete balances at the edge of a dresser just above them. There's no place to stand—the floor is covered with empty milk bottles standing row after row to the trailer's far side. Milk bottles fill moldy cardboard boxes in the hall. Milk bottles stand like nutcrackers on the windowsill. Milk bottles cluster on a sagging bookshelf. And winking dimly at us from under the dusty fabric of a sunken coach: more milk bottles.

Over all of it, glowing softly white in the dim light, are chicken feathers, and that reminds me of how Hank Wistar said Sam stashed his chickens inside when Crash tore the door off his coop.

"Best if you boys wait here," Sam husks as he disappears into the back. Soon, we hear sounds of him rummaging about, and the clinking of more bottles. Milk, I suppose, but maybe not.

When Sam returns he carries a squat, grayish hunk of metal in his arms. A pair of knobs stick out of both sides. A single sheet of yellow paper floats out the top.

"Oh, it's perfect!" I say.

"Don't say that 'til you know if it works," he grunts. "I expect it does."

He drops the typewriter into my outstretched arms, and it's so heavy Frankie has to shoot over to help me hold it, knocking over a dozen milk bottles as he does.

"I best be giving you a ride back," Sam says. "Don't expect you'll make it otherwise."

Frankie and me carry the typewriter into the yard and somehow manage to lift it into Sam's battered truck, where we wedge it safely between us in the front seat. Sam waits until Butch is settled in the bed, then coaxes the engine to life.

As we roll out of Sam's place, past his red, white, and blue mailbox and its new barbed-wire fence, I look at Frankie and can hardly believe our luck.

Later that night, while my family watches Walter Cronkite on the evening news, Frankie and me slip away to the barn to try out our typewriter.

I've pinched a candle from the kitchen and it only takes me two matches to get it lit. It's a fine, cheery little flame that takes to the wick, and in its yellow light, Frankie rolls a piece of paper into the machine and starts to type. The keys seem loud as gunshots in the big dark barn.

Frankie's fingers flow quick over the keys, and I'm impressed he don't have to stop and look for the right letters. When he's done, I lean in and see what he's written:

NOW IS THE TIME FOR ALL GOOD MEN TO COME TO THE AID OF THEIR COUNTRY.

I whistle soft and low.

"Well, we've got our typewriter," Frankie replies, smiling. "So when do we find this fighter jet?"

I bite my lip.

"What?"

"I ain't exactly asked Pete and Will about you coming along with us just yet, Frankie. And truth be told . . . they won't like it."

In the candle's flickering light, Frankie's face changes: the smile leaves and his dark eyes seem to grow glints in them, like sharp rocks deep beneath the surface of still water.

"Because I'm a city boy. And city boys aren't tough at all, are they?"

I don't answer him, but he's right. That's exactly why.

Frankie frowns. "Jack, that is honest to goodness bullshit."

I'm surprised to hear Frankie cussing, but before I can speak a word he goes on.

"All right, so I don't like spiders, or snakes, or being in the middle of nowhere without so much as a streetlight or a car horn to let you know there's other people living on the planet too. Lots of people don't live like that, but that doesn't make them soft. You know what it's like where my family lives? I'll tell you. A week into the riots, four boys from the West Lake housing projects drove into my neighborhood and stopped at the corner store at the end of my block. It's a place to buy sandwiches and cigarettes, and maybe that's what they were there to do. Or maybe they were there to burn the place down. Nobody knows because some men on the rooftop shot them all. Ever wake up to gunshots? It sounds like a car backfiring except it doesn't stop. One of the West Lake boys died that night, and it didn't look good for the other three when the ambulance took them away. Now, my old man is a cop, and he's looking for those men. Alone. Without me. Because he and my mom think I'm safer if I'm here with you. But I want my father safe, Jack. I don't want him getting shot too. And there's nothing I can do to help him here. So I'll go on your adventures. I'll write your stories. But I won't have you think for one second I'm not tough as you."

When Frankie finishes there's tears in those dark eyes, and I'm so shocked and ashamed of myself, it's a while before I can even think to say anything. Here I am sick half to death worrying about my brother, who's alive and safe and still right here at home with me. Meanwhile, Frankie's worrying about his father chasing murderers in a place that's on fire.

Frankie wipes his eyes, still frowning, but the anger's gone out from him, out of his voice now. "And I think that's why I want to help you, Jack. Because I can't protect my father. But maybe I can help you save your brother. Maybe I can help you keep Pete."

The candle's tiny flame sways, and the liquid wax around the wick brims over the edge and goes running down the candle, cooling and slowing as it goes.

"Frankie, I had no idea," I manage, and I feel tears starting in my own eyes now. "I'm sorry. God's honest truth, I'm sorry. And I'm thanking you from the bottom of my heart for helping me."

Frankie sniffs one last time and wipes his nose with his sleeve.

"Forget it."

The next morning I find Pete whittling on the porch. Will sits on the picnic table, reading a newspaper article on Bobby Kennedy, who's ahead in the polls.

I come right out and say it: "Pete, me and Frankie want to come along with you and Will to find that old wrecked fighter jet."

Will, from the table: "No."

Pete pauses, his knife perched at the edge of the stick. He cocks an eye at me through his long, straw-colored hair.

Will again: "No. Pete, they can't come!"

Pete grins and closes his pocketknife. "That's a hard slog into them hills, Jack. A whole county away and likely bombs laying about. Is Frankie tough enough for it?"

Frankie comes around the side of the porch. "Even city boys know not to step on bombs."

Will throws the paper down. "It's miles away over rough country. No way!"

"Frankie's plenty tough!" I tell him. "He'll do just fine!"

Pete turns his green eyes on our cousin. "You ever been camping, Frankie?"

"Never."

My jaw drops. *"Never?"*

Will grins triumphantly and jabs a finger at us. "See? Useless! Pete, tell him he can't come."

"I am *not* useless," Frankie shoots back. "I can carry whatever needs carrying."

I feel the whole thing slipping away. "Frankie has to come!" I cry out. "He just *has* to."

Will draws a deep breath, and I can tell he's about to let loose, but Pete waves his hand and everybody goes quiet.

"If Frankie can prove he's tough enough, then he can come. If not, then he can't."

Will's face darkens. He's been overruled and he's mad.

I grin. "Ha!"

"I'll be the final judge of whether he's tough enough," Pete declares. "And I'll decide what he has to do to prove it." His eyes sweep over the three of us, daring us to argue with him. Will is fuming; I can almost see smoke coming from his nostrils, but he keeps quiet.

Beside me, Frankie says not a word, but his dark eyes are leveled right at Pete.

Pete flicks his pocketknife open again and goes back to whittling his stick.

"What do I have to do?" Frankie asks.

Pete don't even look up. "Nothing too hard. Jump into the Sucker Hole is all. Off them railroad pilings."

My eyes grow wide. *The railroad pilings?*

Will grins. "Hope city boys can swim," he says as he goes back to his newspaper.

"Of course they can!" I insist, hoping hard that it's true. "You'll see."

Frankie is silent, but his eyes jump to me.

"Oh, we will," Pete says. "This afternoon."

I lead Frankie for the barn, walking slow and easy. When we get far enough away from the porch that my brothers can't hear, he whispers to me.

"I have to jump from *where*?"

47

"Just off some old railroad pilings, that's all."

"And what is the Sucker Hole?"

"A nice, deep part of Apple Creek. It's great for fishing. It's great for catching suckers."

Frankie shakes his head. "I'll say."

Chapter 7

The Sucker Hole

The Sucker Hole is dark and green and flat as a windowpane, a still stretch of Apple Creek that lies between the teetering stone pillars of the ruined Coatesville railroad bridge. On either bank, the crumbly stacks lean toward one another like old men in a long talk, moss and tufts of green grass poking through here and there and flicking in the wind like hair on their stony scalps.

The builders of the Coatesville line placed those stones a long time ago. They laid tracks, they raised a bridge, and poor Apple Creek had to amble along underneath it while freight trains thundered across day and night. Then came a war. The railroad and its bridge were stripped, their steel skeletons carried off to cities to be made into guns or tanks or bombs, and all that was left were those two towers—and 'course Apple Creek, same now as it was then or would ever be.

The creek took them in, those lonely heaps of stone, and now herons nest on top of the stacks and fish collect around their bases in thick, silvery clouds—minnows and smallmouth bass and largemouth bass and trout.

Or, as we call them, suckers, which is how this place came by the name the Sucker Hole.

The piling this side of Apple Creek is charred black in places from a brush fire long ago. The moss grew back extra thick and soft, but you can still fit your fingers in between the rough stone blocks. That's extra helpful for the climb, near thirty feet straight to the top.

And that's where Frankie has to make his jump.

Pete pulls off his shirt as he steps out onto the creek bank. "Water looks good today," he says, tossing his shirt onto a fallen tree.

"Looks the same as it does every day," says Will as he kicks off his shoes. He balls up his socks and stuffs them in before unbuttoning his shirt.

Looking at the glassy smooth water, I decide that Pete's right: the water looks extra smooth. Perfect, even. I strip down right quick and lay my clothes next to his on the log.

My brothers and me always swim naked because there's never anybody else around to see us. But once I've stripped down, I turn around and see Frankie with his mouth hanging open, a horrified kind of look on his face.

"What are you *doing*?"

"What's it look like? Swimming!" I ain't yet, but I will be soon.

"Naked?"

"'Course I'm naked. We *always* swim naked."

Frankie stares.

"What on earth *for*?"

Behind us, Pete and Will run into the creek for their traditional race to the far bank. In two seconds, that peaceful green water is roiling with their kicks and splashes.

"*Because*, Frankie, that's how we do it." I sigh. Hot sand begins burning my feet. "Ain't nobody out here but us, so don't be so bashful. Strip on down and get in!"

Frankie shakes his head.

"But, Frankie! You got to! You can't swim with your clothes on."

The sand is *really* burning my feet now. I begin to hop from one foot to the other.

"Look, I'll even turn around while you undress, okay?" I say. "Just leave your clothes on the log next to ours and come on in when you're done."

Pete and Will are racing back to our bank by the time I run into the water. Pete wins. Pete always wins. He comes up from the shallows and shakes the water from his shaggy head, throwing drops every which way. Will comes up coughing, his chest heaving. He's barely caught his breath when Pete scoops a handful of mud and throws it at him, splattering him along his neck.

Before I know it, the three of us are flinging mud fast and hard as we can. I take a stinging slap in the chest. Pete hits Will across the back. I beam Pete upside the head. When it's over we dive under and let the easy current wash us clean. I stay a little longer under the surface, just to feel the smooth silt under my toes and the easy pull of the water. When I come up, I wipe the water from my eyes and look to the bank to see if Frankie's gotten undressed yet.

The bank is bare. Frankie is nowhere in sight.

My heart flips.

Did he leave?

Quickly, I run my eyes along the path along the creek. No sign of him.

Frankie's quit.

I'm just about to swim for shore to see if I can't catch up to him when there's a sputtering sound to my right. Turning, I see Frankie, coming up for air.

"It's cold," he says through chattering teeth.

Will glides over. "So, city boys can swim after all!"

Pete joins him, and now my brothers are circling us like sharks.

"Did you tell him about the eels, Jack?" Pete asks. "Should have seen the one we found last week, Frankie. About this big around." He touches the thumbs and index fingers of both hands together in a wide circle. "Must have been ten feet long!"

I splash at him. "Don't pay him no mind, Frankie. Ain't no eels in Apple Creek."

"Plenty of snakes, though!" Will pipes up. "Water moccasins and copperheads."

"And snapping turtles," Pete adds.

"Yeah, and every one of 'em all scared off thanks to your kicking and splashing," I tell them.

Frankie ain't paying attention. Instead, he takes a deep breath and slips under the surface. Gracefully, he swims to the far bank, coming up for air only twice, making hardly no more than a ripple each time. My brothers and me watch him swim back to us in silence.

"See?" I say triumphantly. "He'll do just fine on the expedition."

"We ain't swimming into them hills, fool," Will snaps. "And just because he can swim all right don't prove if he's tough enough." He looks to Pete. "Let's get to jumping and then we'll see."

Pete frowns. He wanted to swim a while longer before we got down to business. Our cousin comes up alongside us, treading water quietly. "All right, Frankie. Time to climb."

The valley spreads out below us like a painting, Apple Creek glittering yellow diamonds as it ribbons away through the trees. The wind whips across the stony tops of the pilings, blowing hot in my ears and in my hair. Already it's dried the water from my naked body.

We stand at the edge to catch our breath. My arms still burn from that climb, and I've lost feeling in the tips of my fingers from gripping the stones so hard. Frankie's chest heaves and his face is flushed, but if he's scared any about the jump, he don't show it. Pete stands with his hands on his hips, head back, eyes closed to the bright bowl of blue sky above. The freckles on his nose look darker in the sun. He lets the wind throw his blond hair back from his face. He is feeling every part of the day.

Will ain't having any of it. He's all business, with his arms folded across his chest and one foot slapping the stones impatiently.

"Come on, come on," he says. "Get on with it."

"Let him take his time," Pete replies, not bothering to open his eyes. "We got all day."

I see a heron drop from a tree on the far bank and go to point it out to them.

"Hey, you guys—"

Without a word, Frankie steps off the piling and into thin air.

I gasp.

Frankie falls. Arms out, toes together. It feels like forever. And still Frankie keeps on falling, getting smaller and smaller against the vast, deep green of the Sucker Hole.

His splash is a quiet little sound. Pete misses it entirely. By the time he peers over the edge, Frankie has already broken the surface. He treads water for a long minute, his head bobbing up and down in foamy white water. Then he looks up at us, and he waves.

We spend the rest of the afternoon swimming in the Sucker Hole. When our fingers get to wrinkling, we crawl out of the creek and lie on the sandy bank all in a row, like crocodiles, to dry in the sun. After a spell, the Sucker Hole gets glassy-smooth and peaceful again. It's about three o'clock, and in sun that bright all you can do is close your eyes and watch the orange, fuzzy shapes that flit and float behind your eyelids.

I am almost asleep when Frankie asks his question:

"You fellas ever eat an eel?"

"Can't say I have," Pete answers sleepily.

"I have."

That makes me open an eye. "That so?"

"Every Christmas," Frankie tells us. "My grandmother dices them and fries them in a pan."

"Huh."

"Yeah, and you want to know something else?" Frankie asks.

"What's that?" Pete yawns.

"They jiggle."

"They what?" Pete looks at him.

"They jiggle," Frankie says again. "The meat twitches in the pan. It looks like the frying pan is filled with live pieces of eel. Something about the heat makes the meat twitch. They're ready to eat when they stop twitching."

Pete chuckles. "That so? I'll bet they taste like chicken," he says.

We lie in silence for a time. Beyond slow-moving water, Knee-Deep Meadow hums.

Will starts snoring.

I imagine a panful of twitching eel meat and my stomach does a somersault. But then the valley sighs, and I feel its gentle breath move over my bare skin. That sun ain't so bad when there's a breeze blowing. And when the leaves whisper to each other . . .

Pete drifts off next.

It's a little while before Frankie's easy breathing tells me he's fallen asleep too.

I lay an arm across my eyes to block some of that sun, and the orange, fuzzy shapes swimming across my sight go dark . . .

Sun is sinking low in the treetops and long shadows are stretching themselves across the bank when I wake up. Everybody else is still asleep, their easy snores drifting downstream in the current. I lie a while on coarse creek sand and wait for sleep to take me again.

What does sizzling eel sound like? The thought squirms into my head and I sigh. I push it away and turn on my side.

Maybe it sounds like bacon, frying up on the stove? That might be right. Sort of a crackle and maybe even a hissing . . .

I sigh long and easy and try to let myself wander off again. But my mind won't quit, and now I'm wondering if maybe frying pieces of diced eel meat might sound like a girl giggling.

Now, John Thomas, that is surely one of the oddest thoughts you have ever had.

I shift again in the sand but I'm still hearing somebody giggle in my mind.

And across the creek.

I come a little more awake.

Another giggle.

I go suddenly very still.

Holding my breath, I listen—to Apple Creek's murmuring, Knee-Deep Meadow's humming, and my own beating heart, which is getting louder and louder inside my head.

Every boy has a sixth sense that lets him know when he's being watched, and right now mine is buzzing like crazy.

The sound comes again! This time I sit bolt upright, certain now that someone is watching us. I snap my head about the bank, searching, but I see nothing, not a thing—but then movement catches my eye, movement from across the creek: a splash of sunlight on bright colors beneath the trees, white and blue against the darker greens. Floral patterns? Slowly my mind picks the colors apart, and I piece it together that I'm seeing sundresses on Apple Creek's far bank.

Sundresses?

Girls!

Three girls stand on the far bank, pointing at us and giggling.

And us boys are as naked as can be.

My blood runs cold.

"Fellas, wake up!" I shout and roll over to cover myself up. But it don't do me much good because now I'm mooning the three girls across the creek. Their giggles turn to howls.

"Pete! Will! Frankie! Wake up!" I give Will a swat and he sits up slowly, rubbing his eye with a fist.

"Jack, what the—"

He sees the girls and freezes as the color drains from his face.

"Holy smokes!" he cries out as he rolls over too, and now we're *both* mooning those girls. They shriek even louder, and that jolts Frankie awake. Seeing the girls, he instantly flattens himself on his stomach beside us.

"You said no one comes down here!" he shouts at me.

"No one ever does!" I shout back.

"Both of you shut up and get to the pilings!" Will screams as he dives forward, army-crawling as fast as he can for the cover of those stones. Frankie and me scuttle after him, kicking up jets of river sand as we go and showing those laughing girls our backsides the whole way.

The girls on the far bank are just about falling over with laughter now. Something about their laughs sounds awfully familiar, but I don't waste time stopping to look. It feels like a mile to the piling, and by the time I get there I ain't got a shred of dignity left. We flatten ourselves against the mossy stones, gasping for air. Then I realize: there's just three of us.

"We forgot Pete!"

Will cusses fiercely.

Dropping to my hands and knees, I crawl to the edge of the piling and peer around.

And there he is. Pete is still fast asleep on the bank. Flat on his back. Totally naked. He ain't moved.

"Pete!"

He don't hear me. He don't hear anything. In between those awful shrieks of laughter, his gentle snores continue slow and steady.

Across the water, the girls have come out from under the trees. They stand along the bank, hugging themselves in amusement. And now I know why one of those voices sounds so familiar.

Anna May wears a blue blouse and a yellow skirt, and her golden hair is held back in a light-blue headband.

"Oh no," I breathe.

Will tenses. "What?" he demands. "What? Who is it?"

"Nobody," I lie.

He hauls me back from the edge and peers around it himself. He snaps back like a rubber band, a look of complete horror on his face.

Anna May calls to us. "Danger, Will Robinson! Or should I say Will Elliot? Are you just going to leave your brother out there all alone?" She is laughing herself silly, the sound skipping across the water, echoing off the stones. Will balls up a fist and bites down hard on one knuckle. "Oh my God, this can't be happening," he says to himself. "This is a dream. I'm still asleep."

Across the creek her voice twinkles again. "Ooh, and you left your clothes!"

"You're not dreaming, Will," Frankie says bitterly. "And she's right."

Our clothes are on the log where we left them. Thirty feet away.

"You can't just walk around without any *clothes*," Anna May chides, her sweet voice becoming suddenly serious. "It's not decent."

She places her hands behind her tiny waist and leans ever so slightly out over the water as she says it. That warm breeze blows again, and it ripples her skirt. She's lovely. And horrible.

The girls behind her break into fresh peals of laughter. Will sinks to his knees. His face is a sickly grayish green.

"I'm going to throw up."

My mind is whirring, trying to understand it. There's a walking trail on the far side of the creek. That must be it. They must have been out walking and come up on us while we were sleeping.

"Mind that edge if I was you, Anna May."

I stop.

Will freezes.

Anna May goes as still as a statue.

Pete ain't moved from his spot on the bank. He lies the same as before, hands behind his head, eyes shut. But now we all know without a doubt that he ain't sleeping. Pete's awake. And he's *been* awake.

"It's hard to see from where you're standing, but your bank is crumbling," Pete goes on, still lying there. "If it were to collapse, why, you'd fall into the creek. And then I'd have no choice but to swim over there and rescue you."

Anna May leaps back from that bank like she's been stung by a wasp.

Pete sits up, slow and easy like. He waves. Then, taking all the time in the world, he stands up straight and tall. Turning toward the girls, he spreads his arms wide.

The girls stare.

Frankie and me stare. Will is weeping.

"Hey, you girls care for a swim?" Pete asks, grinning. "You're more than welcome. Except the thing is, this is a private beach. And we have only one rule: no clothes allowed."

And there he stands, my brother Pete, naked as the day he was born, holding forth with Anna May Fenton and her friends like he's inviting them to sit down to tea.

Anna May's mouth opens and closes, but she don't make any sound. Then she says in a soft voice, "No, thank you, Pete. We were only . . . taking in the sights."

Pete's smile widens. "That you were." Behind Anna May, her two friends are speechless. They are all staring at my brother.

Anna May frowns and sticks out her chin. "We're sorry to have interrupted your nap. But we will be continuing on our walk now, thank you very much."

Pete gives a slight bow. "You are quite welcome, ladies. But consider this our standing invitation to come back anytime."

Anna May nods her head once, then takes two steps backward until she's joined the other girls. She nods again, and then, ever so slowly, she turns and leads them back to the trail on the far side of the creek.

It's a long time before the girls disappear completely into the trees. They take their time going, and I wonder if they ain't doing it on purpose.

Pete watches them go. Then, once he's sure they've left, he strolls over to the log and gathers up our clothes. Walking them over to us, he tosses them in a heap. "All right, you chickens, it's safe now."

Slowly, I let out a breath I didn't know I was holding.

Pete pulls on his trousers, then tosses Will's shirt at him. "Come on, Will," he says. "You can't just walk around without any clothes on. It's not *decent.*"

Will don't move. He stares into the trees, his shirt crumpled in his lap.

"I can never talk to her again."

"What are you talking about? You'll see her Sunday," Pete tells him in a cheerful voice.

I don't know what ails Will, but I am so impressed at Pete, I can't help myself.

"Holy cow, Pete!" I exclaim as I pull a sandy sock over one foot. "You chased them girls right off real quick!"

Pete runs both hands through his shaggy hair and shakes out some sand.

"I guess so."

"You weren't afraid or nothing!" I turn to Frankie and throw him a big wink. "I bet this'll make a fantastic story, now, won't it?"

Frankie gives me a dark glare and pulls his shirt over his head.

"And that wasn't just any girl!" I go on. "That was *Anna May Fenton*! The prettiest girl in the whole school! Maybe the whole town!" I pull on my other sock. "Why, Anna May might even be the prettiest girl in the whole state!"

"Could be," Pete agrees, buttoning up his shirt. Taking his shoes by the strings, he swings them over his shoulder and begins up the bank for the path home.

"Frankie, what do you think?" I whisper. "Can we put *that* in the newspaper?"

Frankie walks right past me without saying a word, angrily following Pete.

Will is still sitting naked on the sand, a funny look on his face, as if he's just heard a sudden loud noise and lost his hearing. "Never again," he says softly. "I can never talk to her again."

Pete and Frankie are already into the trees, aiming for home. I run to catch up, kicking creek sand as I go. "Come on, Will! And like Pete said, don't worry. You'll see her again on Sunday!"

Chapter 8

THE TICKING TOMB

After the Sucker Hole incident, Will is so mad he don't talk to us for a whole day. He stomps down the stairs next morning, thumping his feet like an elephant, and he scowls all through breakfast so that Dad gives him a frown over the pages of the paper. He's only at the table long enough to shovel down a few forkfuls of Ma's fresh scrambled eggs before slamming through the screen door off to God knows where.

Dad don't even look up from the paper. "Pete, what happened?"

Pete crunches toast. "Sucker Hole yesterday. We were swimming and some girls saw us."

The paper comes down.

"Is that *all* that happened?"

Pete nods. "Yes sir. But Will's sweet on one of them."

Dad looks at Ma.

Ma frowns.

Dad goes back to his paper. Pete goes back to his toast. Ma watches him. You can't ever fool Ma. She knows there's more to it, but she lets it lie.

It'd be different if she knew just who it was we saw.

That afternoon Will catches me as I'm trying to sneak a stack of blank paper out to the barn. I'd steered clear of him all day, but he comes across the yard like a torpedo.

"Don't think Frankie's jumping yesterday means you two can come with us to find that fighter."

"Pete's judging him, not you," I fire back. "You're just mad you were wrong! Frankie's got plenty of courage."

"We'll see about that," Will snaps, and he storms off to where Pete is splitting logs behind the woodpile. I don't like that at all.

I rush and deliver the extra paper to Frankie at the typewriter in the barn. Then it's back to bright sunlight: I got to find Pete and tell him not to listen to any of Will's talk. I'm surprised to see both my brothers marching toward me. Will looks mighty pleased.

"Frankie's got to do another test," Pete says.

I ignore Will's gleeful smile and ask Pete, "Ain't his jump at the Sucker Hole proof enough?"

"This will be a different kind of test," says Pete. "The Sucker Hole tested his physical courage. This will be a test of his *mental* courage."

"Sounds stupid to me," I declare. "Courage is courage! Will's just sore he got spied on by a group of sneaky girls."

Will goes beet red and opens his trap to holler at me, but Pete waves him off.

"I'm final judge, Jack. And I say Frankie's got to do another test."

Pete's mind is made up.

I sigh. "What's it got to be this time?"

Pete shakes his head. "Not now. Tonight. You'll find out tonight."

Will gives me a last nasty smile as they walk away.

It ain't fair. The whole reason we want to go on the expedition is so we can make Pete famous enough that he won't get drafted. Now he and Will are doing everything they can to keep us from going.

I go back to the barn and find Frankie hunched over his typewriter. I tell him.

"It doesn't matter, Jack," he says. "Whatever it is, I can handle it."

"Yeah, but you don't know my brothers," I say. "They'll come up with something really awful. They'll—"

I stop when I see his face.

"Okay," I say.

He goes back to typing.

I wait on pins and needles all that afternoon. At dinner, my brothers carry on like normal, fighting with each other and gulping down Ma's mashed potatoes like it's any old evening. Will is cheerful, and that gets me worried. I watch them both like a hawk all through supper.

When dinner ends, we wash and dry the dishes and then gather around the television to watch Walter Cronkite. On the TV, it's more clips of people protesting in the streets, waving big hand-painted signs. After that, it's boys jumping out of a helicopter in Vietnam, a flare trailing smoke.

I'm feeling crazier than a firefly in a jelly jar when Ma sends Frankie and me up the spiral staircase to bed and my brothers *still* ain't said anything.

"When are they gonna tell us?" Frankie asks me on our way up the steep stairs.

"I got no clue."

It must be an hour that I lie awake, trying to figure it out, while I stare at the cracks in the ceiling and listen to the snakes hunt mice in the attic above it.

"Hey, Frankie," I say suddenly.

"Huh?" His voice is thick with sleep.

"Suppose this *is* the test?"

"How do you mean?"

"You know, the *waiting*. Maybe there ain't no other test and they're just seeing how long we can stand not knowing?"

Frankie turns on his mattress to face me.

"I don't think that's it, Jack."

The good feeling I have whisks away, like a bubble of spit on the wind.

There is a sudden, muffled grating from the ceiling above me, a sound of scales against wood beams. I listen a while more, wondering if the mouse got away or if he's now dinner for a big old black snake.

I yawn. It ain't the most pleasant thought to fall asleep to, but I've had worse.

"Wake up!"

I sit up into a beam of blinding light.

"Ouch!"

"Wake up!" Pete whispers again. The beam of light swings over to where Frankie sits on his mattress, rubbing his eyes.

"What time is it?" I ask. The blood in my veins feels thick and slow.

"Shh!" is all Pete says, and he snaps off the light. He moves to the open window and I see his familiar shape cut out against the stars. Then he's gone, and it's just velvety night filling the empty frame. The gutter rattles. A few seconds later, we hear a quiet thud as Pete jumps to the porch roof below.

The flashlight's left a dull ache behind my eyes, but all the same I'm filled with a sudden, breathless thrill.

"This is it!" I whisper to Frankie as I pull on my shoes.

He meets me at the window, blinking back the sleep from his eyes. There's movement down below: Pete and Will in silvery moonlight. Pete waves at us to hurry.

Frankie's eyes jump to mine. For a second I think he won't do it. Then in one easy movement he is through the window and reaching for the gutter.

We move like clouds across the moon, soundless, down the lane for the ink-dark trees along Apple Creek. Mist blows across the yard, pale fingers clutching at the bare skin on my arms and legs. By the time we reach the trees, my feet squish in soggy shoes.

Pete leads. He don't use the flashlight; he follows the trail by memory. He takes us fast past the invisible tree trunks, and soon I'm sweating in the night's cool air.

Apple Creek lies hidden under a shroud of mist. A handful of stars burns fierce and bright above, and Pete runs us faster in their twinkling light.

We run along the creek bank for a time, through a patch of rubbery jewelweed that glistens in the faint starlight and on past a stand of sycamores. One of their roots reaches up and snatches at my toe and I stumble, throwing my hands out wildly to grab hold of something, anything. My fingers close on empty dark, and I'm pitching over the bank toward that soft cloud that hangs over Apple Creek when Frankie snatches my shirttail and drags me back.

I don't have breath enough to thank him. Pete moves us on, faster.

Where is he taking us? And what sort of test have they got planned for Frankie?

The Sucker Hole's stony towers rise before us, then sink slowly away behind.

Still Pete leads us on.

Beyond the creek, Knee-Deep Meadow opens up, vast and white under the fog. For a moment the curtain parts, as if a breath from the stars has blown it back, and through the hole we can see the valley's far wall. A single orange light burns in that dark: a house across the way. It's visible only a moment before the fog rolls back and hides it from our sight.

Madliner House. As we run, I wonder who among them is awake this hour of the night.

I don't have long to think about it. Our trail turns suddenly, diving away from the creek toward a black hill that rises, silent and solemn, on our left. Starlight gleams on its bare face, the sparkle of Pennsylvania granite. We are running now between the toes of the Appalachians. Trees close in. Our trail hugs that rocky hill close. With the stars hidden, the darkness returns, so thick now that even Pete has to slow down.

Wet branches slap my arms and chest and once something crashes through the undergrowth to our left—something big.

A thought comes to me. A gnawing, anxious idea as to where Pete is leading us. The hairs on my arms rise on end. I remember Will's gleeful grin and my heart sinks.

Ahead our trail bends once more. A clearing. An open space between the hills. Pete slows his pace.

I know where we are now, and I shudder.

My brothers have brought us to the Ticking Tomb.

His name was Hiltch. Jacob Bartholomew Hiltch. And he was born to fight. First the Lenape when their war parties came down out of Pennsylvania's eternal blue forests to burn settlements along the Susquehanna, almost within sight of Philadelphia. Then the British, as a soldier with General Washington's Continentals. Along a dark Appalachian trail, a British musket ball did what the Lenape tomahawks could not, and Hiltch was laid to rest in a graveyard not far from Apple Creek. He was buried in his Continental uniform, with his watch, a gift from his wife.

Hiltch sleeps in his musty grave, and you do not fear him.

You fear his wife.

Hiltch had little enough peace during life that she keeps watch over him now that he's dead. Disturb his rest, stretch out over his grave and lie down flat before his weathered marker, and you'll hear her gift to him, that old watch, ticking six feet underneath you. Ticking—and calling her.

Tick. Tick. Tick.

Then you see her. Hiltch's wife. Hiltch's widow. Dead, but not too much. She's here to kill you.

Your only chance is to get out of that graveyard, over the stone wall or through the iron gate before her icy fingers close around your neck and throttle you.

At least, that's the story as Sam Williamson tells it. Old Sam, who saw her once when he was young, when he and friends came to the graveyard up Apple Creek one night years ago. Sam stretched out over Hiltch's grave that night. It was Sam who disturbed Hiltch's rest and summoned the woman in white. He told us the story around the fireside a few winters back. Pete laughed then. Will said he did not believe it.

But I believed the whiskered old man then. And I believe him now.

We come out of the trees and I see the graveyard lying before us, its leaning headstones poking out of soggy soil like the stony skeleton of some half-buried creature. A wandering stone wall rings them in. Fog washes against it like waves against a shore. There is only one way in: a wrought iron gate that hangs crookedly on its hinges.

Pete aims straight for it.

At Pete's touch, that gate opens without a sound.

He looks to each of us, as if waiting for someone to say they are too afraid to follow him in. When no one speaks, he turns and steps into the yard.

Will goes next.

Then Frankie.

Then me.

That stone wall closes us in among the forest of tombstones. We follow Pete over moldy earth as he threads his way between them. In dim starlight, I read the names on a few: John Trumble, Samson Babb, Thomas Hoopes. Others are so worn from centuries of rain and wind and ice that the names have washed away.

You can't help but feel you're trespassing when you walk through a cemetery at night. It's like you've gone into a stranger's home, unwelcomed. That guilt gnaws at me as we follow Pete deeper into the yard. And with it something else: the feeling that we are being watched.

I throw a few quick glances between the stones. Nothing. Old leaves crunch under my feet, and the noise throws my heart into my throat. It takes everything within me not to bolt for the gate then.

Hiltch's grave is in the far corner.

His stone is shorter than the others. Name's barely visible under the dirt and grime. We form a half circle about the grave and for a long time, no one speaks.

"Do you believe in ghosts, Frankie?" Pete asks.

A chill runs down my spine. Frankie shakes his head.

"Then this should be easy," Pete says. He points to the gravestone. "This here's the grave of Jacob Bartholomew Hiltch. He was killed by a musket ball in the Revolution that went clean through him. Long time ago and not far from here. He was buried with his pocket watch, a gift from his wife. If you lie down over this grave, you can still hear it ticking."

Frankie's eyes dart to mine. He understands now.

"Now, I mentioned Hiltch's wife," Pete continues. "She's a haint. She guards this tomb. She is summoned whenever anybody lies down over her dead husband's grave. If she comes, she'll kill us unless we're able to get clear of this graveyard in time. This is your test: lie across Hiltch's grave for *one whole minute*, and we'll know you're tough inside and out. Do that, and you can come with us to find that wrecked fighter jet."

Fog curls about the tombstones.

Frankie is silent.

My heart pounds inside my chest. *A whole minute!* I couldn't do it. Not for a million dollars. Not for ten million dollars.

Frankie's draws a deep breath. "Start counting," he says. He lies down over the grave, flat on his stomach, and turns his head to one side.

Pete looks to Will. Even in the dark I can tell he's impressed. Will scowls.

"All right, Frankie. One whole minute. Starting now." Pete raises his watch and starts the count.

We wait.

My blood feels like ice water in my veins. My cousin lies before us, his little body beneath a thin veil of fog. The graveyard is so dark, and I turn to the sky, trying to find one of those bright stars for just a little light, but the fog is too thick and the stars are hidden.

"Ten seconds," Pete says quietly.

That feeling of being watched lays hold of me again and I turn to the gate, and I see now that headstones block our way back to it: thick and black, jutting out of the mist at crooked angles. And there's something else: the gate is closed.

My heart skips a beat.

The gate is closed!

Did Pete close it when we came in? Impossible. Pete went in first. *I* came in last, and I didn't shut the gate.

"Pete, the gate's shut."

Will snaps his head up. "Fool! What'd you close the gate for?"

"I didn't!"

"Twenty seconds," Pete says, softly.

At our feet, Frankie is still as stone. He looks dead.

The hairs on the back of my neck rise and it's colder now, so much colder than it should be for a June night.

Did someone else shut the gate? I sweep the yard, but it's just tombstones and shadows and—

"I hear it!"

At the sound of Frankie's voice, I just about jump out of my skin.

"Liar," Will whispers. "You don't hear nothing!"

Frankie's eyes are wide. "I hear ticking!"

Will looks at Pete.

"Thirty seconds," Pete says.

My body is shaking now, and goose bumps cover me from the back of my neck down to my soggy feet. Frankie is lying on top of Jacob Hiltch's grave, summoning his witch of a wife.

Or was she already here, waiting for us? Did *she* close the gate?

"Frankie, come away from there!" I whisper. "You don't have to do this! We'll find another way!"

"What's it sound like?" Will bends over him.

"Super loud! Like a freight train!"

A current of electricity charges down my spine at that. "Pete, call it off!"

Beside me, Pete says softly, "Forty seconds."

I snap back to the gate. A forest of tombstones blocks our way. We'll never make it out in time.

The fog's grown thicker too.

"It's ticking faster!" Frankie whispers.

"I don't hear nothing!" Will insists. "You're making it up!"

Frankie's face is pale, deathly pale. "It's beating like a drum!"

"Pete, call it off!" I cry again.

"Fifty seconds." Pete keeps his eyes on the watch.

Will stares, breathless. "He really hears it." And now I know Will is scared too.

"Fifty-five seconds."

My heart pounds. My skin crawls. I feel the urge to turn again to the yard. But I don't. I *can't*. My eyes are locked on the tombstone of Jacob Hiltch and my cousin lying before it.

Pete says softly, "Time."

The word echoes against ancient headstones, and the four of us hold our breath and listen.

The night around us is silent.

The witch ain't here.

Frankie stays flat and motionless.

"Frankie," I whisper, "you did it!"

He don't move.

Will leans over him. "You hear that? You did it, fool! You can get up now. Unless you *like* lying on a dead man's grave."

But Frankie stays still.

I drop down beside him and lay a hand on his shoulder. When his head turns, he looks at me like he's just woken up from a deep sleep.

"Is it over?" he asks.

"What you talking about?" Will says. "'Course it's over!"

"Couldn't you hear Pete counting out the seconds?" I ask Frankie fearfully.

He sits up slowly. Wet leaves stick to his front. "At first . . . but then all I could hear was that ticking! It just kept getting louder and louder. It wouldn't stop. And . . ." He pauses.

"And what?" Will asks.

Frankie looks straight into his eyes and says in a slow, deep voice, "I *felt* it. A drumming under the ground. As if . . . as if Hiltch was *alive*."

Will stares.

My knees go weak.

It ain't possible. Hiltch couldn't possibly be alive. He's been deader than a doornail for almost two centuries. But Frankie sits before us in the curling fog, his eyes so wide, and I know he ain't lying.

Will looks at him hard. His eyes rise to Pete, then dart about the stones. "Let's get out of here."

Pete shrugs. "Nicely done, Frankie." He drops the watch into his pocket. There's a click and his flashlight's bright beam spills yellow light over our cousin. Frankie's shirt clings to his chest and stomach. There are smudges of moldy graveyard dirt all down his front.

"So I passed the test, right?" he asks.

"I'd say so," Pete says. "And since I'm the final judge, that's all that counts."

Frankie looks to me then. Through my fading fear, realization seeps in: Frankie's passed their test. We are going with my brothers on their expedition.

Pete's flashlight swings away as he begins back through the headstones. Will follows, hands buried deep in his pockets.

"I don't think he heard anything," he mutters. "I think he made it up."

Frankie stands up and tries to brush some of those leaves off himself.

"Frankie, you did it," I whisper as we follow them back to the gate. "You did it!"

"Guess so," he says. "It wasn't that bad, really."

It's incredible. None of us has ever spent a whole minute over Hiltch's grave. Frankie ain't only tough. He's the toughest boy I've ever seen. Who would have thought a city boy would have that kind of guts?

But just then Frankie suddenly stops in front of me. Looking past him, I see Pete and Will have stopped too.

"What is it?" I ask.

No one answers.

Then I see her.

Beyond the beam of Pete's flashlight, standing among the stones, is a woman. A woman in white.

The witch is here.

Chapter 9

MADLINER PLACE

Fear has a taste. It's dead leaves and butterfly weed and moldy earth. It's a funny thing to think as I run through that graveyard in the fog and the dark with my brothers and my cousin and a witch chasing us. But I taste it just the same, even though my tongue is bone-dry in my spitless mouth as I gulp chilly night air—maybe for the last time—and force my rubbery legs to move even faster.

A tombstone rushes out of the dark. I twist away from its shovel shape, my knee scraping rough stone as I go. The next one catches me square in the stomach. I go right over it and land flat on my back, all the wind rushing from me in a sudden gust.

I lie on wet soil with that tombstone leaning crookedly above me. Whoever it belongs to, they'll be sharing it with me. That witch will kill me right here.

A pair of hands seizes my collar. It's Frankie. He drags me up and points wildly through the curling fog to the stone wall.

"Straight through and don't stop!" he shouts.

He don't make any sense. The wall is too high to jump, and we are nowhere near the gate. Then a piece of mist lifts and I see what he means: there's a section of the wall that's crumbled. It's hardly more than a heap of stones.

"Let's go!" he cries and, still holding on to my collar, he starts off through those tombstones once again.

A splash of yellow light sweeps across us: Pete's flashlight swinging crazily as he runs somewhere behind us. So the witch ain't got him yet. Then I hear Will cussing—awful, terrible things—but that's a relief too. If he's cussing, he ain't dead.

Frankie and me run along the wall. There's a white-hot fire in my lungs, its flames licking the insides of my ribs. My knee throbs where I scraped it against that stone. My breath comes in ragged gasps.

"There it is!" Frankie cries.

Mist rolls through the hole in the wall. It rushes past my face as Frankie and me hurtle through that opening and go rushing into black night beyond. Next thing I know we're crashing through high, wet grass and I'm laughing, laughing like crazy though there ain't nothing funny about it.

Trees ahead. Tall and dark and safe. The trail appears on our left and I angle myself toward it, pointing so Frankie can see where to go. Only he doesn't see; he keeps running straight and we bump. We stagger yet somehow keep from tumbling into the sea of fog that swirls about our knees. We keep running, and now thick tree trunks are dashing past us. We're into the woods.

"We made it, Frankie, we made it!"

"Shut up, you fool!"

Will's voice blasts in my ear and I realize he's been right behind us the whole time. Grabbing hold of us both, he shoves us down behind one of the trunks, and all three of us slide into dead leaves and wet earth. At once, I twist to look back, expecting to see that witch coming right for us, her pale bony arms out, fingers grasping—

But the field is empty. The witch is nowhere to be seen. And neither is Pete.

For one horrible instant, I think the witch has got him. Then there's a sound from behind me and a boy-shaped shadow drops into the leaves beside us. It's Pete. There's a few twigs in his moppy blond hair and he's breathing fast, but other than that, there ain't a scratch on him. Before we can say anything, he raises a finger to his lips and motions for us to follow him. In a heartbeat we're moving again—but not down the trail. Instead, Pete leads us up the side of a steep hill.

It's craziness, to my mind. We need to get as far away from here as we can. All the stories say you're safe once you get clear of the cemetery, but I don't want to take any chances.

My heart is still knocking about in my chest as we twist up the face of the hill, rising above the fog until we come to a clearing. Taking cover behind a fallen trunk, we peer down to the meadow and the graveyard below.

Pete looks at us.

"It ain't Hiltch's witch."

His words make no sense at first. But then he points down the hill. The meadow is empty; the cemetery is not.

The woman in white walks among slanted stones.

"The witch!" I gasp.

But Pete shakes his head. "No." And in a tight voice he says:

"It's Mrs. Madliner."

She ain't supposed to be able to walk.

Mrs. Madliner is bedridden. Wheelchair bound. Infirm. But there she is, walking from stone to stone, white robe hanging from bony shoulders and flowing to her feet, which are hidden in mist that's as pale as she is.

"Who is she?" Frankie asks in a trembling voice.

"A neighbor," Will answers. "Crazy as a loon! I'd rather have Hiltch's witch after us!"

But Mrs. Madliner ain't after us. She ain't even left the cemetery. As we watch, she stoops before a gravestone. After a long time, she rises and wanders on.

"What's she doing out here?" I ask.

"She's searching for someone," Pete says. "But I ain't got any idea who."

Mrs. Madliner drifts to another grave.

I shiver.

All I've ever known of Mrs. Madliner are the things I heard from Ma. They were friends when they were little and growing up together. Elmira was the town beauty when she was younger. Pale skin and large, dark eyes that seemed to hold captive just about every boy in New Shiloh. Then one day Arthur Madliner came to town. Where he came from, nobody knew. The marriage was quick—some thought too quick. Then Mr. and Mrs. Madliner moved out of town to the old house across the meadow from Stairways. Elmira was seen less and less. It wasn't long after Caleb was born that word got around she'd taken ill.

I strain for a glimpse of her face, but it's covered by a tangle of black hair.

"How come she didn't say nothing when we saw her?" Will asks suddenly. He's done being afraid. He's angry now.

Pete's shakes his head. "She's sick. Sick in the mind. Maybe she saw us. Maybe she didn't."

In the cemetery below, Mrs. Madliner drops before one of the stones. A sound rises through the fog: weeping.

She stays that way a long time. None of us say anything. We just watch. Then at last Mrs. Madliner rises. She crosses the graveyard once more and passes through the iron gate. We lose sight of her when she walks into the meadow and its wafting mist.

Finally, Pete stands up. Wordlessly, we follow him back down the hill toward the trail.

It's a while before I have the heart to talk again. "Why is she that way?"

Pete answers. "Nobody knows for sure. Ma says she was the same as everybody else when they were girls together. No one knows what happened after she married Arthur Madliner."

"Well, we know *he's* a damn liar," Will says. "His wife can walk just fine."

Pete is quiet for a time, then replies, "I get the feeling he doesn't know."

We walk through trees dark as the thoughts crowding our minds: If Mrs. Madliner can walk, why bother pretending that she can't?

We go slow, each of us listening to the Pennsylvania night around us—snapping sticks and rustling leaves. It's only when I feel firmer earth under us and realize that we've reached the trail home that I begin to relax any. Pete leads us along it, back to Apple Creek, where a fine mist is rising off the water and drifting toward the stars. We go for a time under their twinkling cold fires, but then our bank lifts and lets us see another light in the dark, that same orange ember burning far across the valley: Madliner House.

Nobody says anything, but somehow each one of us comes to a stop.

"Pete," I say then, "why on earth would anybody *pretend* to be paralyzed?"

"People pretend all the time, Jack. Usually to get away from something they're afraid of." Without turning from the house, Pete goes on, "I can't say for sure, but I wouldn't be surprised if Mrs. Madliner's illness was her protection."

"Against what?"

"Against Mr. Madliner. Her sickness came along a short while after he did. Lots of people in town like to talk and say he caused it, and maybe that's so. But I think it became a way to keep him away from her. He hits a lot."

Will begins to nod. "Yes . . . I could see that. Just like that book *I, Claudius*."

I got no idea what Will's saying, but Frankie does. "I read that one. It's about the Roman emperor who pretended to be a harmless idiot so nobody would find out how smart he was."

"Exactly," Will says. "His uncle was emperor and his family were a pack of murderers who'd kill anyone they saw as a threat to their power. So Claudius pretended to be crazy from the time he was a kid so they wouldn't hurt him."

"Did it work?" I ask.

Will shrugs. "Sure, for a little while. Claudius became emperor, as I remember."

"Then what happened?"

Frankie looks at me. "He spent all those years pretending to be something he wasn't, so he could survive his family. And in the end, his wife killed him."

Hours later I'm lying in bed again, staring at that same crack in the ceiling. Nothing moves in the attic now. Not the mouse I heard before. Not the snake that was after him.

Three o'clock. Soul's midnight, so Will says. Time of night you're closest to being dead. Pete and Will are snoring in their bunks. God knows how. A few hours ago, us boys were running for our lives through a cemetery.

I roll over and see Frankie on his mattress. Milky moonlight splashes down on him, and he looks like a castaway on a raft.

Ever wake up to gunshots?

"Frankie?"

I know he's awake, deciding if he wants to answer me or pretend he's asleep.

"Yeah?"

"Did you really hear that ticking at the tomb?"

Silence.

"Does it matter? I passed the test. Pete said we can go with him and Will to find the airplane wreck. And that's good material for story writing."

"That's true," I agree. "You passed, all right. I could never have done that, and I'm grateful. But—"

"But you want to know if I heard ticking from Hiltch's grave."

"Yes."

He rolls over on his mattress.

"Good night, Jack."

Another question I won't ever get answered.

I roll over and try to let my galloping mind tire itself out. Takes a while, but eventually that old horse slows himself down to a trot, then a walk. A faint scraping again from the attic. I decide it's my friend the mouse, that he escaped that old black snake after all.

A little while later Mrs. Madliner comes into the room—floats right over the windowsill and hovers above Frankie's mattress. I realize I've fallen asleep because I'm dreaming now. She's a frightful thing to see, red eyes and white dress that clings to her body, letting me see more of her than I should. Awful as she is, I decide she's better than those popping machine guns in my other dream—the one about Pete in that jungle. I wait for her to melt away into the dark. She shuts off the moon as she goes, and in that inky dark my tired old horse finally lays down to sleep.

Our kitchen smells like coffee and bacon. Morning sunlight spills through the windowpanes and shines through Frankie's ears, making them glow bright red as he eats his eggs at the corner of Grandma Elliot's old table. In that cheery light, the Ticking Tomb and Mrs. Madliner seem like a bad dream, though I know they ain't.

Will's buried in his newspaper, reading an article on Senator Kennedy campaigning in California. I catch his eyelids fluttering, and I know he's fighting sleep. Across from me, Pete's on his third biscuit, honey dripping from his fingers. Of the four of us boys, only he seems completely awake. At the stove, Ma tells him to get a napkin for the last time. When a big, fat yawn takes hold of me, I decide on a nap after breakfast.

The floorboards creak and a second later Dad strides into the kitchen, looping suspenders over his wide shoulders as he comes in. The kitchen shrinks around him, the whole place somehow smaller now that my father has entered it. He kisses the back of Ma's head, then crosses to the coffeepot to pour himself a cup of steaming black liquid. Without waiting for it to cool, he lifts it and drinks. Then he says something that makes my hair stand up straight:

"Arthur Madliner came by early this morning."

At his words, Will's head snaps up from his newspaper and Pete's hand stops with a biscuit halfway to his mouth. A thin strand of honey doodles shapes on Grandma Elliot's table.

Dad takes another long, slow sip before going on. "Storm the other night knocked down that oak in his yard. He needs help clearing it."

Us boys trade looks around the table, but Pete gives the barest shake of his head. I stuff another strip of bacon in my mouth and chew to keep myself from speaking, but the bacon does not taste so good anymore.

"So eat up," Dad continues. "And be ready to go after breakfast."

"Did Mr. Madliner say anything on *Mrs.* Madliner?" Pete asks, dabbing the spilled honey with a napkin, real casual, like he doesn't care a whip one way or the other.

"He did not." Dad drinks more coffee.

Will and Pete trade looks.

"Is Caleb gonna be there?" Will suddenly asks.

"It's his house," Dad says, sitting down and reaching for the bacon himself now. "I expect he will."

I shudder. Caleb Madliner. The bacon turns to hot lead in my stomach.

"You treat Caleb Madliner right," Ma says. "He's different and difficult, but he's got a harder life than you. And no brothers to help him live it."

"Frankie's got no brothers and he turned out fine," I say, before I can think any better. "Caleb could have fifty brothers and he'd still be awful."

Ma gives me a dark look. "Some people fight hard battles, Jack. Just be glad yours are so easy."

At Ma's words, I remember Mrs. Madliner wandering among the tombs last night, weeping like a lost soul. I guess I'd be awful if my mother was that way. Or if I had Arthur Madliner for a father. Now *there* was something to make you rotten. He was creepy to look at, like a pale aspen tree that had uprooted itself and gone wandering for better soil but couldn't find any.

Then there's what Pete said about him last night: *He hits a lot.*

Ma joins us at the table and our family eats together. If my parents know anything about last night, they don't let on. When Dad takes the sports page from Will's newspaper, I decide we must be in the clear. Only now I'm fretting this trip out to the Madliners' will force us to delay our search for the fighter jet another day.

Waterfall of sunshine soaks the whole world in gold as we climb into the pickup. Butch hops up for the ride and blinks his big brown eyes sleepily as he hunkers down by me and Frankie in the bed, his thick fur warm to the touch.

Dad brings the Ford to life, and soon the big tires are crunching gravel as we roll down the dirt lane. Apple Creek flashes at us through gray sycamores, calling to us. We turn onto Hopkins Road's smooth pavement and Dad gives the engine some gas. Warm wind makes Butch's fur ripple, and there's a sweet scent of honeysuckle in my nose. I imagine us stopping a while at the bushes along the road's edge, breaking the fragile green stems and drawing out the tiny, delicious drops . . .

But Dad keeps the Ford moving.

Almost a mile later, we come up on Sam Williamson's place: his trailer with its sagging porch and corrugated roof; his red-white-and-blue painted mailbox. Sam himself is sitting in a rocker on the porch, dressed in his same long underwear and wide-brimmed hat. He lifts a hand at us as we go by, and Dad gives the horn a tap.

Lonely Sam.

I watch his colorful mailbox drift into the distance for as long as I can, until green trees slide in between us and the little cheerful mailbox is gone. Then I feel Dad hit the brakes as he turns off Hopkins Road and onto a bumpy dirt lane that leads up a hill through dark, lonely trees.

The old white house does not stand at the top of its steep, rocky hill. It *leans*.

The walls are a dead, chalky white, and cracks run in the plaster along the wind-bitten north face overlooking the valley. They remind me of bone.

The trees don't get too close; they stay back, making a wide ring around the place, and as our dusty Ford leaves their protection, Butch raises his nose for a sniff, his pointy ears standing up straight.

Black, empty windows stare at us as we climb down—like deep, cold, fishless lakes.

"I like what they've done with the place," Pete says. When he slams his door, the sound is eerily loud, and it echoes off the house.

We follow Dad across the yard to the northwest corner. Coming around the side, we see that this was where the great oak tree stood. It alone had the courage to stand so close to the house, and it stands no more.

The great gray trunk lies across the yard. The top is hidden in a violent plume of green leaves. Branches, broken and blistering white in morning sun, lie trapped under the trunk, pinned by its incredible weight, or curling into the sky like the fingers of a dead hand.

There is a man beside the tree.

Tall. Lean. Black hair twitching in the wind. Mr. Madliner shakes Dad's hand when we come up.

"Right good of you to come, Gene," Mr. Madliner says. "Hate to trouble you with this." There is no feeling in the words.

"No trouble, Arthur," Dad answers him. "She was a terrific tree. Sorry you had to lose her."

Mr. Madliner casts coal-fired eyes over the giant that so narrowly missed his house. That's when a funny thought comes to me: maybe the old tree *wanted* to come down, not across the yard but on top of the house—just come crashing down with all its old strength. Maybe it knew what evil lurked there and had simply had enough. Watching Mr. Madliner look with such hate at the tree, I can see it being that way.

His eyes drift toward us boys, and my stomach tightens as I wait for it, wait for him to tell Dad what we all guess he knows about last night: *Gene, did you know your boys was out late spying on my wife? In a graveyard, no less?*

He doesn't.

"Bring the axes, Caleb," he says instead.

Like a ghost, Caleb comes out from the side of the house. I did not see him there before, waiting in the house's shadow. His dark hair falls in greasy swaths, covering most of his angular face. He's skinny under a faded flannel shirt. He crosses the yard in long, awkward steps, like a fawn fresh on its legs, carrying an armful of frighteningly clean and bright-looking axes. He drops them at his father's feet, where they lie, gleaming in the grass.

Mr. Madliner draws a breath, and I hear it rattle around inside him. Then, in that same toneless voice, he begins to explain how we'll cut up the oak. Listening to his odd, unwavering voice, I know it for sure: he don't know about last night.

"We'll trim those branches first, cutting each into logs," Mr. Madliner says. "Those leafy boughs we will dump over the side of the hill, down to the ravine. Then we'll cut the trunk into pieces. Gene, you and your boys take whatever you can haul. The wood will be good and dry come wintertime. It should burn well."

He explains a few other things, but I don't listen. My mind is reeling. I look over to Pete, but he shakes his shaggy head ever so slightly in a wordless warning.

We take up our places along the oak. Looking along the trunk, I try to guess how high it stood, and I figure it must have been at least eighty feet. I lay a hand on the rough, gray bark, warm in the sun.

"It died with a scream."

I turn and look at Caleb Madliner, who is suddenly standing beside me.

"What do you mean?"

"When it came down, it screamed," he says simply.

That doesn't make any sense to me, but I don't bother asking him again. I don't want to hear him. Just then, from farther on down, I hear the first sounds of Dad's ax biting into the bark. Caleb lifts his hatchet to do the same, and as he bends, a piece of his long, greasy hair slides away from his face and I see the dark purply-green bruise around his right eye.

Mr. Madliner may be a wiry willow of a man, but he sure packs a wallop.

We swing the axes all morning.

When the sun climbs directly overhead, we break for lunch: cold sandwiches and a pitcher of milk that tastes funny.

We sit and eat on the steps in silence. With the old oak gone, we can look out over the whole valley. That's the only nice thing about Madliner House: its view of everyplace else.

I wonder where Mrs. Madliner is inside the walls of cold stone behind me. Is she watching us at this very moment? Does she even remember last night? Or is she lost in her own mind?

I'm halfway through my sandwich when Butch begins barking.

It's a yelp, really. A high, funny sound. I know most all Butch's barks, but I don't recognize this one right off. My dog's got a different bark for cars, for deer, dinner, even people. Out in the yard, he is giving that strange bark and doing what looks like a funny little dance.

"What's got into him?" Frankie asks.

"Snake," Pete observes from where he stands on the porch. "He's found a big old black snake."

I squint and try to see. For just an instant, I catch sight of something sleek and shiny—a glimmer of sunlight on scales, a line of quicksilver ribboning for the trees.

"That snake probably had his home under those oak roots," Will says. "I bet we woke him up with all our chopping."

We watch Butch follow the snake across the yard, bouncing on his paws, nose to the dirt, tail swishing back and forth.

"Butch," I call out, "leave that old snake alone."

Butch ignores me and keeps up his yipping.

Then Caleb Madliner does a funny thing.

Without saying a single word, he gets up from where he's been sitting on the porch and picks up one of the hatchets we'd left in the yard. Walking his funny walk, he carries it over to where Butch is still bouncing, still barking into the grass. Caleb Madliner lifts the hatchet.

Thunk.

Butch's barking stops. Caleb's killed the snake.

Leaving the hatchet stuck in the dirt, Caleb turns, walks back to the porch. He goes back to eating his sandwich. It's a minute before he looks up and sees all of us looking at him. He turns to me.

"What are you staring at?"

"What'd you do that for?"

"I couldn't kill your dog, could I? How else was I supposed to get him to stop yipping?"

He takes another bite from his sandwich.

After lunch, Dad drops the tail of the pickup and lays two boards against it so us boys can load up the Ford with as many logs as it will carry. Late afternoon sun pours down around the top of Madliner Hill as we grunt and heave them logs up into the bed, but even the day's changing light doesn't make the place look any nicer. Instead, the bleached bone-white walls turn sickly yellow and the shadows from the surrounding trees get longer, weaving across the yard like a web.

At last it's over and us boys are spent, covered in wood chips and bark. Dad, Pete, and Will climb into the cab and Frankie, Butch, and me set ourselves on top of those logs in the bed. When the Ford rumbles to life underneath us, I think I've never been so happy to leave a place.

We've just about reached the safety of the trees when, in one of those dark windows, movement and a glint of sunlight on shiny metal catch my eye, and I see her. She's sitting in a silvery wheelchair that shines back the sunlight, her face peering through one of those old panes so it's like I'm looking at a framed portrait. Her black hair is pulled back, letting late-afternoon sun break against a hard nose and jutting cheekbones. Mrs. Madliner's eyes are dark and empty as the space between stars.

I am not even sure that she sees us, but I do it anyway.

I lift my hand and I wave.

Chapter 10

CRASH CALLAHAN

Atop the logs in the pickup bed, Frankie and me hold Butch between us, not talking until we see Madliner House draw back among the trees, shrinking out of sight. Frankie's face is pale, like the ends of the freshly cut logs. My stomach feels twisted in knots, and it stays that way until we turn us onto Hopkins Road once more. Dad keeps it slow on account of the logs in the bed, but that honeysuckle breeze is still blowing, warm and delicious, and soon as it hits us I feel my body begin to unwind, all the tightness lifting off and floating away like last autumn's leaves on the wind. Frankie leans his head back against the cab, closing his eyes, one hand absently petting Butch. My dog is a sight: pink tongue hangs out his open mouth, flapping as we go. I rub my knuckles between his ears, the way he likes.

Up front, Will turns the radio on and goes hunting through heavy static for music. Dad lets him, and soon Jimi Hendrix's electric guitar crackles on summer air as Pennsylvania rolls on past us. On our right, Knee-Deep Meadow beams golden and bright. Beyond its yellowy grasses, Apple Creek ripples under the sun.

It's too late in the day now to start after that fighter jet, but maybe we can get a swim in after all, wash our bodies and our minds of the Madliners.

There're some animals you just don't go near. A possum that looks dead. An old raccoon stumbling through your yard in the middle of the afternoon. A mama snapping turtle looking to lay her eggs. You steer clear of them because they're dangerous. There are people the same way. If they come looking to make trouble, that's a different story. But otherwise, you don't have anything to do with them.

That's how I feel about the Madliners. I don't fault Dad for taking us there. Mr. Madliner came and asked him for help, and my father is the last man who will refuse someone help who really needs it. But I still wish he'd just said no.

I'm grateful when Frankie interrupts my thoughts.

"What's that?" He's still leaning against the cab, but now he has one hand shielding his eyes as he squints down the road behind us. A yellow cloud is rising over it and there are shapes rolling beneath it, shimmering in the heat, like water.

Butch's toenails scrape against the logs as he gets up.

Jimi Hendrix's guitar is still wailing from our radio, but there's a new sound on the summer wind now: a deep growling of pumping pistons and firing cylinders. Butch answers with a low growl of his own, and his ears twitch.

The shapes under the cloud get sharper. I see spinning wheels and sleek metal frames. Faces above that gleaming wall of metal. Red bandanas snapping in the wind . . .

I watch, hypnotized, as Crash Callahan's motorcycle riders disappear into a dip in the road. For an instant the riders are hidden, leaving just that cloud of dust and the roar of engines and whooping voices that I feel in my chest and behind my Adam's apple to tell us they will soon be upon us.

"Jack, grab the dog!" Dad calls from the cab. His voice cuts through my trance like a knife through butter, and I grab hold of Butch's collar right as the first rider rockets out of the dip.

I'd know him anywhere because it's old Crash himself.

We've seen him every year at the autumn festival at Red Root Mountain. Crash is the closing act. As the crowds watch and cheer, he rides his motorbike down a cliff and crashes through a burning hay bale. The festival ain't over until his performance.

Crash comes sailing out of that dip and stabs into the sky like a fallen angel clawing for heaven. Long hair streams back from his sun-burned face, and his lips are pulled back over yellow teeth in a wild grin. His tires spin on empty air until he lands on the road, his bike bucking underneath him like a bronco. His riders come right behind him, howling like wolves.

They sweep down on us like lava.

"Boys, hold on!" Dad shouts.

Two riders pull up on our left, sunlight burning off the metal monsters between their knees. Another three slide up on our right. Then two more sweep in front of our Ford. Suddenly, we're surrounded. Boxed in. More riders roll up—ten, fifteen, now twenty—and our Ford rushes on in a sea of snarling motorcycles.

Raw, leathery voices call out to us.

"Hey, fellas, where you off to?"

"Here doggie-doggie-doggie!"

Butch lunges toward the edge of our truck. I try holding him back, but the oak log I'm crouching on rolls under me and I go with him, swinging like a busted chain.

"Ride him, cowboy!" a rider shouts.

I taste something warm in my mouth and realize I've smashed my lip on the log. Arms around my chest lift me: Frankie pulls me up.

Butch leans over the edge, snapping at the rider. I can't hold him so Pete clambers through the cab's back window. With his blond hair snapping in the wind, he shouts at us to get down as he puts his arms around Butch and drags him back.

Crash Callahan has pulled up alongside Dad's door. He leans over and raps his knuckles against it.

"Where to, pop?" he asks. "Going to the picture show?"

Dad stares straight over the steering wheel like he don't even see him.

"You deaf, man? I'm talking at you!" Crash jams his fist into the door's metal. Will jumps off his seat and shouts, but Dad shoves him back down and keeps right on ignoring Crash.

Crash don't like that, so he spits a blob of white saliva that darts somewhere behind him into the cyclones of yellow dust. He lifts his hand and waves. Sunburned faces parade past us in a fresh scream of metal as the riders roll on.

Oak logs slide under me again. Dad is slowing us down. The last of the riders seem to fly on even faster, leaving us behind in their cloud of yellow dust.

We come to a stop in the middle of the road and listen as the roar of Crash's horde grows fainter and fainter.

As fast as they appeared, the riders are gone.

Will is swearing up a storm in the cab.

In the back, Frankie's sprawled over the logs, his glasses hanging from one ear. Butch barks, struggles against Pete to get loose, to chase the men on the motorcycles.

I run my tongue around the inside of my mouth, checking to make sure I've got all my teeth. I do, but I've cut my lower lip bad. I go to spit blood over the side of the truck. I miss and it dribbles down my shirt instead.

"They're headed for Sam's place," Pete tells Dad.

My stomach turns over at that: Crash and his gang are off to torture lonely old Sam again.

But then I catch sight of my father in the rearview mirror. His eyes are icy blue.

"Hold on," he says as he buries the gas pedal.

Five minutes later, we come up on old Sam standing in the road in front of his trailer, hatless, his curly hair blazing in afternoon sun like a silver halo around his square head. The .22 rifle gleams dully in his hands.

Dad gives a tap on the horn as we come rolling slowly up to him, leans out his window, and says in a soft voice, "Sam, you all right?"

"They took Myrtle's mailbox."

The massive head jerks to a dark hole at the road's edge. A few clumps of dirt sit by it, fingers of green grass peeking out of them, waving in the breeze.

Dad puts a hand on his shoulder. At his touch, old Sam turns and we see his tomato-red cheeks and steel-wool beard are streaked with tears.

"They tore Myrtle's mailbox right outta the ground," he cries. He sways, and Dad's hand tightens on his shoulder. "I been down with the hay fever. I didn't hear them coming . . . I ain't good for much when the hay fever gets me."

Dad is silent.

"A man's got his dignity," Sam says. He looks skyward. "I'm sorry I let 'em take it, Myrtle. You know how I am when the hay fever gets me."

"Better climb up here, Sam," says Dad. "We'll drive down a ways and take a look."

A quarter mile down Hopkins Road we find what's left of Myrtle's mailbox. The four-by-four post is scraped up and splintered but otherwise fine. Somehow grass still clings to its earth-darkened point. But at the other end, a heap of brightly painted metal blossoms like the petals of a red, white, and blue flower: the mailbox crushed and twisted beyond repair.

Sam stoops and takes it in his arms, standing there a minute. When he climbs back up on the logs, fresh tears leak from the corners of his eyes. He lays the mailbox over his knees.

Then, on a breeze that smells like honeysuckle, we hear the distant thunder of engines.

"They're coming back!" Will cries out.

Sam's fingers tighten around the mailbox, the knuckles bone white.

Dad looks at him. "Sam, seems them boys on the bikes are coming back."

Sam nods grimly.

"They done you wrong," Dad tells him. "And I think we can help you fix them for it. Only one condition: no shooting."

Sam sits still on his log. "How you figure to fix them?"

"I'll tell you when you promise on Myrtle's grave that twenty-two will not have any part of it."

Sam chews his dip and thinks. He spits—a jet of brown juice that arcs over the truck into the road.

"On Myrtle's grave."

In the cab, Dad allows himself a slow smile.

"Just hold on," he says.

He brings the Ford to life once more and turns us around, giving the truck as much gas as he safely can with such a heavy load in the bed. We're almost back to Sam's trailer when Dad suddenly brakes again, bringing us to a stop. Twisting in his seat, he says to Pete, "Quick now, drop the tailgate."

At Pete's touch, the tailgate drops down with a clang.

"Now," Dad says, "start rolling them logs out the back."

That puzzles me. We spent half the blame day loading them logs *into* the truck. But with fresh light in his watery eyes, Sam rises, his road-mapped face crinkling into the fresh creases of a crooked smile as he shuffles to the back of the truck and kicks one enormous log over the tailgate.

Thud.

Dad gives the Ford a little gas, turning the wheel ever so gently as Sam kicks another log over.

Thud.

Thud. Thud.

Frankie taps my shoulder and motions toward the tailgate. Together we climb over and roll out a log. Pete joins us. Next thing I know, Will comes through the cab window to help.

Thud. Thud. Thud.

Dad drives the truck in a gentle S shape, slow and easy all the way back to Sam's, with us rolling logs out the back the whole way.

With every log, Sam gets cheerier and cheerier.

"Ooh-wee," he breathes to himself. "Ooh-wee, the Hoodlums are in for a surprise!"

When at last we reach the place where Myrtle's mailbox stood, the truck bed is empty. Giant, fat pieces of Mr. Madliner's oak tree lie scattered all across Hopkins Road.

From up the road, that motorbike roar is getting louder.

It's a good view of the road from Sam's front porch. Dad and us boys crouch behind the railing, but Sam sits in his rocking chair, Myrtle's mailbox on his lap, rocking himself with one foot. True to his word, Sam has leaned the .22 against the side of the trailer.

It ain't long before we hear those familiar raw and leathery voices on the wind.

"Somebody got Butch?" Dad asks.

"I got him," Frankie says.

"Hold him tight, son," says Dad, "because here they come."

Up the road, another yellow cloud is rising above the trees. The metal growling grows louder. Another minute, and that wave of glimmering steel comes rolling over the horizon, looking so even and so perfect that I'm breathless at the sight of it.

They ride in a tight pack, almost a perfect square of sun-seared faces and blackened leather, hot sunlight dripping from their metal machines.

A rush of fear and doubt seizes me and suddenly I think Dad's plan won't work. The riders have too much time to see the logs, too much time to slow down, to maneuver—

GRUNTCH.

With a squeal of anguished metal, the first rider rams a slice of solid oak. He flips like a pancake, somersaults into the meadow as his bike roars away under him.

A cry goes up from the swarm behind him, a frantic voice: "Hold up! Hold up!"

But it's too late.

Pop! Another rider lifts into the air, shooting like a cork. His motorcycle slides by, its front tire nothing but rags.

The riders begin to shout.

"Spread out! Watch out!"

But we've scattered logs all across the road. There's nowhere to go.

That shiny steel wall breaks against those fat oak logs and melts into a pile of steaming metal. Riders are tossed from their seats. Motorcycles grind into solid wood, crumple, and die. One roars on even after its rider is thrown into the field. It runs almost to Sam's front porch before it finally catches a log dead-on, rises, and goes end over end, tires still spinning, straight into the trees.

"Ooooh-weee, take that, Hoodlums!" Sam shouts from his rocking chair. He slaps his knee and lets loose a raspy laugh.

In the meadow the riders—now just staggering men—look up in confusion and disbelief. Amid the din of gasping motorcycles, we hear their cries of surprise and frustration.

Then comes a single, ear-splitting shriek. It comes from up the road. It comes from Crash Callahan.

He is still on his bike, still rolling down the road. Astonishment blazes across his red face at the sight of his horde lying wrecked and dazed and humiliated before him.

Crash jams on his brakes and slows, weaving in and out of the logs and busted motorbikes, leaning over the road at impossible angles. He rides through a sea of his gang's wreckage, licking his lips, howling in defiant rage.

He roars right up to us.

"Nice work, old man! We'll be back. Tonight! And tomorrow night! And *every* night for the rest of your life!" He spits again.

Before any of us can say anything, the rifle is gleaming in Sam's hands again. There's a crack like lightning and Crash's front tire pops.

"Come back anytime!" Sam hollers. The rifle cracks again. Crash's back tire pops. *"Anytime!"*

With a face like paper, Crash guns what's left of his bike and takes off down the road, his tires flopping like rags.

But the shooting is too much for Butch. At the sound of those rifle blasts, my dog bolts. He bounds off the porch, right into the sea of defeated motorcycles and angry men. There's just one problem: he takes Frankie with him.

Dad dives for him, fingers snapping shut on empty air. "Let go!" he shouts.

But Frankie can't let go. His arm is looped through Butch's collar. Facedown, he's dragged alongside my German shepherd—right into the road.

Dad charges after him.

"Sam, cover us!" Pete shouts as he charges too.

Sam's rifle cracks like corn in a hot skillet. He pops tires. He clips branches. He rains leaves down on the men in the road and at the edge of the field. He makes the dust spit at their feet.

Between that and my dog, the riders decide enough is enough. Those that can, right their bikes and pour back up the road in a last thunder-roll of choking diesel and dust. The rest take off running through Knee-Deep Meadow.

And now I'm running too: jumping steaming piles of motorcycle wreckage, chasing after my dog and my cousin. At first I don't see them in the swirling dust of the road. Then I see Butch, without his collar, chasing the last of the riders into the high grass.

Ahead of me, Dad and Pete jump over the motorcycles that lie panting like dying animals in the dust, running for the shape of a boy lying facedown in the dirt.

Frankie! A lump rises in my throat. But when I get close, I see he's sitting up. He holds Butch's busted collar in his hand, looks as if he's wondering what it is. He's a mess. He's got grass in his hair and stones down his shirt. One shoe is missing. Somehow he's still wearing his glasses.

"You all right, son?" asks Dad.

Frankie runs his hands over his chest, his arms, his legs.

"I think so," he coughs. He looks around. "Where'd they all go?"

Except for the logs and the wreckage of the motorbikes, the road is empty. Butch's barking comes now from halfway across the meadow. There ain't a single rider in sight.

"We chased them off!"

Will and Sam come up, shattered glass crunching under them. Old Sam is red-faced and smiling ear to ear. He slaps his knees several times, laughing as he looks about him.

"Ooh-wee," he wheezes to himself. "Look at all this, Myrtle. We fixed 'em good, didn't we? Ooh-wee."

He drops to one knee and lays a hand on one of the motorcycles. It's hot to the touch, and he snaps his fingers back real quick.

"How much you figure Hank Wistar will give me for these parts?" Sam grins again and slaps his hands against the singeing metal.

I help Frankie to his feet and brush him off as Pete and Will lift one of the bikes upright. Pete swings a leg over it and sits with his hands on the bars. "How do I look?"

Dad stands with his hands on his hips. His blue eyes sweep over the road, the logs, the steaming motorcycles. He smiles.

He looks down and kicks at a piece of glass.

"Well," he says, long and slow. "Let's get this mess cleaned up."

There is a kind of tired a boy can be when even breathing seems too much work. I feel that way as I lean against Stairways' cool stone and let a heaviness like lead settle into my arms and legs.

A slow fire burns in my muscles, a deep, dull ache that is somehow so satisfying and so good. I borrow a breath from the summer night and let it out, long and slow.

We lifted those old oak logs in and out of our truck in three different places—at Madliner House, at Sam's, and finally at Stairways. From the porch, I can see the logs stacked beside the barn, tall and dark, there to wait, there to dry in preparation for winter.

They will burn well.

My stomach tightens as I remember Mr. Madliner's words. There was something uncomfortably gleeful in the way he said it, like he looked forward to a time of burning for the great old tree.

I push that man out of my mind and focus instead on the good pain in my shoulders and neck, the pain that comes from working with people I love and who love me.

I doze for a time, there against the solid stones of the house where I was born. Fireflies are glowing in the yard when I wake. I sniff and smell something that wasn't there before: cigar smoke.

Dad is in the yard under the tree, watching night come to the valley he loves so much.

Gathering my last ounce of strength, I get to my feet and cross the yard toward him. As I go, I see a mistiness curling along the base of our hill, rising off Apple Creek, blanketing the tree roots. Soon, those long white fingers will drift across our yard.

"Dad?"

"Hm."

"What's a man's dignity?"

I did not even know the question was in me.

"Why do you ask?"

"Today on the road, when Sam was so sad about his mailbox, he said, 'A man's got his dignity.' I was just wondering what it means, is all."

Dad nods and his cigar trails lines of silver into the blue-black bowl above us. The first stars are coming out.

"Dignity is your value, Jack. It's something you and every living person have just because you are."

"Is that all?" I ask.

"Isn't that enough?"

I'm quiet.

"That's plenty," Dad tells me. "In fact, it's everything. The dignity of others is how we know some actions are good and others bad. It's how you know it isn't right to steal, or to kill without grave reckoning, or to lie."

"You get all that from dignity?"

"You do."

Dad looks down at me, and it seems he's standing very tall.

"Crash Callahan is dragging more than Myrtle's mailbox through the dust. It's Sam's understanding of his own self-worth."

"Oh."

Above us a shooting star traces its way across the night sky.

"Can you lose your dignity?" I ask after it disappears on the other side of the world.

Dad puffs a long time on the cigar before he answers.

"I don't think so," he says slowly. "You might forget you have it, but you can never lose it." The end of the cigar glows brightly. "How's that?"

"That's good." I yawn.

At the base of our hill, the mist has thickened.

"Are you going to make it all the way up those stairs?" Dad asks.

I nod my head, but Dad knows what I want, and I don't complain when he lifts me up in his arms and carries me across the yard to the house.

Chapter 11

Bobby

A river of black tar oozes under a fiery sky. On the far bank, boys in uniform line up and wait patiently beneath dark trees.

I am in the jungle again. My feet are rooted to the bank, like I'm ankle-deep in dried concrete.

A scream builds in my throat—and sticks there, like I've swallowed an egg whole.

The first boy comes into that open clearing and stands still as a statue. Waiting.

I lurch forward, and discover my feet *do* move. I take a slow, dragging step for the edge.

The shots begin upriver, angry fireflies flashing from a tangled mesh of vines and roots. A sudden metallic rattle.

That first boy falls stiff as a board, end over end, down into the dark river. He disappears without a splash.

"No!"

No sooner does the word tear from my lips than that awful machine-gun rattling begins again. Its murderous wail drowns me out, and a second boy slips below the surface.

Pete will be up soon. He's in line right now, waiting his turn.

I leap. For a moment I hang between water and sky. The river is thick and warm as blood. I fight my way through it for the far bank, clawing to get my head above the surface so I can shout while I swim. When I do, I see the bank is much higher than the river. I'm going to have to climb.

A familiar shape strolls to the edge of that cliff. Tall with broad shoulders. Moppy head of hair. My brother.

"Pete! No!"

A mouthful of warm water gurgles my words.

But Pete hears me. He stops and bends slightly from the waist, looking down into the river, searching for me.

"Run!" I try to scream, just as that rattle begins again.

There is a single mosquito tapping against the inside of my bedroom window when I awake. I watch it strike the glass, buzz off angrily, circle about, and come around again, only to fly into the glass once more.

I draw a long, deep breath and let the air out into the feeble light. Dawn soon. Sights of the river and that fiery sky fade.

Inside, I'm still screaming.

Time's running out. Pete's eighteenth birthday is just a few weeks away. Frankie and me need to make him famous before then. Famous people don't get drafted. Famous people don't get sent off and killed.

I peel damp sheets away from me and kick them in a bunch down to the foot of my bed. Morning air is cool on my skin. I draw another deep breath.

Frankie. Frankie's here. Frankie knows how to write. We've got him a typewriter. And he's passed all of Pete's tests, so he can come along on the search for that old fighter jet. Maybe we could even start the search today.

An itching on my wrist. A red bump. That mosquito bit me sometime in the night.

It's still buzzing over by the window. Once, he dips down to the windowsill, and I think he'll finally get out of our room. But he dips too low, and instead of flying out into the coming day, he buzzes around Frankie's head.

Enough.

I look around for something to swat him with, but all I see is Will's *Saturday Evening Post* magazine on the floor by the bunk, the one with Senator Kennedy's boyish face on the cover. That's no good.

Today is some sort of political decision day in California. Bobby Kennedy is expected to win. If he does, Will says, he'll be the Democrats' candidate for president in the fall. Will's been waiting for it all week, and last night he fell asleep reading the magazine.

I can't use Will's magazine to kill a mosquito.

But then the itch on my wrist comes again, worse than before.

The mosquito circles Frankie's sleeping face.

I decide.

Glancing carefully at my sleeping brothers, I hop down and take the magazine. I roll it up and tiptoe on creaky floorboards over to the window.

The mosquito jumps up, misses the window again, and taps the glass once. Twice.

The third time, Will's rolled-up magazine is right behind him.

Splat.

When I bring the magazine away, I see I've smashed him good. He's smeared to the glass in a sticky mess.

"Gotcha," I whisper.

Then I look down and see the blood and bug juice on Will's magazine.

If I'd been smarter, I'd have rolled the magazine with the front cover facing in. Those bug guts would have splattered across the Winston cigarette ad on the back cover. Instead, a blotch of blood has smeared right across the front—right across Bobby Kennedy's smiling face.

Uh-oh.

Quickly, I try wiping it with my finger.

It smudges.

I press a little harder. Soggy paper slides under my thumb. I stop.

A sudden sigh from my brothers' bed sends me shooting back to my own. I toss the magazine and dive into my bed, pulling up sheets still wet with my own sweat.

I roll over and pretend to be asleep. That mosquito bite on my wrist itches like mad, but I don't scratch it. I lie still.

I stay that way until I hear Will roll out of his bunk, cross the room, and stagger sleepily down our creaky staircase to the bathroom.

I lie in bed a while longer. Pete gets up next, throws a flannel shirt over his bare shoulders before taking the stairs two at a time down to the kitchen. His thundering wakes Frankie.

Outside, Butch barks. Day has come to Stairways.

Even still, I wait until I hear them all downstairs, hear the clinking of forks and dishes. I give it another two minutes, then make my own way down those spiraling stairs to join my family in the kitchen, looking as innocent as I know how.

It's us boys and Ma at breakfast. Dad's gone to work early at the game preserve. And since Dad's not here to holler at him, Will talks about the election and how Bobby Kennedy's going to win it.

"Today's the day," he says. "Kennedy wins California, then it's on to the White House!"

I haven't seen Will so happy in ages. He bounces on his seat as he chews.

"I thought the election wasn't 'til November?" Frankie asks.

I expect Will to frown. Instead, he shakes his head and patiently explains. "That's the general election between the two parties. Today is the *primary* election for the Democrats in California. Every state has primaries. They're smaller elections before the bigger one. They have them so people in either party can choose who they want for the big election in November. If Kennedy wins today, it's almost for sure he'll be the Democrats' nominee."

Frankie nods. "I get it."

I don't. I've never understood any of Will's political talk, or why he and Dad have such nasty fights over it.

And I don't really care at all about the primary election in California.

I *do* care about finding that old wrecked fighter jet. I'm just about to ask Pete if we can go today when Ma ruins it.

"Today we're going into town," she says.

I sigh. "What for?"

"You need new pants. Will needs new shirts."

"Can't it wait 'til tomorrow?"

"It could," Ma says, "but it won't."

Will spreads raspberry jam across a biscuit. "Terrific," he says. "I want to stop by the newsstand and see if there's any early results from California."

"That'll be fine," says Ma. "*After* we get your shirts and Jack's pants."

"Do we have to go?" I ask again.

"John Thomas," says Ma, her voice getting sharp. "I already told you. *Yes.*"

I eat my eggs and sulk.

Another wasted day.

"If you don't fuss any, maybe we'll get some ice cream," Ma adds. "*Maybe.*"

That helps. Some.

Next to me, Pete leans back in his chair and takes a sip of coffee. I don't know how he can drink it, but he does. No cream. No sugar. Just like Dad.

"Hey, Will, I got a question," he says suddenly. "Suppose old Bobby Kennedy *loses* today?"

Will frowns. "He won't. He's going to win."

"Sure," says Pete before he sips more coffee. "But what if he doesn't? That's possible, right?"

I smell their fight brewing in our kitchen the way you smell a storm coming in the late afternoon. So does Ma, and she ends it before it can start.

"Pete, you stop. Let Will be." She rises. "And come to think of it, you could use some new shirts too, so don't you wander off anywhere."

"No ma'am. Nothing I love more than new-shirt shopping."

The rest of the coffee goes down the hatch.

I sigh. That's it. Ma is dragging us all into town to shop. Of all days. Fine, then. Tomorrow. Tomorrow, we'll begin our search.

We come out of the five-and-dime into Main Street's bright sun. It's about three in the afternoon. Automobiles bake at the meters along the sidewalk. Across the street, a man in a blue uniform writes a ticket and slips it under the windshield wiper of one.

"John Thomas, you're growing like a weed," Ma sighs. "You'll be too tall for these in a month." She shifts the package under her arm: three pairs of pants for me, two shirts each for Will and Pete.

A car crawls past us, shiny green in the hot afternoon.

"Can I have a dime for a paper?" Will asks.

She hands him a folded, dusty-looking dollar. "Bring me the change."

Will powers ahead of us; Mr. Murray's newsstand is at the other end of Main Street.

"Can we get ice cream now?" I ask.

Ma sighs again. "I suppose."

"I'm going to get mint chocolate chip," I decide.

"Butter pecan," Frankie replies.

Pete and Ma don't walk fast enough, so we leave them and take off ourselves down Main Street. A second car rolls by. This one is cream-colored and full of teenagers.

"Busy afternoon," I say to Frankie, and it seems to me he's got something stuck in his throat because he coughs at that.

We pass Mr. Wistar's hardware store, then Mr. Hudspeth's barber-shop. His door is tied open with a piece of string, and I wave as we go past.

Ernie's Luncheonette & Homemade Ice Cream Parlor is across the street. There's a bell above the door that rings as we come in. Chilly air washes over us, stirred by a pair of fans that spin lazy circles overhead. It smells like melted chocolate, peanuts, bananas, and butterscotch. Afternoon sun pours through stenciled windows and gleams off a black-and-white tiled floor and the red booths along the wall. I guide us over to one and set my pocketknife down on the table to show it's taken before taking Frankie over to the glass counter.

"Afternoon, boys," says the man as he comes off his stool. As he puts down his newspaper, I recognize Bobby Kennedy's smiling face in the black-and-white photograph.

Frankie and me have each tried two samples of ice cream when Ma and Pete walk in, sending the tiny bell above the door into its dance again.

"Four cones, please," says Ma, opening her purse.

The man takes the dipper from a jar of cold water and rolls brightly colored balls of ice cream out of the tubs behind the glass. He stacks them three each onto the cones.

We eat the ice cream in our booth. It's delicious, but I can't eat it fast enough, and soon I've got mint chocolate chip dripping down my chin. Ma passes me a napkin.

Beyond the stenciled windows, the cream-colored car of teenagers cruises by again.

"Didn't we just see them?" Frankie asks.

"They're driving Idiot's Circle," says Pete as he crunches on his cone.

"What's that?"

"Imagine you're a high-school guy with a car and nowhere to go," Pete tells him. "You pick up your girl and drive her around town in a loop. Down Main Street, back up Second Street, and down Main Street again."

Frankie frowns. "And that's all?"

"That's all."

I take another lick. "Sounds stupid. Riding around in a car for hours."

Pete smiles. "Depends on the girl."

Ma gives him a look.

"Where's Will at?" I've gotten down to my own cone now. "He's missing ice cream."

"Probably jabbering at Mr. Murray about his hero, Bobby Kennedy," says Pete.

"Let him be," Ma commands. "It's good to have heroes."

We finish our ice cream cones to the hum of the tired ceiling fans. Will never shows up. It's not until we step back into the blazing afternoon that we see him again. He comes up the street, a rolled newspaper tucked under his arm.

Ma holds out her hand for the change.

"Radio reports are good," Will says. "Kennedy is going to clean Humphrey's clock!"

He don't even seem upset that he's missed the ice cream.

We start back up the street, with him telling Ma about polling numbers so far.

At the next block that cream-colored sedan full of teenagers rolls up beside us. They wait at the light while we cross and I recognize a familiar, beautiful face behind the windshield in the passenger seat.

"Hey, look!" I point.

In the passenger seat of the car, Anna May's long hair is the color of summer. She's curled it so that it cascades down her long neck, cupping her round shoulders. We ain't seen her since the day she and her friends found us sleeping naked at the creek. I was too flustered to notice how she looked then, but now her blue eyes meet mine through the windshield and it seems all the breath goes out of me.

Anna May smiles, and for an instant us boys stop in the middle of the street.

Next to Anna May, behind the wheel, is a boy: Everett Scott. He's big, bigger even than Pete. Brown hair curls down a wide, fat forehead and stops above tiny brown eyes.

When he taps the horn, I jump and the kids in the back of his car laugh. Everett lifts a sausage-shaped finger and points at the traffic light above us.

"It's green, kid," he says.

Those are the only three words Everett Scott's spoken to me my whole life. But in that moment, I hate him.

We move out of the street, letting the big car slide past us, the engine muttering as it goes. Anna May turns in her seat, craning her beautiful long neck to watch us as Everett Scott carries her off. She didn't laugh like everybody else when he honked the horn.

Will watches her go, the newspaper hanging limp at his side.

"She going out with him?" he asks.

"Looks like it," Pete says.

Will frowns.

Then, without saying a word, he turns and walks away.

The room flickers from the television set. The announcer reads from a card.

"Exit polls show Senator Robert F. Kennedy will win the California primary tonight. The senator has long considered a presidential run and is now in a strong position to win his party's nomination for the November election."

Dad lets out a bushel of air through his nose.

Will's knees bounce up and down.

"He did it," he whispers. "He did it!"

Dad sighs again and seems about to speak. Ma glances at him and shakes her head.

The news program ends. An advertisement for detergent comes on. Dad gets up and walks over to the set and shuts off the TV then. Our room goes dark. Without a word, Dad goes out to smoke his cigar.

"Congratulations, dear," Ma says to Will once he's gone.

I look over to Frankie on the couch. He's asleep. I don't blame him. The whole election is boring.

Ma wakes Frankie and we begin for the stairs. Pete passes me, on his way out to the porch. I stop him.

"Pete?" I ask. "What we doin' tomorrow?"

He shrugs.

"Can we start the search for that old fighter jet? Frankie passed his tests. He's ready."

Cicadas hum in the yard. Through the screen door we smell Dad's fresh cigar.

"You're right, Jack," Pete says. "Frankie passed the tests. He's earned it."

"Then we can go tomorrow?"

He nods his shaggy head.

I hold back my smile until Pete is through the screen door. Then I climb the steep stairs for my room.

Frankie is on his knees at the windowsill, saying his prayers.

"Tell him thank you from me," I say. "Tomorrow we're going to find us an old wrecked fighter jet!"

Frankie's dark eyes flash. After a long minute, he nods his head.

"I'll be ready," he says.

"You already are," I tell him as I climb into my bed.

Something ain't right.

I lie awake in my bed and wait for my mind to catch up with what my body already knows.

Pink sky outside my window. Trees are still dark. The morning around me is silent.

And that's how I know.

Stairways ain't ever this quiet, not even so early in the morning.

Ma and Dad should be awake, in the kitchen together. But I don't smell Dad's coffee. I don't hear nothing sizzling on the stove.

Quickly, I look to my brothers' bunk. Both of them are still sound asleep. Same with Frankie on his mattress.

Quietly, I slip out of my bed and steal down the stairs to the kitchen.

My parents are at Grandma Elliot's old table. Dad has his arm around Ma. Her face has a hard look to it and her eyes are red around the edges. She's been crying.

"What's going on?" I ask them.

My parents see me.

"Is Will awake?" my father asks.

I shake my head, but then a groggy voice behind me says, "I'm right here."

Will is at the bottom of the stairs. His hair sticks off his head at angles.

He looks at our parents, then at me. "What's wrong?"

Ma gets up. She moves toward him, arms out.

But Will steps away, a look of alarm on his face.

"Tell me what's wrong!" he cries suddenly, his eyes wide.

Dad's chair scrapes across the linoleum floor. In a low voice he tells Will:

"Son, Senator Kennedy's been shot. He's dead."

Chapter 12

TROUBLE IN THREES

He isn't getting up, that man in the dark suit and tie. His sandy-haired head stays down, resting on the kitchen floor, and for once that face looks so peaceful. The man's eyes are half-shut, like he's taking a nap, and his body under the suit appears to be draining, losing its shape, the arms and legs splayed out more like a scarecrow than a senator. He seems to be relaxing more and more by the minute.

Everyone else is screaming.

Waves of people crash against each other. Some try to get closer. Others push them back. One woman shouts loud enough that a microphone records her panicked voice. My family and all of America hear her wailing on the evening news that night.

"Not again! Not again!"

Bobby Kennedy lies in a pool of his own blood, shot in the head by a man disguised as a cook in a hotel kitchen. He is dying on a million TV screens across the country. All we can do is watch.

Bobby Kennedy, like his brother the president, is dead.

And it's just like it says in the Book of Ecclesiastes: Nothing under the sun is new.

Will is gone.

Just started across the fields by himself the day after Kennedy's killing, his long legs carrying him away over the spine of our hill in the early morning light.

I'm through the screen door and almost off the porch after him when Pete stops me.

"Let him be, Jack."

"But, Pete, he's hurting!"

"It's a time for hurting. Let him be."

I do like Pete says and watch Will slip over the horizon.

Day breaks over the world and it burns hot and fierce. Knee-Deep Meadow's golden yellow burns brown. The valley's far wall is lost in haze. It stays lost all day in murderous heat. But Will does not return. The sky goes orange in a dusty twilight, and the pines burn black against all that bright color. Shadows pool at the bottom of our hill, preparing for their long march to our house. Still Will ain't come back.

He don't show for dinner or for Walter Cronkite on the TV.

Night comes down around our stone house, hot and humid. Dad greets the dark in smoky silence on the porch, his cigar burning slowly between his fingertips. Seems he's taking a while with it tonight.

I stay and wait with him.

There's flashlights on the wall inside. We could grab them and go looking for him. But Dad stays in his chair and so I do too.

When the cigar burns down to just a stub and Will still ain't back, Dad makes a move like he's going inside for the night. He drops the stub, crushes it out under his shoe. But instead of heading in, he reaches into his breast pocket and pulls out another. He bites off the end, puts it between his teeth, and lights it. Fresh blue smoke spills through his knuckles. In yellow porch light, the scar on his hand shines a ghostly white.

"Go on up to bed now, Jack."

I hadn't been tired till then. But after Dad speaks, a great weariness invades my body and I feel like my bones have all turned to lead. It's a great effort to even pull the screen door open. A greater one still to climb the stairs to my room.

Frankie is sprawled on his mattress, his arms and legs splayed out. At the sight of him, my mind runs right back to the TV and bleeding Bobby Kennedy lying that same way on the hotel floor. I push the thought away as I fall into my own bed.

It's a jumpy kind of sleep, like you get when you're sick with a fever. It must be hours later when I come all the way awake again, my whole body trembling, the sheets clinging to me, and the dead face of Bobby Kennedy that has somehow become Will's face staring at me in the dark.

Will's bed is still empty.

I sit, awake in my bed, and shiver in the warm night until a few minutes later, when I catch a whiff of the breeze coming through my open window:

Dad's cigar. Still burning.

The days after Kennedy's killing come hot and dry, with the sun hanging like a ball of white fire over our valley. Tree leaves scorch and crinkle. Islands appear in the middle of Apple Creek; the fish retreat to their darker holes.

I'm first one to spot the dust clouds rising at the bottom of our hill.

I raise a holler to Dad just as Kemper's big black car comes out of the trees.

Kemper's horn blares twice, but he never gets out. Through the dusty windshield he checks around for Butch. Then the tiny eyes fall on me. As best I can with my dry mouth, I spit.

Dad takes his time coming around the barn. Hands in his pockets. Walking easy. Real easy.

My father is mad.

Kemper rolls the window down and sticks out one arm. His small fingers clutch an envelope, and he waves it at my father like a flag of truce. Dad stops just out of reach of it and stands still beside the idling car.

"Days are numbered, Gene," Kemper says. "Take a look and see for yourself. A judge has ruled that the county can have this land if they want it." He pauses, adds, "And we want it."

"If," Dad says.

"When," Kemper corrects. "Read it. Sell this place while you can. I'm giving you a last chance. This is the best offer you can get, and it's not half as good as what you could have had last time. Chase me out now, I promise it won't ever be this good again. Sell the house now. Half-price. Or I'll take it from you and you'll get next to nothing."

It ain't a big stone, just the closest one I can find, but I throw it hard as I can.

It dings off the side of the big car.

"He said no, the answer's no!" I shout.

Before I know it, I've grabbed another.

"Even my dang dog knows what that means. Why can't you figure it out?" I let fly again. This time my stone lands right on his windshield and leaves a thin spiderweb when it bounces off.

"Jack!" Dad whirls.

I'm on my hands and knees looking for another stone when Pete appears, grabs me from behind. My brother lifts me right off the ground and swings me away under one arm, carrying me toward the barn.

I fight him furious, but he's holding me upside down and all the blood rushes to my head and it's no use. I give up and just let the tears roll up my forehead to the earth that swings side to side above me.

Pete carries me past our barn to the woodpile, flips me over, and sets me down on one of the logs.

Standing back, he folds his arms.

"Why don't he just go away and stay away?" I bawl. "Why's he keep coming up here and botherin' us like he does?"

I'm embarrassed now. The tears run like water from a faucet. Pete watches while I double over and blow my nose into the dry grass between my knees. "And how come Will's gone all weird? I know he's sad somebody shot Bobby Kennedy, but that ain't any fault of ours. Why's he got to go off all alone and leave us?"

I am running out of tears at this point, but still sobbing so that I can hardly sit still.

Pete waits. When I'm done talking, he walks to the other end of the pile and picks up the sledgehammer and a few of Dad's thick metal wedges. He walks slowly back to where I sit and drops them into the dry grass in front of me.

"Get up," he says.

He places the wedge, thin end first, against the center of the log I've been sitting on. He taps it lightly a few times with the sledge until its edge has bit into the wood.

He hands me the hammer. "Here."

The sledge is awful heavy for me by myself, but Pete helps me steady it. I strain with all my might and I manage to lift it, slowly.

There's a sharp cry of metal on metal. The sledge strikes the wedge at an angle, slides away. It ain't as good a hit as it could have been, but the wedge has sunk deeper into the wood. A tiny crack has formed around it.

Pete helps me lift the hammer again.

I drive that wedge slowly the whole rest of the way into the log.

At last there's a sound like someone's ripped a piece of cloth, and the log comes apart into two halves.

Wordlessly, Pete kicks one out of the way, takes the wedge, and sets it into the center of the other half.

"Again," he says.

I'm so focused on it I barely notice the sound of Kemper's engine, or the dust from his car as he slides back down our drive for Hopkins Road.

I bring the hammer down again. I jump when I see orange sparks shoot from the metal and catch my breath as they fall. The grass is awful dry, but the sparks die in the dust.

I wipe the sweat from my forehead and lift the hammer again.

My back is to the barn, so I don't see Dad come up. I know he's there just the same.

I give the wedge a last slam. It's dead on, but the wedge doesn't go deep enough to split the log. I take a long breath and turn to face my father.

He stands bareheaded in the sun, forehead shining with sweat. He's still got Mr. Kemper's envelope in one hand. He folds it and stuffs it into his pocket.

I wait for him to speak, wait for that incredible fury he held back from Kemper in the drive. Dad controlled his anger then, but I didn't. I let loose with my words and those stones, and I embarrassed him worse than he could have himself.

I can't look him in the eye, so I stand there and wait.

For a long time Dad doesn't speak. Then he steps forward and puts out his hand for the sledge.

I step aside as my father takes up his place at the log. In one fluid motion he swings the sledge, his powerful shoulders rolling under his overalls. The sledgehammer wheels in a giant arc over his head and comes smashing down, like a thunderbolt.

White wood shines in the sun. The wedge drives clean through the log and sinks six inches into the dirt.

Pete crouches and rolls another log into place.

Dad swings again. He splits it in two again, then hands the sledge to Pete.

Pete swings a few, then hands the sledge to me.

And that's how we spend the afternoon, splitting wood, Pete and Dad and me.

The next morning we watch Bobby Kennedy's funeral on the television. Before it begins, the network broadcasts the word **SHAME** in large blocky letters, and then we see the stone steps of St. Patrick's Cathedral in New York City. Hundreds of people, black and white, young and old, wait in line to pass inside and say goodbye. After the Mass, the flag-covered casket is carried down the steps by gray-faced men, followed by a stream of weeping family and friends. President Johnson is there. So is Nixon.

Dad shuts off the TV.

Martin Luther King Jr. killed in April. Now Bobby Kennedy. I can't help wondering who will be next.

They say bad luck comes in threes. If you had asked me, I'd have said things couldn't get worse, what with Bobby Kennedy's killing in California and that worm Kemper and his county council trying to steal our land to sink Apple Creek under a reservoir. But the day after Kennedy's funeral, things *do* get worse.

Frankie and me are at the creek, skimming some of those smooth pink and blue river stones, when we hear Ma calling for Frankie from the front porch, shouting that his mother's on the telephone.

You've never seen a boy move so fast.

I trot after him, catching sight of my mother's face as I push through the screen door. A hard look is on it, her eyes flinty sharp and her lips closed tight with no color to them. I know right then: something's happened.

By the time I get in, Frankie is standing at the phone in our kitchen with the receiver pressed tight against his ear. Aunt Effie's voice comes squeaky to me, and I don't catch everything she says, but I can tell something ain't right.

"But how is he?" Frankie asks, still catching his breath.

Aunt Effie's voice comes through the receiver in a thin squeal. Hard to hear her now, but a tremor seems to pass through Frankie, as if his whole body is water and a heavy stone's been dropped into it, sinking deep and making waves as it goes. With a sudden chill, I remember Uncle Leone's been looking for the murderers of them boys at that corner store, and I wonder if maybe he's found them. Or if they found him.

The thoughts swimming through my mind scatter like minnows when Frankie suddenly starts shouting into the phone. "Let me come home! Let me come home!"

Aunt Effie's voice gurgles over the phone again, and I think I hear her crying now.

Frankie is trembling, but he goes on listening as his mother talks. He stares at the plaster on the kitchen wall, touches it with his fingers. I watch my cousin make his whole body slowly go calm, the water smooth once more. Then Frankie whispers to his mother, "I will."

He hangs up.

Ma is at my side now, though I don't remember hearing the screen door.

We wait.

Frankie's still staring at the wall. Then, in a voice as dry as that plaster:

"My dad's been shot."

My breath catches in my throat, but before I can speak a word Frankie goes on in that same funny voice, slowly, as if he's stamping it on his own mind. "He was at a traffic light. Someone walked up and started shooting. Most of the bullets went into the car. One hit him in the leg." Frankie's voice seems to be drifting away from him, like it's leaving him, heading home. "He's hurt, but alive . . . He's in the hospital now."

I draw a deep breath. "Come on, then. We've got to get you back to that train station."

He shakes his head once, a quick jerk. "I have to stay." His dark eyes move first to Ma, then to me as he repeats it. "He wants me staying *here!*"

My mouth drops. "But what on earth does your dad want that for?"

"Because he loves you." Ma's voice is full of command, of truth. To deny her words would be like telling someone the sun don't come up in the morning or go down at night. She moves to Frankie, puts her arms around him. "Your father is a strong man, Frankie, and he will recover," Ma tells him, her voice softer now. "And he will do it easier knowing you're not in danger."

Frankie bows his head, and now the tears are running down his cheeks. Ma holds him a minute longer, and I'm surprised to see tears in her eyes too.

When Frankie lets go, Ma sends him upstairs to lie down. I listen to him climb those spiral stairs and wait until I hear the door to my bedroom shut before asking her.

"Was it those men Uncle Leone was looking for? The ones who killed them boys in the car?"

"It was him being a policeman in a policeman's car," Ma says. "Nothing more than that." She wipes the tears away with the hem of her apron. "Let him be a little while. Then keep close. Understand?"

I tell her I do, but as I push through the screen door, out into the furnace of a day, the truth blazes like a torch in my mind: I don't understand any of it. Not why anybody would kill anybody for looking different. Or light fires. Or shoot a policeman. I make for the creek, looking to quench the fire burning in my mind. Next thing I know I've stripped down to swim.

Creek is low, and I bump my knees against the sandy bottom, but I keep right on swimming to the far bank. Push my feet into white clay, turn around. Back again.

I want it all to be over—the war; the shooting and the killing; the mobs, the riots, the fires. But I know it won't be over. Not anytime soon. And most of all, I know there's nothing—not a single blessed thing—I can do about any of it.

Day burns on above me, and when I lie down in my bed later that night, after a dinner where both Will's and Frankie's chairs sit empty, I feel the sun's cold-fire kisses along the back of my neck and all down my arms and legs, burning me still.

I bust into tears when I wake up and see Will lying in his own bed. I run over and climb in and give him a big hug, bawling my eyes out the whole time. Will doesn't shove me off right away. But he don't hug me back.

He don't have to hug me. He just has to be home.

Chapter 13

BONNIE AND CLYDE

Sadness drops like a curtain down around our stone house in the days after Kennedy's funeral and the news of Uncle Leone. Frankie keeps to our room most of the first day, but he shows for breakfast the next, appearing his normal self though maybe his eyes are redder around the edges.

Will comes to breakfast, but he don't eat. He barely sleeps, though he lies in bed most of the day. Sometimes he reads—a dusty book of Greek poetry. Or that *Saturday Evening Post* with Bobby Kennedy's picture on the cover. Slowly I realize that Frankie is mending but Will ain't. He may be back, but he ain't better.

Afternoon of the third day, Will grabs that *Post* magazine and that blue-and-white Kennedy campaign pin off his bookshelf and carries them down to the barn. He clangs around inside until he finds a shovel, then he marches out into the meadow and buries both the magazine and the pin. Then it's straight back up to the bedroom.

Pete and me watch from the porch. "What'd he do that for?" I ask.

"He's saying goodbye," Pete replies. "It's something you do when people die. It helps with the sadness."

"Oh," I say. "How long you figure before Will's done being sad?"

Pete shrugs. "A while."

I don't like that. I don't want Will to be so sad. But there's something else bothering me. Will won't go anywhere or do anything. That includes looking for that fighter jet. Our expedition has to wait until Will feels better. That means Frankie's story has to wait too.

"Can't we do anything to make him feel better faster?" I ask.

Pete shakes his head. "Some things you can't rush, Jack. This is going to take a whole lot of time."

We ain't got a whole lot of time. Pete turns eighteen in less than a month.

If I'm going to save Pete, I must first save Will. And to do that, I've got to find a way of helping him to feel better.

Dad beats me to it.

Normally Dad likes to work at whatever is ailing him until it's fixed, the way you sand down a piece of wood so nobody gets any splinters or caulk a window to keep the winter wind from coming in. But Will's sadness ain't a piece of lumber or a cracked windowsill. His hero is dead. And there's no work Dad can do that will change that.

Dad knows it. So he comes up with something different.

He crushes out the stub of his cigar and comes through the screen door to where we're gathered in the living room.

"Everybody get your shoes on," he says. "We are going to the movies."

The drive-in movie theater is just outside New Shiloh.

Rows upon rows of cars are parked side by side, their dark and cooling headlights pointing toward the giant glowing screen. The night smells like roasted peanuts and popcorn.

The concession stand at the lot's far end is an island of boards and glass and yellow light in the summer dark. It draws us boys like moths through the crowd of teenagers who sit on the hoods of old Chevys, barefoot in blue jeans and tie-dye T-shirts, eating, drinking, talking, waiting for the movie to start. Some of them smoke smelly cigarettes, and I pinch my nose as we go past.

From the big speakers at the end of the field, scratchy music begins.

"Fellas, the movie's starting," I tell my brothers.

"You can go back and watch with Ma and Dad," Pete says. He keeps moving through the sea of automobiles.

Every kid in the valley is here tonight, but there's only one he and Will care to see. I don't care about finding Anna May Fenton. Pretty or not, she's only a girl. This is a real, live *movie*—and we are about to miss it. The feature tonight is *Bonnie and Clyde*.

The crowd is thinning by the time we get our popcorn. Most kids have already got their hot dogs or popcorn and are returning to their cars. But Pete and Will are still searching the crowd for her.

"This is stupid," I say. "We came to watch a movie, not hunt all over creation for—hey, look!"

Two rows down, Anna May Fenton is disappearing into the sea of automobiles. For an instant, we see her against that bright screen. She's lovely in that electric dark.

The boy with her is anything *but* lovely, because it's Everett Scott again. That big galoot we saw after getting ice cream.

"Ugh, him again." I grimace.

"Is she really going with him?" Frankie asks.

At first nobody answers.

But then Pete says, "Hard to tell, Frankie. Maybe she is. But maybe she ain't." Then Pete's face lights up, as if he's just gotten an idea. "Say, Will, why don't you go say hello? You still got some time before the movie starts."

Will looks at him for a long moment. He knows what Pete's doing. So do we all.

Down at the front of the field, the music is getting louder.

Will waits just a second longer, then without a word he wanders down the row of cars too.

Pete watches him go.

The opening credits are running on the big screen now. The movie has started.

"Can we *please* go back now?" I ask. I'm whining now and I know it.

"Lead the way, Jack," Pete replies.

"Where's Will?" asks Ma when we get back. She and Dad are sitting in the cab, windows down, the radio tuned into the right station to get the sound for the movie.

"Trying to steal Anna May Fenton away from her boyfriend," Pete says as he climbs up. "I give him good odds. Poor old Everett. If his brains were dynamite, he couldn't blow his nose."

"Anna May Fenton?" Ma asks. "The preacher's daughter?"

She looks at Dad, but he ain't paying any attention. He's watching the movie.

Frankie and me sit on the roof of the truck. We get a good view from up there—of the screen and the cars around us. There's a boy and a girl kissing in the one next to us. They're in the back and all hunkered down so nobody walking by can see. Reminds me of what Pete calls the drive-in: "the passion pit." We watch them a while, passing a greasy bag of roasted peanuts back and forth, but then Clyde shoots a man and those gunshots pull our attention back to the movie. Now our eyes are glued to that big screen that's blazing a hole in the soft dark.

Something about the movies lets you forget where you are and go into a whole different world. You just float, and time goes by without you hardly even knowing it. You forget.

I forget about the boy and the girl next to us.

I forget about Uncle Leone's shooting and Bobby Kennedy's killing.

I forget about Kemper and his plan to flood our valley.

I even forget about the war. Just for a while.

The movie lays hold of me, sight, sound, even touch: under me, the truck's cool metal trembles with each gunshot.

There are plenty of those. That Clyde, in his blue suits and wide-brimmed hat, is a real killer. But awful as he is, it's Bonnie, his partner in crime, who is the more frightening. Cold as ice. Cruel. Beautiful—and deadly.

At last, I feel the movie coming to an end. It's the end for Bonnie and Clyde too. On a dusty road that looks a lot like Hopkins Road, they pull over to help a man with a flat tire.

It's a trap.

I hear Ma's gasp from below when the policemen begin with their machine guns. It's loud and sudden, and it makes both Frankie and me jump. The boy and the girl in the car next to us stop their kissing to watch Bonnie and Clyde get shot to pieces.

Those machine guns rattle on, blasting out of the speakers from a thousand cars across the lot. After a horrible minute, they're both dead.

Next thing I know, the screen is blank again, swaying like the sail of a giant ship against the night sky. The closing credits roll.

Frankie turns to me then.

"What'd you think?" he asks.

"There was a lot of shooting," I say.

"Pretty great, huh?" he asks.

"You bet," I reply. We clamber down from the roof. My legs feel funny from sitting so long. And my bladder feels like a balloon about to bust.

"I have to go to the bathroom."

"Take this on your way," says Ma, handing me an empty pop-corn bag.

Pete stays with Ma and Dad so it's just Frankie and me wandering our way through the narrow alleys toward the fuzzy yellow light of the concession stand.

When we get there, we find Will worse than I've ever seen him.

He stands at the edge of that pool of yellow light, leaning against the fender of a parked car. A crowd of kids pulses around the concession stand.

His head is down. A sweep of shaggy hair hides his eyes. My brother looks about to cave in on himself. The body under his clothes is crumpling before my very eyes. One hand steadies himself against the hood of the car. When we last saw him, he was walking after Anna May and Everett. He must have found them, and whatever words were passed had hurt him bad.

The sight of him brings the cry from my lips: "Will!"

At my sound there's a flurry of movement from the kids at the stand. A shape peels away from them. A big shape. It starts across the gravel.

"Will, what's happened?" When he don't answer, I turn to Frankie—but he's looking away from me, toward the mountain-like shape that's marching toward us. I suck in a breath as Everett Scott comes up, all two thousand pounds of him.

"Will Elliot!"

My brother's got a beautiful name, but the way Everett says it makes it sound like something gross.

Will flinches at the sound, but he don't look up.

There's a sudden charge on the night air. The hairs along my arms rise on end as I watch Everett storm over to Will. He means to fight him, though why I can't say.

"You think you can try stealing my girl right in front of me?" Everett asks. "You Elliot boys are something else!"

There's pure venom in those words. Everett is huge, even taller than Pete, thicker around the middle, like a tree trunk. He's a fish-smelling grizzly bear of a boy—and he's rolling up his sleeves.

The crowd of kids comes over to us now, feeling the coming fight. They draw closer, though not too close, and make a ring around us.

Frankie tugs my sleeve. I look and I see her now. Anna May Fenton standing on her tiptoes on the walk under that yellow light, tilting her head to see over the crowd.

Right in front of us, Everett is steaming like a bull.

"You Elliots can live like animals if you want back in your *holler*. But when you come to town, you're around actual human beings. You straighten up. You need help straightening up?"

Anna May shouts from the stand. "Everett! You stop it right now!"

Everett ignores her. Will looks sick. His face is gray. He's still leaning against that car, his head still down. He won't so much as look at Everett. Everett is disgusted with him, but he's got an audience now, and he's still hoping for that fight. He tries to bait Will again.

"I said animals," Everett goes on. "But I'm wrong." He scrunches up his nose. "I meant trash."

I drop that empty popcorn bag.

This is it, I think. If Everett Scott wants a fight, why, then Will is going to give it to him. Nobody calls our family trash—*nobody*.

Only Will don't answer him. He just stands there.

"Go ahead, Will," I say then. "Let him have it."

But he doesn't. My brother just stares at dirt.

And that's when I know for sure that my brother is truly broken. Whatever happened before the movie, when he went after Everett and

Anna May, it's defeated him. His spirit's been crushed. His fire is out. Will is like a dead star.

Hot tears well up in my eyes then because I know this will be the worst. Will won't ever recover from this. For the whole rest of his life, he will carry the shame of that night Everett Scott insulted him and our whole family and he did nothing about it. This will be worse even than losing his hero. This will be like dying, but worse, even: it'll be a killing of the soul.

"Leave him alone!" I cry out. "You big dumb bully!"

I feel the eyes of the crowd fall on me now. Everett grunts.

"Real cool, Will. Let your kid brother stick up for you."

All I can do is stand there, and so help me God, tears start running down my face.

Everett smirks at that. "That's it, candy-ass. Cry."

"Will," I sniff. "Are you just going to let him say those things about us?"

Then, finally, Will speaks.

"Go back to the truck, Jack," he says in a voice so weak I almost don't even hear him.

My jaw drops. For a moment I can't even breathe.

Everett snorts. He ain't getting his fight. Will don't have any fight to give.

Everett lets out a bunch of air, like hot steam escaping the valve of some greasy machine. His enormous bulk turns to go.

That's when Frankie steps into the circle. Our city-boy cousin. His face is smooth, but I feel the electricity coming off him.

"Hey," Frankie calls out. "You with the face."

Everett stops.

"Yeah, you," Frankie taunts in a voice that's different from his usual one. Thicker. A city voice. And angry.

"You like to talk," Frankie says. "Talk to me, tough guy."

Everett looks at him, amazement slowly spreading across his ugly face. The other kids begin whispering to each other.

"Frankie . . . what are you doing?" I whisper. Everett Scott is nearly twice as tall as him. My cousin has to tilt his head back to look up at him.

Frankie ignores me, but he calls out to Everett again: "Because if I was as dumb as you, I'd keep quiet so people couldn't find out."

One of the kids in the crowd gives a low whistle. "Hey watch it, Everett! That's a live one!"

The kids in the crowd laugh.

Frankie ignores them. He's bouncing on his feet now, shifting back and forth from one to the other, that electricity crackling.

Everett takes a step toward him. "Shut your mouth, kid, or I'll do it for you."

At that moment, Anna May squeezes past the kids and comes into the ring. She rushes over to Frankie.

"Everett Scott, you leave this boy alone. He's only a boy!"

"He talks plenty good," Everett tells her.

Then Frankie does something that amazes everyone. He laughs. It's a chilly sound, somehow, in the summer night.

"Is that how you talk, tough guy? *Plenty good?* Man, you sound like a frigging caveman."

Everett wears a look of stunned surprise. The crowd goes totally still. Then Frankie finishes it:

"You're *stupid*, Everett. Dumb as a sack of rocks." And he smiles.

Everett hits him. Just whips the back of his hand straight across Frankie's chin.

Our cousin flops over and hits the ground—hard.

The crowd gasps.

"Everett!" Anna May screams.

"Frankie!" I shout.

Everett stands, bewildered, staring at his own upraised hand, like he's wondering how it got there. He's still staring at it when Will comes off the hood of that car.

My brother hits him like a torpedo.

I don't see their fight; mostly I listen as I bend over Frankie to see if he's still alive. Everett really cracked him good. Anna May kneels beside me in the dust. I catch a whiff of her perfume over the smell of stale popcorn.

Frankie groans.

"Lie still and don't move," she tells him.

"Is he fighting?" Frankie asks.

"Can't you hear it?" I ask him.

Behind us, Will's voice lashes out even worse than his fists. He's swearing up a storm.

Frankie smiles. Blood dribbles down his lips.

"You've cut your lip," Anna May tells him.

"I'm fine," Frankie says, sitting up. "I want to see it."

It ain't much of a fight no more. Everett Scott has his hands up in front of his face, trying to protect himself as he stumbles backward. Will comes at him like a freight train, his fists swinging wide and low in a never-ending stream of blows and punches that drives Everett straight into the crowd.

And Will is still swearing. Oh my, but it's lovely. Such an awful cussing you've never heard.

Everett trips and goes into the dust. He don't try getting up—it's too dangerous for that—so he rolls over on his belly and crawls like a beetle fast as he can toward the stand. The kids in the crowd scatter.

Will lets him go. And now he stands alone in the circle, his chest heaving, hair hanging in front of his eyes. He's got a fat lip. One eye is getting dark.

He looks at the crowd. The crowd stares back.

"Holy smokes," someone says.

Will spits.

Then, as the whistles and cheers go up from the kids around him, he turns and in an unsteady way walks over to us.

Will drops into the dust beside us. "Frankie, you okay?"

"Peachy," Frankie answers.

"He really hit him," Anna May says. She dabs at Frankie's chin with the hem of her dress. "I'm so sorry. He's just a little boy. I can't believe he hit him."

"He ain't a little boy," Will says. "He's tough. Right, Frankie?"

Frankie nods. "Yeah, real tuth."

He wobbles when we get him to his feet. More blood dribbles down his chin and onto his shirt.

"Jeez, he's a mess," I say.

"Not as bad as Everett," Frankie says, and now he grins.

On the other side of the lot, Everett is stumbling off. The crowd of kids is thinning out again. One of them walks by and says, "How 'bout that? I bought one ticket but got two shows!"

Will looks at Frankie's shirt. "Ma's gonna pitch a fit," he says, as his face falls. He's realizing now that he's going to have to explain it all. He sighs. "Come on."

We begin to move toward the cars.

"Where we taking him?" Anna May asks.

"My family is back here somewhere," Will tells her. "You can go now, Anna May. He's all right." He pauses. Then: "Thank you."

"Let me at least help you walk him back," Anna May says. "I want to make sure he's all right. And you're not in such good shape yourself."

"I'm fine," Will snaps. "Why don't you go take care of your *boyfriend*, Everett? He's the one needs helping."

I expect Anna May to run off right then and there. But she doesn't.

"You listen to me, Will Elliot," she fires back. "Everett Scott is *not*, nor was he ever, my *boyfriend*. After tonight, I am never speaking to him again. And if you don't let me help you now, I'll never speak to *you* again either!"

Will takes a big breath, as if to say something back. And stops.

"Fine," he says.

"Fine," she says back. "Now, which way?"

"This way," I sigh. "Follow me." I lead them down the narrow metal canyons, past shiny fenders and foggy rolled-up windows, toward our family's Ford.

Will and Anna May quit their talking. They walk either side of Frankie, each with a hand on his shoulder.

I try to make sense of what all just happened. I can't. One minute, Will's completely defeated. Next, Frankie's talking like nothing I've ever heard. Everett smacks him. Will clobbers Everett. And now Anna May is walking with us back to our truck. I just can't figure it out.

All I know is this: Will's back. *Really, truly* back. My brother is back. As if it wasn't just poor Everett Scott he was whaling on at the concession stand, but his own sadness.

I look at Frankie, walking wobbly-legged next to me. Did he *want* Everett to hit him? I shake my head. That's utter foolishness.

Why on earth would you ever want to get hit in the face by Everett Scott?

Midnight in the kitchen.

Frankie sits in a chair with a pack of ice on his lip. Will beside him, a piece of ground chuck wrapped in white paper pressed to his eye. Dad stands over them, arms folded across his chest.

Pete and me watch from the doorway.

We've dropped Anna May back at her house in the new development on the other side of the train tracks. Dad walked her to the front door and explained to Pastor Fenton why it was us bringing her home and not Everett.

But Dad ain't said a word since, and now all four of us are waiting.

Not Ma. She went straight upstairs soon as we got back. She would have no part of it. Whatever would happen, it would be just the boys.

Dad looks at Will with icy eyes, but he ain't spoke yet. That means there's still hope for him.

A bottle of whiskey sits uncorked on the counter. Frankie nearly choked on his spoonful. Will just took his in one gulp.

"Dad, I got hit in the face too," Pete says.

"Be quiet," Dad tells him—and he does. Then, turning to Will, he says, "Talk."

Will does. He tells Dad everything.

When he's finished Dad lifts one eyebrow. "Is that it? This Everett boy hit Frankie and you hit him?"

"That's it."

My father's blazing eyes fall upon me.

"That's just how it happened, Dad. Honest."

"Gosh, Will," says Pete. "If I thought it would get me some time with Anna May, I'd have licked old Everett ages ago."

"Pete, I told you to be quiet," Dad tells him.

"Yes sir."

Dad's stern gaze returns to Will. "You goin' to fight this boy again?"

Will frowns. "Only if he wants it."

Dad frowns, but I know he likes what he's heard.

"Not even Everett Scott is that stupid," I say.

Dad sighs. "Rest of you boys go on up to bed now," he says, looking at me and Frankie. "Pete, you too."

Frankie slides off his chair. Will stays still on his. Dad is going to talk to him alone. That piece of ground chuck is starting to thaw. Bloody water trickles down between his knuckles.

Pete and Frankie and me go as far as the second landing before we stop to listen. But the voices in the kitchen are too low for us to hear. Then the floorboards creak and we hear them moving for the front door. The three of us head up to the bedroom and make for the window. But by the time we get there, Dad and Will are crossing the yard, heading into the fields.

They're going walking together.

"Well, shoot," I say as they disappear into the dark. "How we gonna hear what they're saying now?"

Pete climbs into his bunk. "Forget it, Jack," he sighs. "It's gonna be a long one." He looks over at Frankie. "How's that lip, Frankie?"

Our cousin is lying on his mattress with that ice packet pressed to his mouth.

"Not as bad as Everett's," he says.

Pete is right. It is hours before I hear Will come up the steep stairs and into our room. By then, Pete and Frankie are asleep.

"Did you get in trouble, Will?" I whisper.

"Not exactly," he answers.

"That's good."

I wait.

"Dad wants me to talk more," Will says.

"About what?"

"About anything I feel like . . . He says he'll listen."

Away in Knee-Deep Meadow, the crickets play. Their soft song drifts through our open window.

"You gonna do it?" I ask him.

Again, Will takes a long time before answering. "Yes. I think so."

I wonder what that will be like. Will talking *more*. "Well, if you didn't get in any trouble and all you have to do is talk . . . then it sounds like you got off pretty easy."

"Yeah."

Will lowers himself into his bunk.

I wait for a bit, trying to decide if I should say it.

"Hey, Will?"

"What?"

"Just one thing. Next time . . . don't wait so long to hit somebody who says such nasty things about you . . . about us. Okay?"

He sighs. "Okay."

"Promise?"

"Promise."

"Okay."

"Good night, Jack."

"Good night, Will."

I roll over. Our room is quiet now. That cricket symphony is still playing across the creek. It's beautiful.

"Hey, Will?" I got one more question.

"What, Jack?"

"You sure whooped old Everett good, didn't you?"

Will don't say nothing.

"I mean, you really clobbered him 'til he couldn't take no more."

Will sighs.

"Not even Pete could have whooped him no better. You really laid into him."

Will sighs. "Go to sleep, Jack."

I quiet down, but in my mind I live it all over again. Will's swinging fists. His beautiful cusses. It was a thing to see.

Then there was Anna May there too. She's pretty, for sure, but there's more important things to be thinking about. Like that old wrecked fighter jet.

Sunday morning again, and that means church.

This time we drop Frankie off at Saint Peter's Catholic Church in town so he can pray with his people before we drive down to Main Street Lutheran. Saint Peter's looks more like a castle than a church, with iron-colored stones and narrow stained-glass windows and a statue of old Simon Peter himself out front holding an enormous key. As Frankie passes through the arched doorway, I see what must be a thousand candles glowing softly in smoky dark inside, and it seems to me mysterious and awfully old but also very pretty. Will says something about Catholics sure liking their smells and bells, and we drive off across town to our church.

Low clouds over the cornfields look like they're fixing up some soft summer rain when we arrive, which suits me just fine as it keeps everything that much cooler inside.

Services begin with us all singing, and from our pew I see Anna May Fenton over with the choir, in a green dress with tiny pink flowers all across it. About a minute or so later, I catch her looking at us. Let her look. I imagine she's feeling mighty foolish about ever spending any time with Everett Scott. She's still looking our way once the song ends, and that's when I see she ain't looking at us, really, but at Will, and *just* at Will.

I glance to Will to see if he's taken any notice. He's redder than a turnip.

We sit for Pastor Fenton's sermon, and this time he's talking about holding on to what's true in a time of so many confusing changes and telling us to keep our eyes aimed at the Lord. I don't think Anna May's listening, because every time I look her eyes are aimed right at Will, who's more focused on the white paper pamphlet in his hands than I've ever seen him.

When services end we all lift one last "Amen" before filing out of our pew for the front. I'm hoping to walk with Dad to Mr. Hudspeth's, but he stays a while talking with Pastor Fenton. Ma goes to her church-lady friends, and I'm amazed to see Pete go along with her.

I turn to ask Will if he wants to go up Main Street, but he ain't next to me no more. A minute later, I find him out front with the other kids, standing at the edge of their circle, hands in his pockets, like usual. Only this time, Anna May is standing next to him. Not right next to him, but closer to him than anybody else.

Lordy.

"Come on, Will," I say to him. "Let's go on down to Mr. Hudspeth's 'fore it starts raining and we can't."

Will squints skyward and rocks forward a little on his toes as if that could help him see them clouds any better. He bites his lip. About five feet away, Anna May is looking at the sky too. She don't say a word. She stands very still.

Will seems to be wrestling with a thought. He takes a big old breath of June air and blows it out through his lips.

"Well . . ."

"Well, what?" I ask.

The cornfields begin rustling. The same breeze finds its way over to us and pulls playfully at Anna May's green dress, swishing it around her shoulders, her hips.

". . . I guess we can."

"'Course we can. Let's go."

I start off the steps, but Will stays rooted where he is.

Behind him, inside the church, Ma is coming, her church ladies following like chicks. Trailing them are Dad and Pastor Fenton.

Will's head suddenly snaps toward Anna May.

"Hey, Anna May?"

"Yes, Will?" she says real fast.

"Do you—?"

It ain't just a thunderclap that comes then, it's an explosion. With it, the sky opens, and it seems like every drop of water in the county comes down over the church parking lot. The kids scatter. Ma's church-lady friends flood on past us and let out a whoop as they make for their cars, holding the white paper pamphlets over their heads.

I watch Main Street disappear into silvery sheets.

"Damn it all," I say, even though we've just gotten out of church.

Will shuts his eyes and tilts his head back. Anna May ain't moved, but she seems to be standing farther away now than before.

"Damn it all," Will breathes, softly.

Dad, Ma, and Pete come up, Ma telling us to come on because we're going to pick up Frankie and warning me not to dawdle, as if there's any place to go now. I follow my family into warm summer rain. The cracks in the pavement are already filling up with splashing water, but I still hear Anna May when she says it, her voice faint over the rain.

"Damn it all."

Chapter 14

The Expedition

When I wake up the next morning, my mind is still so wrapped up in Will's wonderful fight that at first I hardly hear what he says when he tells Frankie and me:

"We're going hunting for that fighter jet today. Pack your things and be ready by high noon."

Will heads down the stairs to the kitchen, leaving me in my bed and Frankie on his mattress, both of us dazed and sitting like fools with our mouths open.

Frankie looks at me.

"We're actually *going*!" he says.

The realization comes like the boom after fireworks, after the flash and dazzle's disappeared and it's nothing but spidery white clouds drifting through the night. We're going on an expedition to find that wrecked fighter jet.

"This is it, Jack!" says Frankie. "The big story! The one to *really* make Pete famous. *Peter Elliot Discovers Wreck of Long-Lost Fighter Jet.* That's the title that saves your brother!"

I can hardly move, can hardly breathe.

"Well, come on!" Frankie says, climbing off his mattress. "Will said high noon! What do we need packed by then?"

A million items cross my mind but I can't speak a word, and then it all comes out, and it comes out as a laugh, and it's all I can say but somehow it says it all.

At noon we meet in the yard in front of Stairways. Everything we need is in a pile before us: walking sticks, pocketknives, a spool of fishing string, a compass, canteens, two cans of beans, a book of matches, a coil of rope, fishing hooks, a roll of tinfoil, flashlights, blankets, an old fire-blackened skillet, a cardboard box of pancake mix, and a half-dozen potatoes. Butch eases over to sniff the potatoes, and I have to push him away.

Pete sets down a giant can of grape juice so big it looks like an artillery round for a tank. No clue where he got it.

Will frowns at it, then turns back to the map he's got splayed over one knee. It's Dad's map and I know he ain't asked permission to borrow it. With a worn-down stub of a pencil, he begins drawing.

"We'll go north along Apple Creek, past Devil's Hole, and pitch camp tonight here."

He draws an X. The map crinkles.

"Old Sam says the crash site's somewhere east of there. We'll cross the creek and start the search tomorrow morning."

We divvy up the equipment and load our packs. Pete grunts as he lifts his; that tank-round of grape juice swishes somewhere inside.

My brothers don't know it, but I've packed a little something extra too. Will may have pinched Dad's map, but I pinched his Kodak camera—and *two* rolls of film.

There ain't a doubt in my mind whose sin is greater, but I figure it's worth it.

143

When Frankie submits his story to the newspaper, it's going to have *photographs*.

There's no feeling like the kind you get when you begin a journey to find something you ain't ever found before. Us boys were always going places in these hills, crawling through streambeds or climbing haystacks or sneaking across railroad bridges or wherever to find Lord knows what. But whatever things we found—arrowheads, old snakeskins or snakes still in their skins, or salamanders, or four-leafed clovers—we'd seen them all before.

None of us has ever laid eyes on a fighter jet.

Every boy loves the idea of flying. Some want to be astronauts, like Neil Armstrong or Buzz Aldrin, and that's sure something special. But astronauts don't fly into a battle in the sky. That's why us Elliot boys love fighter pilots. They're *fighters*.

And though we tell Ma that we've decided to go camping for a time with Frankie, when my brothers and cousin and my big galoot of a dog set off to follow Apple Creek north for the ten thousandth time, it ain't like any time before.

We are going farther than we've ever gone before.

Up north, Apple Creek twists like a python between high, rocky hills. The path gives out, and Pete has to find us a narrow deer trail along sharp outcroppings. We follow it for a mile until it gets slashed by a deep, dark gorge.

Pete leads us down into the gorge and then up the far side, but the walls are so steep we have to go hand over hand, grabbing hold of tree roots that poke through the pale clay until we reach the top, covered in mud and out of breath—only to see another deep gash waiting for us, and down we go again. The land is crossed with ravines, some with piles of dry, dead leaves in their bottoms and others with trickles of water gleaming in the dark.

It's slow going for us. Butch loves it. He trots along the ravine bottoms, stirring up clouds of silt and the hair along his legs getting wet and bristly.

Once, Frankie slips and slides almost thirty feet on his backside all the way to the bottom. When he gets up, there's streaks from the seat of his pants all the way up his back to his neck, so dark I know they ain't ever coming out.

Pete and Will bust out laughing, and even though I try not to, I can't help it.

"Why we going this way, anyway?" Frankie asks, red-faced. "Are all these rivers on your map?"

Will tells him that it was heavy rains collecting between the hills that cut these grooves.

"They change over time," Will says. "But these canyons are a bad place to be when the heavy rains come."

Looking about, I can see he's right. I imagine torrents of water rushing down these dark ravines to join the creek. With all that extra water flowing into her, Apple Creek, normally so calm and gentle, becomes a raging monster.

"Isn't there any faster way?" Frankie asks.

"No rush," Pete tells him. "That wreck ain't going nowhere."

Pete may be right, but it ain't the wreck's going anywhere that worries me. It's *Pete's* going somewhere.

Days are ticking down till he turns eighteen, and Frankie and me ain't got one story published yet.

I try wiping some of the mud off Frankie, but it's no use and I tell him so.

"Forget it," he says, and I do and we start to climb the next wall again.

When we leave those rocky ravines behind, we come to a forest of fir trees standing like sentries at the creek's edge.

Pete calls a break and we set our packs down in a dusty clearing beside a piece of deadwood that's been stripped of all its bark so that it gleams white as one of those old bones Butch likes to chew on. We sip metal-tasting water from our canteens and listen to the hum of summer around us: cicadas in the trees overhead and across the creek.

Will lays Dad's map out over the bare trunk and he and Pete hunch over it, murmuring to each other in their way. Pete checks his compass.

Sweat trickles down the back of my neck, between my shoulder blades. It ain't just hot; it's humid, like heaven's dropped a hot, wet towel over the world. I take another long sip from my canteen, becoming more and more aware of a fogginess inside my brain. A tingling.

Pete snaps his compass shut. The signal to rise.

With backpacks clinking, we take to the trail again.

Pete finds another trail—a narrow passage between the firs—and keeps a steady pace. Soon we fall into a rhythm, and I figure that we're marching.

Left, right. Left, right.

Step, step, step.

Pete, Will, Frankie, me.

And Butch.

That goof trots easily alongside me, stopping every so often to cock a leg or lap creek water or bite at flies that float around his muzzle. He sniffs at the base of one of those dark trees, then bounds off to the top of the rise in front of us, scouting ahead.

The ground rises under us; Apple Creek is falling away. We are coming into rocky hills.

Midafternoon now. The day is hot, silent, still. The straps from my pack dig deep into my shoulders. The air feels thick and close, like there ain't another soul for miles.

Butch waits for us at the top of the rise. There Pete suddenly stops.

"Son of a gun."

Below in the creek stands a boy. The hem of his long cotton shirt trails in the current. He's got a pole in one hand and a burlap sack slung over the opposite shoulder.

He wears a wide, floppy hat made of black felt, and it covers most of his face and shoulders.

Even so, I know who it is, and I begin to feel dizzy.

It's Caleb Madliner.

He wades slowly through Apple Creek. Every few steps he tests the bottom with that pole, putting one end down, tapping, feeling, searching.

"What is *he* doing out here?" Will whispers.

Nobody answers. Nobody knows.

I feel like someone's punched me in the gut. Caleb Madliner is here. The boy who wanted to kill my dog. I reach for Butch's collar, hold him close.

Frankie squints. "What's he doing with that stick? Is he looking for something?"

My heart jumps. All at once I know that's *exactly* what he's doing. He's plumbing the streambed, feeling for anything metal. Caleb Madliner is looking for our fighter jet.

Looking to my brothers, I can tell by their faces they've had the same thought.

"So it's a race," Pete says quietly. A thin smile tugs at the corners of his mouth.

My rage boils over. "Doggone it, I don't wanna race Caleb Madliner!"

"Shh!" Will hisses. "Too bad. We already are. Nothing to do now but win it."

He looks at Pete. "Think we can sneak past?"

"We can try," Pete says. "Go cross-country and try to get out ahead of him. We'll lose time. It won't be easy."

"Let's do it," Frankie says then.

Pete's thin smile breaks into a grin. Without a word, he turns and heads into the trees.

The pack on my shoulders feels full of bricks. But there's a new fire burning in my chest and legs now. Caleb Madliner is hunting our treasure, the thing that can save Pete. And there's no way in the world I'll let him beat us to it.

Pete sets a faster pace now, and nobody talks as Apple Creek falls farther and farther behind us.

There is no trail, no path. We crash through a patch of skunk cabbage, fat, rubbery leaves slapping at our legs and a horrible scent hanging over us. Will cusses and Frankie covers his nose at the stench, but I'm too fired up to care about their stink.

After the skunk cabbage come the stinging nettles. I can't ignore those. Fiery pinpricks stab our legs like needles. Tiny white splotches appear on our skin where we've brushed up against the poison plants. When we come out of it at last, our legs are on fire.

Frankie collapses against a tree, wincing back tears and rubbing his calves. Will finds a stand of jewelweed and, quick as we can, we cut ourselves stalks of it and rub the clear liquid juice down our throbbing legs. The pain lessens, the fire dying down to coals.

"I ever mention how much I *hate* Caleb Madliner?" Will says.

You're not supposed to hate anyone, and in his heart I doubt Will really means it. But truth be told, in that moment I feel the same way. When we start again, Pete takes us at a slower pace.

An hour. Two hours.

We go until that ball of white sun overhead begins burning orange and sinks a little lower in the sky. Pete calls a halt then, and he and Will look over the map once more.

"How you holding up?" I whisper to Frankie.

He takes a long draw at his canteen, swishes it around some. "I'll be all right. You?"

I tell him the same, but he narrows his dark eyes at me.

"You don't look good, Jack."

"You ain't so pretty yourself."

"No, I mean your face is pale."

He reaches out a hand and lays it against my forehead—and snaps it back fast. A look of alarm crosses his thin face.

"Jack, you've got a fever!"

"Hush your mouth," I whisper quickly. "I've got no such thing." I look over my shoulder to where my brothers are murmuring over the map. "I'm just hot from the heat and all this walking, that's all."

"I can't believe with all we packed, we forgot medicine! Maybe Pete brought—"

Before he can get up I've got him by the arm.

"Don't you dare, Frankie! I'm feeling just fine. Maybe a low fever, but that ain't nothing to get upset about. We're *this* close to finding that wrecked fighter jet. Fever or no, I can deal 'til then."

He looks at me hard. I can tell he don't like it, but just then Pete comes over.

"Some good news, fellas," he says. "Give me one more mile, and we're done for the day. We'll make camp and have us some dinner over an open fire; what do you say?"

I look at Frankie as I answer for us both. "Sounds dandy."

We rise and hoist our packs upon our backs once again. Maybe I do feel a little fuzzy behind my eyes then, but I give a big smile to Frankie to show how fine I really am.

Pete turns us back to old Apple Creek, and it feels like we're coming home. That fuzzy feeling inside my brain lets up a little.

It's only by chance I look back down the way we came and spy a flash of cottony white against dusty greens. I squint but it's gone, and now I start to wonder if maybe I'm seeing things and Frankie is right after all about me being sick.

I push that thought away. Plenty of time for fevers later.

Pete has us pitch camp on the dry pebbly creek sand beside a calm stretch of Apple Creek. The four of us are washing off the day's sweat and dust, the stench of the skunk cabbage, and the smoldering burn of the nettles when Frankie finds it: a twisted piece of scorched metal, half buried in the silt in the shallows, a dial of the kind you'd turn on a radio. Gray and speckled with rust. Wires stick out the back.

No one speaks for a moment, as we pass it back and forth to each other.

"Is it . . . part of it?" Frankie asks.

"Yes," Pete answers. He scrapes mud with a fingernail, revealing what looks like the face of a clock. He reads out a series of numbers in the gathering dark.

He looks up. "This is an *altimeter*."

Will whistles, soft and low. "So our city boy found the first piece."

Frankie's dark eyes flash. "How close do you think we are?"

"Close. I imagine this washed down from upstream," Pete answers.

We stare up Apple Creek, flat and black in the coming night.

I can *feel* it. That great gray hulk of twisted metal and magic, lying hidden somewhere upstream. Bone-tired as I am, suddenly I am filled with a fierce urge to start right away, just go crawling through the mud in the dark to find it.

"Tomorrow," Pete says, as if reading my mind. "At first light."

We make camp by the creek.

Pete lays out the bedrolls, then sinks the can of fruit juice into the creek to cool before sending Frankie and me off to collect kindling for the fire. Will takes his fishing line and disappears into purple twilight.

When we return with armfuls of deadwood, I see Pete's arranged several smooth river stones in a circle on the sand. With a few handfuls of our kindling, he lights a small fire. He builds it up good, feeding the flames tiny twigs, one by one, until blue smoke drifts across the creek. Then Pete produces another can—tomato soup—and places it near the edge of the fire to warm.

A fat, yellow moon rises behind black trees. We stretch out on the sand as Pete pulls a harmonica from his shirt pocket and begins to play.

Will returns with something hanging over his arm. Firelight shines off the scales of an enormous trout.

"Didn't think I'd get him." Will grins. "I got him."

Soon that trout is sizzling in the skillet.

Potatoes wrapped in sleeves of tinfoil bake in the coals. I catch a whiff and it makes my stomach growl. Pete cuts open the can of tomato soup and passes it around.

The moon's reflection bobs on the water, and I begin to relax. The smell of woodsmoke. Hot soup in my stomach. Pete's playing soft as the frogs join in. The ache in my shoulders from carrying that pack all day melts away. My mind goes easy. The knots in my soul are being loosened one by one.

I pass the soup to Frankie and remember the can of fruit juice cooling in the creek. I get up and go over to lift it from the water, feeling the cool metal in my hands. Pete cuts a hole in the lid and lets Frankie and me take the first sips.

We eat our dinner on the creek bank under the moon and a handful of blue stars.

When we're done, Frankie passes the airplane dial around again. Each of us takes a long time holding it in his hands, as if we might absorb some of its magic through our skin.

"Somewhere just around the corner," Pete says, turning it over in his fingers, letting orange firelight play across the scorched metal.

"What happened to the pilot?" Frankie asks.

"Far as anybody knows," Will replies, "he died."

We're quiet for a time. So it ain't just a lost wreck we're searching for, but a burial site. Hallowed ground.

Butch ambles over, and I give him the last of my baked potato.

"How about a song, Will?" Pete says then, as he starts up his harmonica once more.

Will shakes his head.

"A story then," Pete says. "Shakespeare? One of your old Greek myths?"

Will looks at Frankie. "You ever hear the Beowulf tale?" he asks.

Frankie shakes his head.

Pete grins, kicks off his shoes, and leans back on the sand. Frankie and me do likewise as Will sits himself up and begins the story of Beowulf and his band of warriors. Heroes is a better word for them, for they answer a call for help from an old king whose people are being attacked by a monster named Grendel.

Will's a marvelous storyteller, and the way he tells it, we're right there with Beowulf and his men as they lie in wait for the creature around their campfire, pretending to be asleep but really ready to jump up and fight the moment he appears. And when Grendel comes, it's a big battle until Beowulf tears the monster's arm off and beats him to death with it.

Will finishes the story and I have to ask him.

"Is that a true story, Will?"

He drains the last of the tomato soup from the can. "No one knows for sure."

The four of us sit quiet on cold sand. It's the same dark that presses against us and our tiny campfire as before, but now there's the possibility of something hideous hiding in it and our fire has died down to a few glowing coals.

"Can we put another piece of wood on?" I ask.

"It's late now, Jack," says Pete. "Best to let the fire be and get some sleep."

Frankie and me lie extra still in our rolls.

At first I'm too scared to sleep, even though I know Grendel ain't real and that it was all just a story—and an old story at that. But then the weariness settles into my body. My bones become heavy.

It's not too much longer after that when I let my eyelids close over our bank, those glowing embers, and the black water—and the shape at the edge of the trees that seems to melt into the dark just as I leave the world.

Chapter 15

Fever!

When I wake, dawn's rose-colored fingers are peeling back the curtain of night from the sky, but even that watery light is too much for my aching head to handle.

I'm running a fever.

No doubt about it.

I'm running a fever, sure as I'm breathing.

How bad? Have to hide it. Can't let Pete or Will see.

My brothers are still asleep. Gray lumps in the gray light. So is Frankie, his glasses hanging crooked off his nose, mouth wide open at the sky like he's trying to taste the coming day.

I lie still, and through my headache I am able to taste it too: wet dew on my blanket and on my clothes; the blush of warm sunlight on my face; across the creek, a mourning dove . . .

I let its newness flow through me, into me, over me, try to let it heal me.

I get up on one elbow and feel the blood rushing hard in my temples. I wince, but I stay up.

My clothes are wet from sweat too, and in the early morning cool I shiver.

How long before Pete and Will wake? How long before they decide to call off our expedition because I'm too sick?

The whole thing is something fun for them, a great adventure. They don't know it's something more, that it's Pete's ticket to safety, to staying out of the draft, to staying out of Vietnam and those murderous jungles.

Mist curls over Apple Creek's glassy surface, white, ghostlike.

The creek. Cold and clean. I crawl out of my bedroll and across damp sand to it and, cupping my hands, bring that water to my face and the back of my neck. I wash in the creek in the early morning and feel the thrumming between my ears let up just a little.

Pete's voice startles me.

"First one awake has to make breakfast," he says from his place, still with his eyes shut.

I sigh. "Yes sir."

Slowly, tenderly, I draw a few twigs of deadwood out from the pile Frankie and me gathered last night and start the fire. A few of the coals on the bottom still have life to them, the faintest red glow. I breathe soft and easy on them, and soon I'm rewarded with a cheerful snippet of yellow flame.

"Two eggs over easy, a side of Canadian bacon, and a cup of coffee, black," Pete tells me.

I sigh again.

Will rolls and I realize he's awake too. "Short stack of blueberry flapjacks for me."

We take only what we need for the search. Everything else we leave on the bank. Pete says it's base camp and wants to give it a name. Will ain't pleased.

"What on earth for? A camp's a camp!"

"This ain't just any old camp. This is *our* camp. And it's got to have a proper name."

Neither notices as I sneak Dad's camera out of my pack and into my back pocket.

"We're wasting time!" Will shouts.

Pete shakes his head. "Not without a name." His eyes fall on me. "Well, Jack? What'll it be?"

I think fast.

"Camp Beowulf."

Pete smacks his hands together. "Camp Beowulf! Established in the year of our Lord nineteen-hundred and sixty-eight—"

"For heaven's sake, Pete—"

"Hush, Will, I'm commemorating the camp—by the Elliot brothers, Peter, Will, and John Thomas, and their city-boy cousin, Frankie."

Pete picks up one of the fire-darkened sticks and shoves it into the sand. I don't know what that was supposed to do, but somehow it did it, and we've commemorated Camp Beowulf now and forever.

"Okay, Will," says Pete, brushing the sand from his hands. "Which way?"

Will sucks in a long breath through his nose.

"North, northeast half a mile. That should put us right on top of it. Keep your eyes open for anything like the piece Frankie found last night. They'll lead us to the big wreck. And watch your step for any unexploded bombs or missiles. They should be easy to spot too. Any questions?"

Frankie and me shake our heads. Even if we had any, we wouldn't ask. The magic has got us, the draw of that fantastic fighter jet. It's time.

"Then let's go!"

We follow Apple Creek a quarter mile north and cross at a sandbar where the water is ankle deep and crystal clear in the early light. Climbing up the far bank, we pass through a stand of pricker bushes and come at last to the other side.

Dark trees stand like old gray men at attention. We pass through their gloom and heavy quiet, spying into their deep timbers as if they're cages for some living thing.

That lost fighter jet might as well be alive—a creature of living metal, sending out its pulses, like a heartbeat, for us to follow. I can almost smell jet fumes and burnt rubber on the thick, stifling air.

At Pete's command, we spread out and walk slow through the spiderwebbing shadows, casting our eyes over ground covered with old leaves, dead leaves, rotting leaves, looking for anything that don't belong: a flap of torn cloth, a gleam of metal, the shine of glass.

No one speaks, and even Butch seems to understand in his animal way that we are very near to the place where a man has died.

What was that night like? Blasts of stinging ice and howling dark. A sound like the world was ripping in two and a sudden flash of fire raging against all that bitter cold. Then silence.

Like it's silent now.

The deeper we go, the less daylight there is trickling down through the treetops.

A thick dead-leaf perfume hangs on the air. Musty. Almost too much. A sudden sense of floating inside my head, and I have to place a hand against one of those old gray trunks to steady myself.

My brothers don't see. They have all gone ahead, already tiny shadows under the trees. Like me, they're thirsting to make the next discovery, hoping to repeat Frankie's miraculous find from last night.

To my right, a stand of waist-high ferns catches a bit of sunlight that's leaked in from above. It's a cheerful splash of color in all that gloom, and I head for it, hoping I'll come across pieces of the airplane on my way.

I don't.

Just strips of old bark and rotten logs.

A bead of sweat runs down my forehead. Fever's back.

I sigh, a muffled sound in that closed-up air.

I'm sweating more; I don't care. That fighter-jet excitement is in my blood. We're close, so close to the discovery that will save Pete's life.

I feel for Dad's camera in my pocket. The reassuring square box is there. And the two rolls of film . . .

The film!

I stop dead in my tracks. Both rolls of film are in my pack—at Camp Beowulf. I forgot the film.

"Oh no."

My voice sounds funny, as if I'm hearing myself from far off.

How far back was camp? A half mile?

I turn around.

There's no choice now but to go back for it. I might miss being there when the next discovery is made, maybe the one that leads us to a trail of still more fantastic pieces—a long, glittering trail of twisted metal leading us straight to the wreck itself.

I could kick myself for my foolishness. But there's no other way. We've got to have pictures. We need pictures of Pete standing triumphantly alongside the plane, pointing, smiling. The *newspapers* need those pictures of Pete.

I'm close to Apple Creek, can hear its sweet babbling, when I realize that my clothes are clinging to my body like a second skin and I'm sweating all over, trembling all over. It seems my shoes are filled with sand, heavy, dragging.

Dimly, I realize the fever has laid hold of me.

And the trees . . . all those tall gray trees, so close, so near. Before, they looked like a cage for some wild animal. Now I realize they are *my* cage.

I stagger forward a few more leaden steps and stop when a shape appears in the trees before me. It's white and moving toward me.

Shadows cover the head and face. No. Not shadows—a hat. A black felt hat.

In some back corner of my mind, maybe the last part of my brain that ain't burning up with fever-fire, a single clear thought rises: call for help.

With the last of my breath I give the greatest cry I can, and then the world rocks like a seesaw under me and then everything goes dark.

It's a dream, that much I know. I am somewhere very high, hanging over the ocean. And far, far below I see waves gently rolling. They're singing to me, singing my name, over and over. Their song is beautiful, like a lullaby.

But I know if I go, I will never wake up again.

"Stop that hammering."

The sudden sound of my own voice startles me. But still that hammer keeps coming, sending streaks of white-hot lightning crackling through my skull.

"Ain't nobody hammering, you fool." That's Will. But he's afraid. That makes *me* afraid.

"He's awake!" Frankie's voice is very close, very loud.

Cool metal touches my lips. "Drink, Jack." And there's Pete, low and stern.

That lightning comes again, searing my brain, but I sip at the canteen like my brother tells me just the same.

"That's a good boy."

"What happened?" I ask.

"It was your darn fever," Will says. "Why didn't you tell us you were burning up?"

I open my eyes, but even the weak sunlight under those trees is too much for me. It stabs into my brain like a knife. I shut my eyes quick, but not so quick I don't see someone else there with my brothers and my cousin, someone in a white cloth shirt and a black felt hat . . . Caleb Madliner!

"What in the world is he doing here!"

I sit up but it's like a bomb goes off inside my head, and it hurts so bad I cry out.

"Sit back, Jack!" Pete commands. His hands on my chest, pushing me down. There's nothing I can do now but lie there with my eyes shut tight and tears leaking down my cheeks.

"You should be thanking Caleb," Pete's voice goes on. "He found you and then he found us."

I'm whimpering from my headache, but my mind races. Caleb Madliner has caught up to us. Has he found the wreck yet? And then a more horrifying thought: Where is Butch?

My heart knocks against my ribs.

"Where's Butch?" I ask, and now I really am crying.

"He's right here," Frankie says.

I sniff at that.

"Jack." Pete's voice is still stern. "You tell Caleb thank you for finding you."

I swallow. "Thank you, Caleb."

If Caleb makes a reply, I don't hear it. And with my eyes squeezed shut, I can't see him. I'm fine with that.

"What's wrong with me?" I ask. "It hurts to see."

I feel Pete and Will turn to each other. Their gaze meets somewhere above me. Then I become even more afraid: they don't know.

"We ain't sure. You've got a bad fever," Pete says. "We've brought it down some. But we've got to get you back to Stairways and the doctor right away—"

"Did we find it?" I ask suddenly.

Did my brothers find the wreck? Or has Caleb already found it?

"The only thing that matters now is getting you home," Pete tells me.

"Did we find it?"

"Jack—"

I force my eyes open and ignore the pain. Around me I see my family, my dog, and Caleb. And at his feet is the burlap sack. It's full. That drawstring pulled tight.

"What's he got in his sack?" I cry, even though I already know what's in it. Airplane pieces. Nasty old Caleb Madliner has beaten us to the crash site, and now it's his.

"Jack, hush," Will tries. But I won't be hushed. It's all over. The dream of finding the fighter jet, of saving Pete. It's all over, and it's all because of me and my stupid fever.

And then *he* speaks.

"It's none of your business what I got," Caleb says. And he smiles.

I want to leap upon him, knock that black felt hat off his head, but then I feel Frankie's hand on my shoulder. His dark eyes look into mine.

"Nobody's found anything," Frankie tells me. "Now, you listen to Will and *hush*."

Frankie's back is to Caleb. Quickly he raises a finger to his lips and signals me to be quiet.

I blink. Slowly I realize: He and my brothers didn't find the wreck yet. But they don't want Caleb knowing.

Frankie's hand stays on my shoulder until he sees I understand.

"How are we gonna get him back?" Frankie says then, looking to Pete. "He can't walk."

"We'll have to carry him," Pete answers. "But that's not what's got me worried."

As if to prove Pete's point, a low rumble comes from the west. Thunder.

"Think fast, Pete," Caleb says. "Storm's coming. A mighty storm. Can't you feel it?"

I despise him, but even so, I know he's right. The air under the trees has gotten cooler. The hairs on my arms are standing on end.

"Where will you take them?" Caleb asks Pete. "The creek will surely flood, and your little camp will wash away within the first hour."

Pete's got the corners of his mouth turned down. He's thinking hard.

Will whips out Dad's map, throws it on the leaves, and drops down over it. "We need to get to high ground," he says quickly. "Maybe some-place west. There's hills west of here." He's scared.

Pete stands very still, looking west. The thunder comes again.

"I know a place." Caleb ain't moved. He sits same as before. "North of here."

Pete is silent.

"North? Don't be foolish!" Will snaps. "We need to head *south*. Toward home. We ain't taking Jack farther *north* with a fever and a flood coming!"

Caleb's coal-black eyes never leave Pete.

"North. Not far. High ground. A cave."

Will goes white as a sheet of paper. *"There?"*

Caleb smiles again. "Scared?"

Will's face flushes scarlet red. He stands up. "Pete, he's talking non-sense! That's crazy."

But Pete's already decided. Will knows it too, and that color drains from his face once more.

There's a fierce light to Pete's eyes as he says, "We make for camp. Pack fast. Then we head north to the Rock."

Frankie looks at me. "But Jack can barely walk!"

Pete drops down next to me and, in one smooth movement, lifts me into his arms.

"Let's go."

The sky is green around the edges when we come out of the trees. Bruised clouds of purple and black turn and turn above us. A warm wind blows, whipping the creek, now a silvery green, into little white-caps of foam. Grendel is coming.

We abandon Camp Beowulf in a clatter of pans and cussing and kicked sand. The packs are loaded, Will and Frankie taking two each. Pete carries me.

Will tries one last time. "There's got to be some other place!"

"There's no time," is all Pete tells him.

I know why Will's scared. I'm scared too. I've only heard of the place we're going. A place where one of earth's stony ribs has torn through its skin. A jagged black rock, weather-worn, carved by time to look like the head of a man—but not just any man, an Indian warrior, proud, sad, and vengeful.

Lightning cracks the bruised sky. Through that fresh cut in the heavens comes a sound like the hissing of an enormous snake. Then sheets of rain.

It's started.

"Follow me, Elliots, if you don't feel like swimming!" Caleb shouts over the wind. Without waiting, he lurches into the storm.

Pete cradles me in his arms, close to his warm body as the wind hurls rain against us.

"Hold on tight, Jack."

He begins to run.

Chapter 16

The Cave

Caleb leads us inland and uphill, weaving between the dripping trunks. Cradled in Pete's arms, I see his white shirt bobbing like a ghost in the stormy dark. He never looks back.

Behind us Apple Creek boils under sheets of merciless machine-gun rain. Uprooted trees ride the current like crocodiles, rushing past on foamy water. The creek is rising.

Thunder tears the night in two and I twist in my brother's arms, trying to find Butch, trying to see that he's with us, not scared senseless and running blind toward rising water. But it's too dark and I cannot see my dog.

Branches and leaves slap at us and fallen limbs lunge across our way. Pete dodges them, jumping, ducking, leaping. Soon his breaths are ragged gasps, but he don't quit.

All at once we burst into open space and we're running along a shelf of rock that rises into the night. There's nothing above us now but the storm, and it hurls rain and each drop is like ice on my feverish skin. Through it, I see Will and Frankie behind us, coming out of the trees, and finally Butch, bounding alongside them, barking like mad.

Pete's heart pounds like a jackhammer through his chest, and I am afraid it's going to burst it's beating so fast. I struggle to climb down, to let him rest, but he just holds me tighter, his muscles locking me against his body, and all of a sudden we're flying, dashing through electric air as he jumps from one rain-splattered rock to another, and then another and another, up the mountain.

A ball of blue lightning explodes over us, and suddenly the Indian is there in the rain-slashed night. In the place where his mouth should be is a black hole: the entrance to the cave.

Caleb disappears into the Indian's mouth and is gone.

Pete don't even slow down. Ducking his head, he dives into that dark and the warrior swallows us too. Pete's arms go loose and I slide onto the wet rock floor. I hear him collapse beside me, his breaths echoing off the walls.

I reach for him in the darkness of the cave and my hand touches his heaving chest, and I feel his heart, still pounding away underneath. I want to tell him how sorry I am, but my body shakes so fierce I can't make any words.

Pete lays a hand on top of mine and gives me a weak squeeze.

Barking outside. Frankie and Will crash out of the night, soaking, coughing, cussing, Butch right behind. My dog finds me in the dark, his coat dripping wet, and starts licking my face and whining, as outside thunder crashes again.

Will shrugs off the two packs he's carried the whole way, then turns over and throws up.

Beyond the mouth of the cave, the storm roars like a wild animal. But there's something else in the air now, a terrible, high-pitched shrieking that sounds almost human. Sticks and leaves blow in from the night. Butch whines again.

"What's that?" Frankie asks in a trembling whisper.

From the inky black, Caleb answers him.

"It's a twister."

Outside, the shrieking grows louder.

"Get to the back of the cave!" Pete shouts.

We scramble blindly in the dark over the rough rock, but the cave ain't deep. At its far end, we huddle against cold rock and a mesh of old roots and wait. I wrap my arms about Butch and hold his soaking body close.

"Hang on!" Will shouts as suddenly the cave is filled with a screaming wind.

It's Frankie who remembers the rope. As that howling cyclone reaches its fingers into our cave and whips our clothes about our bodies and snatches at the hair on our scalps, our city-boy cousin crawls to the entrance and finds it in Will's pack. Ignoring our shouting, or maybe because he don't hear us, he stays at the edge, tearing through the pack. Lightning flashes and we see him, a blackened cutout of a boy, kneeling before a torrent of water and wind and light. When the lightning comes, the cave's mouth is empty and I'm certain he's been sucked out, but in another flash of electric light he appears out of the dark right before me.

He's got the rope with him.

"Wrap it around you!" he shouts. I do and an instant later the rope tightens and I realize: he's lashed us to those roots.

There comes a sound like the world is ending, a terrible crash that shakes the rock walls. The ground trembles under us and I think: *This is it. This cave is our tomb.*

It's a second later that Will's pack picks up and sails right out of the cave. The others go right after it, one after the other, and now that awful, shrieking wind is tugging at me, tugging at Butch, trying to drag *us* out too.

But that rope around my chest holds; the twister can't have us.

"Hold on!" someone shouts.

That shrieking gets even *louder*, and I shut my eyes and start to pray, pray that my family won't die, that they and even Caleb Madliner will live through this, even if I don't.

A wave of peace, a touch of sadness come over me. And just when I decide that I'm ready to go, that horrible shrieking begins to fade. The wind begins to lessen until, with a last furious breath, that twister blows itself out.

We press against cold rock, barely believing we're still alive. Even when Frankie lets that rope go slack, nobody moves until, slowly, he crawls to the mouth of the cave and peers out into the night.

Rain hammers the mountain and lightning splits the sky once more, but the twister is gone.

Rain pitter-patters against the Indian's rock face. Away south, thunder rumbles. The storm has passed. From far below comes a sound like a soft wind rustling in the grass. But it ain't wind. It's water. A whole lot of dark, fast water.

Apple Creek is flooding.

Cold and wet, we sit in the dark: five boys and a dog with no food, no blankets, and no fire. It's the fire I need most. My fever's back and my wet clothes and that cold air have me shaking like a leaf on a tree.

"Anybody got a match?" Pete asks. His voice sounds weak, haggard.

"In my pack," Will answers, sounding every bit as tired. "Miles away now."

There's a scratching sound and suddenly a single yellow flame cuts a hole in the dark.

Caleb Madliner holds a lit match in his fingers. Where he got it, I don't know. At first we see only his floating head, and it's horrifying.

Then, in flickering light, the walls of the cave, the tangle of roots, and some scattered, curled leaves.

Frankie grabs two fistfuls for kindling, but Caleb turns the matchstick around in his long, bony fingers, watching the tiny strip of cardboard wither and curl inside the flame. He lets it burn down to his fingertips before dropping it on the leaves.

We gather as many sticks and twigs as we can find in the cave. When the fire is a tiny pyramid of twisting flames we sit close around it, and for a long time we do not talk.

"Too dangerous to travel now," Pete says at last. "Sleep if you can. We will try in the morning."

We stretch out best we can in the cramped cave. Pete is so exhausted he drifts off almost at once, and it ain't long before Will joins him. I curl up on my side against the wall, but I know there won't be any sleep for me tonight.

A thought gnaws at me, terrible as it is true: *I've killed my brother.* Oh sure, Pete is still breathing just across from me in the cave, but he might as well be six feet under. My plan has failed. We came out here to find that fighter jet, to make Pete famous enough that he wouldn't get drafted, that he could stay safe. But my fever has ruined our expedition. Pete's run himself half to death, and we all almost got carried off by a twister.

My brother is as good as drafted, and I know what that means. I listen to the dull roaring of a flooded creek below us and I think of that *other* riverbank, the one from my dreams, where boys line up and wait for the machine guns to rattle.

Hot tears run down my face. It's all my fault. And since I am not even trying to sleep, I just lie there and watch our little fire slowly burn down.

But I'm not the only one.

Caleb Madliner sits against the far wall, staring into the flames. The fire's taken him somewhere else in his mind, and in that place he don't feel the rough stone or the cold air blowing in from outside. He's in a trance.

I've always been frightened of people in trances. You never know what they'll do while they're visiting that faraway place—or worse yet, when they return and find you lying across from them in a narrow cave in the middle of nowhere.

I watch him from under my eyelids as I pretend to sleep, watch him watch the fire burn. Don't know how much later it is when he finally draws a deep breath—like he's coming up from being underwater a long time—sits up, and looks about himself. That red firelight reflects in his dark eyes, which sweep over us and then to a place in the back of the cave where the light don't reach, to a shadowy place beneath those old roots.

Funny how your mind puts things together sometimes. Watching him, I suddenly remember that his burlap sack was nowhere to be seen the whole time we sat around the fire. All at once I figure out that he's hidden it back there among those roots. He must have done it as soon as he came into the cave, just before Pete and me.

But what's he hiding? Has Caleb found pieces of that old fighter jet after all?

As I watch him flatten himself against the wall and pull his black hat low over his eyes, I know what it is I'm going to do.

The fire has died down to just a few embers by the time I move, crawling on my hands and knees right past him, to the back of the cave, where I feel coarse burlap under my hands.

I'd like to blame it on the fever. I know I can't. I know full well that what I'm doing is stupid, that I'm taking an awful chance messing with someone crazy as Caleb Madliner. But I know more than that too. I know it's wrong to be snooping on people—even people like him. I do it just the same.

The sack's heavy and I find I need both hands to draw it forth from its hiding place. Quiet as I can, I work that drawstring loose, the threads rustling softly as they come free, and it's a tiny little sound but one so loud in that stony dark that I suck in my breath and wait for Caleb to spring up.

He don't move a muscle.

Caleb's sack lies open before me on the cave floor, but there's just one last problem: it's too dark to see.

Getting down to my last good idea, I tiptoe back to the fire and, with a few hushed breaths, heat up those coals. I find a twig with a few dry leaves clinging to it, light them, and creep once again to the back of the cave. Sweat pours down my face now. My heart is slamming against the inside of my ribs.

A wild and terrible idea rises in my mind as I reach for that sack a second time, the thought that I could *steal* one of those pieces. My heart skips a beat. Oh, it's a sin to steal, but if it saved Pete's life, wouldn't it be *worth* it? A way to save the whole expedition. A way to save my brother.

The whole weight of that mountain bears down on me as with trembling hands I lift that flap and—

Two round, black eyes stare into my soul.

All the breath leaves my body in a rush of fear.

Staring back at me is a great-granddaddy of a snapping turtle, the biggest I have ever seen, with folds of pale skin and an enormous triangle head and a beak mouth that's opening wider and wider, showing a vast satiny-white cavern within.

The creature rises on knock-kneed dinosaur legs and hisses, and then a cold voice from behind me says:

"Does he look hungry to you, Jack?"

Dad told me stories of a man he knew as a boy, Dutch Billy, who used to hunt snappers in the slow-moving parts of Apple Creek. He only had seven fingers.

He'd catch the snappers alive and bring them back and turn them loose in his cellar. And whenever he wanted one, he'd just go down and grab it by the short, fat tail and take it out back, where he'd waggle a piece of rebar in front of it until the turtle chomped down. Since snappers never let go once they bite, Dutch Billy would just pull its head out from under the shell and hack it off with an ax. Even then he'd have to toss the rebar, with the bloody stump of a head clamped down on it. Never could get those jaws open once it was dead.

I remember all of that as I stare into reptile eyes that gleam right back at me in fiery light.

The hand that closes over my mouth buries my scream before it even begins. Caleb is there, his arm pinning me against him, and with his other hand he grabs my wrist and squeezes until I drop that burning brand.

"Should have left it alone, Jack," he whispers.

In the wavering light, that ancient snapper takes one lumbering step forward, its head gliding out toward me. And slowly, ever so slowly, Caleb stretches my hand toward it, moving my fingers toward that pale, gaping mouth.

"Like I said, he's hungry, and you've got fingers enough."

It must be a nightmare. A feverish nightmare. I'm dreaming. I shut my eyes hard as I can but when I open them again, that snapper is there just like before and my fingers are sliding closer and closer to that awful mouth. I'm awake. Caleb Madliner is feeding my fingers to a snapping turtle while my brothers and my dog sleep not ten feet from us.

The snapper lifts its enormous head and hisses once more, and I know it's preparing to bite when I get a last, desperate idea.

I bite first. Hard as I can on the hand over my mouth. Caleb gives a startled cry and his grip goes loose for just a moment, but it's all I need. With every ounce of strength in my little body, I burst away from him. Then I scream.

A lot happens then.

Everybody comes awake.

Caleb seizes the sack and yanks the string shut, closing the loop over the hideous head.

Butch barks.

In my blind rush to get away from the snapper, I crash into someone—Will, who falls into Pete. All three of us Elliot boys go down in a heap on the cave floor.

Caleb springs for the cave entrance, but Frankie is just climbing to his feet and he's blocking Caleb's way out. Without hesitating for a moment, Caleb swings that burlap sack and its awful contents right at him. Frankie ducks just in time, the sack sailing over his head through empty air. But now the way to the cave's mouth is open, and I look up just in time to see Caleb Madliner leaping through. Before anybody can do or say anything, he's gone into the night.

I'm babbling like a fool, and it's a good while before Pete and Will and Frankie are able to make any sense of what I'm saying. When I finally do tell them all that happened, they're stunned. Then furious.

Will grinds a fist into his palm. "I'll whip him for this. I always wanted to have at him too."

Pete don't say a word, but the way his jaw is set and the look in his eyes, it would be downright dangerous for Caleb Madliner ever to come near him again.

"It's my fault, Jack," Pete says. "I'm the one who decided to follow him up here. I should have known."

Pete builds up the fire best as he can with what's left of the kindling, then, giving us stern orders to stay put, he goes out to gather what firewood he can find from the branches blown down by the twister. When he comes back, he works the fire, finally getting it up to a good, hot flame that gives plenty of light.

Frankie stands at the entrance, looking into the dark. "What if he comes back?"

"Then he'd make my night," Will says.

Pete shakes his head. "He won't. He will try to cross the creek and get back to his house on the hill." Pete snaps a branch over his knee and thrusts the broken ends into the fire.

"Will he make it?"

Will huffs. "Who cares? After this, it'd be just what he deserves for him to drown in Apple Creek."

Nobody has anything to say to that. Truth is, we're out of gas. All of us. Pete knows it. For the second time that night he tells us to try to get some sleep. Tells us he'll stay awake and keep watch.

I am so worn out that I think I really will sleep this time. As I lie down again, though, I can't help but think of that snapping turtle in the sack. Despite the fact that it almost bit my fingers off, I can't help feeling sorry for it.

I feel sorry for anything that has to be that close to Caleb Madliner.

Chapter 17

The Raft

A fine mist blows over the mountain when we wake the next morning, cool and soft and chilly. I wander out into it to do my business.

For the first time, I see what the twister's done to the world. Trees are splintered bony white, their arms flung far and wide across the forest floor. Standing at the edge of that rock shelf, I see something else lying down there too: Caleb's black felt hat. Must have blown off when he was running out of the cave last night.

I unzip and pee thirty feet straight down onto it before going back inside.

Pete crouches over the ashes of our fire and tries to breathe life back into the coals. He looks different in that gray light; older, like he's aged a bunch of years in a single night. Guilt sticks me in the gut. My brother's lost some of his strength because of me. I'll be the death of him.

A tiny wisp of smoke curls through his fingers. Dead coals come back to life. Pete smiles and it's his old smile, that grin he gets when he's pleased with himself. He gives Butch a scratch behind the ears and looks up at me as I come in.

"How do you feel?" he asks.

"Fine," I lie. I've never felt worse in my life. Forget the fever. Forget the snapper. Forget the stiffness from sleeping on cold rock. I have ruined our chance to save him.

We warm ourselves by the fire, but there's no food, so after kicking it out we make our way slowly down the mountain to see what's become of Apple Creek. It's a torrent of gray, frothy water. Clumps of long grass rush by in the current.

"That's one good thing the twister's done for us," Pete says, tilting his head at several fallen trees. "It's given us a way home."

"What's that?" Frankie asks him.

"Floating."

The raft comes together by noon. It isn't much to look at. A mess of branches bound together by that rope of Frankie's and some monkey vines that Will drags down out of a stand of pine trees. But it floats. That's all we care about.

On Pete's orders, I sit with Butch while they hack and bind it all together. I am miserable, shaking, and feeling fuzzy inside my head.

When it comes time to shove off, Frankie and me take up our places in the raft's center. I hold Butch so he won't get skittish and swamp us. The raft dips under some when Pete and Will climb on, pouring cold water into our laps. I am sure we're about to sink, but then Pete and Will spread out and we come up out of the water again and suddenly we're moving, riding the current. With a pair of long branches, my brothers steer us farther out into the creek.

We get a last look at that old Indian warrior as we go. I am not sad when he slips behind the bend. I never want to see him again.

"Sure beats walking," Pete says. "Just nobody drown."

Farther along, the water flattens out. With our little raft just about steering itself, Pete lies back across those knotted branches and shuts his eyes. Next to him, Will hunches over Dad's map. He's had it in his back pocket this whole time and it's soaked clean through, but he stares at it just the same, trying to find out where we are. Won't be easy. Apple Creek's banks are completely washed over, the trees seeming to grow right up out of the water. There's not a landmark to recognize anywhere.

As if I wasn't feeling bad enough already, the sight makes me think of Kemper and his reservoir. That worm will flood our whole valley worse than this if he gets the chance.

Of us all, only Frankie seems to be anything other than miserable. Covered head to toe in mud, with the seat of his pants soaked from the water that trickles over the branches of our dingy little raft, he leans on one elbow, lost in his own thoughts, watching the world slide by. Peaceful. How different a sight he is from the boy we found on the train platform.

I am surprised at what he says.

"I hope Caleb is all right."

"That's downright charitable of you," Pete says tonelessly from his corner of the raft.

I'm about to tell Frankie that I don't care if Caleb's drowned body is stuck in a tree somewhere when someone appears in my mind, clear as morning sunlight shining off the creek. It ain't Caleb; it's my mother. Standing on the porch against a stormy sky. She looks at me.

Don't you ever do anything to make somebody feel like their life is no account to you, hear? It's the worst thing you can do to a person. It's a kind of killing, a killing of the soul.

At the memory of my mother's words, I'm ashamed. I'm ashamed because I know I have done things to make Caleb feel his life was no account to me. A boy who gets hit by his father. A boy whose mother is insane, likely *because* of his father. And in that moment, I know Frankie is right to hope he's safe.

"What do you think is wrong with him?" Frankie asks.

"With Caleb?" Will looks up from his map and furrows his brow. "Caleb's crazy. That's all."

Frankie chews his lip. "Don't you think something *made* him that way?"

Will shrugs. "Maybe. Maybe not. But it don't matter. You saw what he tried to do to Jack. And that ain't all. He's crazy in other ways. Did you know he likes to light fires?"

Frankie shakes his head.

"He's a firebug," Will goes on. "He lights fires for fun. It does something to him, puts his mind a certain way that he likes."

The raft creaks and groans. Creek water splashes through the planks again. Sun comes out, making the creek sparkle around us. The day is getting beautiful, but I shiver just the same.

Frankie asks another question.

"How do we bring this thing ashore when we get where we're going?"

Will frowns, thinks, laughs. "You know something? I don't know. In fact, I haven't a clue. We could float right past Stairways, on through town, for all I know. We could drift down into the Chesapeake and then right on into the Atlantic Ocean."

From my place on our wobbly raft, I wonder if that's really possible. I remember hearing somewhere that every drop of rain that falls eventually ends up in the ocean. I suppose Apple Creek eventually finds its way there too.

"We really are a ship of fools," Will says, laughing once more. "Hey, Pete, what's your plan for getting us ashore?"

Pete don't bother to open his eyes. "Just enjoy the ride." He yawns. "And don't interrupt me when I'm thinking."

Will sighs and looks back to Frankie. "We'll figure something out when the time comes."

We do. We swim.

Pete doesn't want to just abandon ship, though. He wants to sink our little craft—"scuttle the ship and give her an honorable death at sea." And he wants to name our little raft first.

"What about the USS *Swiss Cheese*?" says Frankie, as water splashes through onto his pants again.

I don't care what fool name we settle on. I'm feeling awful and resenting how cheerful they all are. Even Butch looks happier now that the sun is out, and we're so close to home. But I'm nursing my own guilt deep down. It's a fire worse than the fever.

"Jack, you're good with names," says Pete. "What'll it be?"

"I don't care," I mutter.

"Sure you do. Tomorrow you'll wish you said something."

I keep my mouth shut but Pete stands up then, and the whole raft tips under us.

"I will not leave this deck until we get a name. I swear I'll go down with the ship if you don't say something."

That does it, and I think for a minute. Most boats are normally named for girls, and so I say the first name comes to mind.

"The *Anna May*."

Will turns bright red. Pete beams. "That works. Now, somebody be brave and give old Butch a scoot overboard. Make sure he's pointing the right way. We're aiming for *that* bank. Just holler if you start drowning."

Pete yanks at a few of the ropes. The USS *Anna May* sinks in six seconds, spilling us into chocolate-colored water. We climb out upon a familiar creek bank. I can just about see Stairways up the path. We're home.

There's no joy in it for me. None at all. Our expedition is a failure, all our equipment is lost, and Pete's days are numbered.

And there's one other thing too: my fever's burning me alive.

Old Doc Mayfield has been our family doctor long as anybody can remember. He towers above my bed, and the top of his head almost brushes the ceiling of our bedroom. Doc Mayfield is the tallest man I know, and when he listens to my heart he has to bend almost into a U shape to hear through his shiny metal stethoscope.

He listens to my chest through cold metal and runs his fingers under my jaw before asking me to quit my shirt. Ma stands next to him, watching with arms folded. There's just the barest trace of a frown on her pretty face. She's worried.

When we first came up from the creek after getting back, Ma was fit to be tied. She'd been worried sick about us being out in the storm and the flood. Once she got over that, she was fixing on being mad at how dirty we all were. And then she saw me and all that anger went right out of her.

Funny how being sick can get you out of a lot of trouble.

"Jack, I'll bet you spend a lot of time outside," the doctor says to me. "That so?"

I nod.

"In the summer these boys only come inside to sleep," Ma tells him.

"Don't blame 'em," Doc Mayfield replies. "A place like this at their feet. Almost paradise. I'd be out in these woods all day and all night if Marjorie would let me."

He hands my shirt to Ma. When nothing looks out of the ordinary on my front, he asks me to roll over. Ma lets out a sharp gasp then.

"It's how I figured," Doc Mayfield says.

Ma sighs. "Oh Lord."

"What is it?" I ask, suddenly fearful.

He puts a hand on my back, right between my shoulder blades. "Son, you've been bit by a deer tick. You have a bull's eye wide as a dinner plate across your spine. That's telltale Lyme disease. Judging from this, you've had it about two weeks."

"Am I gonna die?"

He laughs. "Sure, in about seventy years. But not from this. Though Lyme disease is nothing to fool with."

He looks to Ma. "It'll be fevers off and on for the next week. And he's going to be mighty weak. Bed rest. No running around, inside or out, for two weeks."

"Two weeks?"

"Sorry, son. But unless you want to get real sick, you'll do like I say." He looks at Ma. "Adelene, if I can trouble you for a cup of coffee, I'll take a look at those other three. If one of them has got it, there's a chance the others do too."

Doc Mayfield leaves a bottle of pills for me, then goes downstairs to check over Pete, Will, and Frankie. An hour later I hear his tires crunching gravel down the lane.

Left alone in my room, I stare out the open window at a sky that's perfectly clear and blue and think how horribly unfair it is that I have to be in bed for two weeks. It's too much to take. Our failed expedition. That awful night in the cave. Pete's soon-to-be drafting. I begin bawling real quiet to myself.

I hear footsteps on that spiral staircase outside my room. I've just about stopped my crying when my father comes in, a cup of chicken soup steaming in his hands. His blue work shirt is stained with sweat and dirt. Dried mud is caked along the sides of his boots. He's just come back from working at Mr. Halleck's.

Dad sits next to me while I take a few spoonfuls of the soup, just sits and is quiet. His face is tight with worry. His oldest boy about to be drafted. The county trying to take his land. And me with my fever. I figure Dad has a lot to be worried about. But he ain't crying. So I won't neither. But when he lays a heavy hand on my knee, that's too much and I start my blubbering all over again.

"Dad, it ain't fair. It's *summer*."

My father is quiet for a moment. His clear blue eyes meet mine and he sighs.

"Life's not fair, Jack. You ought to know that by now."

For three days I battle that Lyme disease and the worst fever I have ever known. It pounces on me all of a sudden. It leaves me shivering in scorching afternoons and burning up in the dead of night. In all that time, I don't do a thing except lie in my bed and watch the sun come up through the open window and wait for it to go down again. Then, on the morning of the third day, I beg Ma to let me sit outside on the front porch. She agrees on condition that I not set one foot off it. So I sit on our porch, wrapped in the quilt Grandma Elliot made for me just before she passed, and sip watered-down lemonade through a straw.

I've got aches in my arms and legs and all down my back. Just walking from the screen door to the chair takes almost all of the energy I've got. I am feeling pretty sorry for myself when Pete, Will, and Frankie come onto the porch. In Frankie's arms is every board game we have.

"You feel up for playing a few?" he asks.

We burn through every last one of those board games.

Then, Pete comes up with the idea to hold contests to entertain me. The three of them start in on sit-up contests, push-up contests, chin-up contests, and then, when they really start running out of ideas, *talking* contests. Each one of them memorizes a speech and recites it for me, and I get to be the judge and decide who gives it best. Pete does Edgar Allan Poe's "The Raven," and Will does something out of Shakespeare that has a lot of old-fashioned words I don't understand. Frankie recites a poem about baseball. I like them all, but I go with Frankie because he's the only one who's able to get the whole way through without having to look down at the page.

But after all that, I can tell they're getting bored as I am, and I tell them so.

"Look," I say. "It's awful nice of you fellas to spend all this time with me. But just because I'm sitting here missing summer doesn't mean you have to. I wish you'd go down to Apple Creek and swim yourselves silly."

Pete and Will narrow their eyes at me.

"Nothing doing, Jack," Pete says. "We like being right here with you."

"You trying to get rid of us?" Will asks.

"God's honest truth, you three are getting crazier than I am. I'll be fine on my own for an afternoon."

I can tell they really want to go and I'm glad when they finally do trot off toward Apple Creek and leave me on the porch by myself.

It's not ten minutes later the screen door wheezes and Ma comes out onto the porch. She's wearing her apron and there's flour on her hands.

"Where'd those boys run off to? Did they up and leave you?"

"I told them to go swimming. I didn't want them cooped up here all afternoon."

"Don't you lie for your brothers' sake," Ma says sharply. "They know we have company this afternoon."

I blink. "We have company?"

"Land sakes, John Thomas, you're not *that* sick. I told you this morning, I'm having the ladies from church over for bridge tonight."

I swallow.

"Well," Ma sighs, "at least you'll be here. I'll get your nice shirt for you to wear. You don't have to say anything; just wear it and be polite and smile."

The egg timer above the stove goes off and Ma goes back inside.

She don't usually get to entertain on account of us living so far outside of town. When she does, she goes all out. For her friends in the bridge club, she bakes a loaf of fresh bread and then puts a pot roast in the oven to cook while she mixes a salad with those cucumbers and lettuce from her garden out back. Then she sets the picnic table and gets the duplicate bridge boards out from the cupboard under the stairs.

I'm bored being sick, but not so bored that I want to sit through a bridge party. I'd rather be in bed. I'm about to ask Ma if I can go up and lie down, but then the first car comes up our lane.

I'm too late.

And now I'm wishing like mad I hadn't told Pete, Will, and Frankie they could go to the creek. And I got no idea when they'll be back.

It's dusk and the bridge ladies are long gone by the time they get back. But it's only two boys coming slow through purple shadows: Pete and Frankie. Will ain't nowhere in sight.

"Where's Will?" I ask Pete as he comes onto the porch. Pete just shakes his head and goes through the screen door without a word.

That gets me spooked, so I turn quickly to Frankie and ask him the same question.

I can tell he's been swimming. He's got sand on his arms and he smells like the creek.

"Hard to say," Frankie answers me, sitting down.

"Is he all right?" I ask quickly.

"Yeah, sure," Frankie assures me. "Nothing bad happened."

I relax some at that, but now I'm itching to know.

Frankie pours himself a glass from my pitcher of lemonade. After a long, slow sip, he sits back in his chair and cocks one eye at me.

"We went swimming at the Sucker Hole," he says. "We jumped off the pilings for a while. Then we raced. Pete won every time, but Will came close once—"

"They always do that," I interrupt. "What happened to Will?"

"Hold your horses!" Frankie says. "We'd just finished racing when suddenly a voice calls out to us. A voice from across the creek."

He sips lemonade.

"Who was it?" I ask.

Frankie looks at me. "Anna May Fenton."

My eyebrows shoot up. "Her again? What was *she* doing at the Sucker Hole? Did she bring a whole pack of girls to spy on you again?"

Frankie shakes his head. "It was *only* Anna May. Nobody else. And she wasn't spying. In fact, she called out to announce herself. And when we looked up, there she was on the far bank, walking backward toward us."

"Backward?"

"Backward," Frankie says, "so she couldn't see us. Then she says, 'I don't mean to embarrass you, so I won't turn around. I'll stand here until you get your clothes on.'"

"Are you fibbing?" I ask. I look at him close.

Frankie puts a hand over his heart. "God's honest truth."

"So what happened next?" I ask suspiciously.

"Well, Will thought it was a trick, but Anna May called out again. 'No, it is *not* a trick,' she said. 'But if you don't want to talk with me then I'll just leave.' Well, that did it. We got ourselves dressed real quick. But even then, Anna May wouldn't turn around. She said, 'I'm embarrassed for my sake now, so if you don't mind, I'll just stand like this until I've said what I have to say.'"

"And what *did* she have to say?" I ask.

Frankie shakes his head. "She only wanted to talk to Will, so she asked Pete and me to leave."

"You mean you didn't hear what they said?" I ask incredulously.

"No, of course we did," Frankie replies. "Soon as we were out of sight, Pete and me doubled back so we could listen."

This is the oddest thing I've ever heard. I imagine it: cranky old Will on one side of the creek and beautiful Anna May on the other side standing with her back to him.

"So what'd she say to Will?" I ask.

"She asked him why we hadn't been to the Sucker Hole for a while. She said she'd been coming every week since the day she found us sleeping there, hoping to see us again."

"Anna May came to the Sucker Hole every week hoping to see *us*?"

"Not us," Frankie says seriously. "Just Will."

My mind does a somersault. This is shaping up to be the weirdest story I've ever heard.

Frankie goes on, "Will asked her to turn around so they could talk face-to-face. Well, she did. But then a funny thing happened: they stopped talking. Both of them just stood there staring across the water at each other. It seemed to last forever. It was downright boring, until Anna May took a tiny step forward. That did it. The bank she was standing on was all worn away beneath her. It was nothing but baked mud. She took that step and it crumbled!"

"She fell in the creek?" I gasp, sitting up. "What'd Will do?"

Frankie laughs. "You've never seen a boy move so fast in your life. Will swam over and got hold of her and pulled her out."

Will rescues Anna May from drowning—and I missed it!

"And then what?" I'm on the edge of my seat.

"She was embarrassed," Frankie says. "And she was crying. And there's poor Will trying to wring out the hem of her dress. It didn't do any good because they were both soaked. Eventually she stopped crying and the two of them went back to staring at each other." Frankie sits back. He sighs. "And then he kissed her."

"*What?*"

Frankie nods.

"On the lips?"

Frankie nods again.

I can't believe it. Will not only rescued her; he kissed her.

"What happened next?" I ask.

Frankie shrugs. "Will asked if he could walk her home. Last we saw, the two of them were walking down the trail together. Will never even looked back."

I'm quiet for a while as I try to make sense of it all. Of all days to miss being at the creek! Will kisses Anna May at the Sucker Hole, and I'm stuck with Ma and her church-lady friends playing bridge.

Still, it *is* strange, to think of your older brother kissing a girl. It's just something I ain't ever thought of before. Anna May is pretty and all . . . but to kiss her?

Frankie don't seem at all bothered by it. He sits with his hands behind his head and a dreamy look on his face. Over in Knee-Deep Meadow, the crickets start up.

"Do you think they're having a good time on their walk?" I ask Frankie.

"I imagine they are, Jack."

Will returns later that night, when the moon is low over the meadow and everything seems soft in milky light. He crosses the porch planks slowly, easily. He don't say a word to us, just smiles kind of gentle and goes right on in.

All through breakfast next morning we wait for him to say something, anything, about it. But he doesn't. He just eats his eggs and drinks his orange juice. Afterward he wanders off somewhere with a couple of sheets of lined paper and a pencil behind one ear. We watch him drift toward the meadow.

"I can hardly believe it," I say. "Will Elliot writing love letters."

Pete leans against the railing, watching him go. "I guess sometimes things work out."

"Think we'll ever see him again?" Frankie asks.

"He needs a stamp if he's going to mail that thing," Pete says. "He'll be back."

Next afternoon, it's just me on the porch, sipping my lemonade and watching our valley gleam golden and beautiful under the sun.

Things are duller than ever now that Will's in love. He disappeared early, walking toward town. Pete decided he needed some money and went to pick up a few hours at the gas station. Dad's at the game preserve. Ma is in town. I figure I'll ask Frankie to play another game of Battleship, but he just shakes his head and takes off across the flagstones for the barn.

"Sorry, Jack. I've got writing to do," he tells me.

I got no idea why he's even bothering anymore, but I let him go anyway. No use making Frankie miserable about our failed expedition.

Alone on the porch, I start to get mad about it all. I know I shouldn't, but a good part of me just wants to blame it all on Caleb Madliner. If we hadn't run into him in the creek that day, well, maybe we'd have had time enough to find that fighter after all. I'm chewing that over in my head when I hear another car coming up the lane.

It's a police car. State trooper. But he ain't got his lights flashing or his siren sounding. It pulls up in front of our barn, and I see there are two people in the front seat. Only one of them gets out of the car, though.

It's Kemper.

He glances about the yard. Then when he's certain Butch ain't coming for him, he begins to study our house and yard with his black ferret eyes. He stands there a long time, blinking in the sun. The way he looks at our land makes the skin go tight across the back of my head.

Then he sees me. He scowls.

"Your parents here?" he calls from the drive. The voice is squeaky.

"No, they are not," I tell him. "Whatever you've got to say, you can to me."

Behind him, the police officer rises from the car and looks about. He rests his hands on his belt and there's a sound like a little metal jingle.

Kemper crosses the drive for the porch.

"You the one threw those stones, aren't you?" He licks his lips as he comes and looks around him again, like he's checking to see if anybody else is here.

When he gets close, he puts one polished black shoe on the porch step. Then he looks me over. I feel his eyes on my faded shirt, the one that used to be Will's. Those eyes jump to the patch on my pants, the one Ma sewed on after I cut up the knee running.

"You see that policeman behind me?" Kemper jerks a thumb over his shoulder so that he's pointing to the barn, not to the police officer in the drive, but I don't bother telling him that.

"He's here to protect me while I deliver this to your daddy." He draws a white envelope out of his suit and waves it at me. "It's a notice of a public hearing to consider a proposal to create a reservoir on this land. Do you know what that means, boy?"

Cold fire ignites in my veins. I keep silent.

"It means your daddy should have sold to me when he had the chance. Now it's over for him and your family. Or it will be, soon as the council votes."

Kemper tugs at his suit jacket, then leans over from the waist. He looks directly into my eyes.

"How would you like living in a trailer? A little box on cinder blocks down by the tracks? That'd be quite a change from all this space, wouldn't it?" He looks to the yard, to Apple Creek and the meadow beyond. "Because that's about all your daddy will be able to afford if he holds out any longer on selling."

I feel the tears welling up at the corners of my eyes.

"Maybe you ought to tell your old man to stop thinking only about himself," Kemper says. A bead of sweat streaks down the side of his head, glistening in the sun. He dabs at it with a perfectly clean white handkerchief.

I swallow. Then, in a voice that's hardly more than a whisper, I tell him, "You're a small man, Mr. Kemper. You've got no guts. You leave that letter here if you want, and I'll give it to my father. But you won't get one inch of our land."

Amazement flashes across his face. Then anger. The monstrously huge Adam's apple does a dance along his pencil-thin neck, and he draws up and snorts. Then he tosses the envelope on the porch boards and turns back for the police car without saying anything. The officer lowers himself back in, and soon their wheels are making dust down our lane.

I sit a long time in my chair, Grandma Elliot's quilt wrapped around me and that white envelope lying on the floorboards just a foot away from me. I don't touch it. I won't touch it.

It seems like I'm fighting too many battles, and not one I can win. Fevers, floods, and failed fighter jet expeditions; now a nasty man from the county hell-bent on taking our home.

Most of all, it seems like I'm fighting time. Pete turns eighteen next week. I know there'll be another letter in the mail soon after that, one from Uncle Sam addressed to "Mr. Peter Elliot." That letter will change his life—and all our lives—forever.

And there's nothing I can do about that neither.

Chapter 18

The War Council

When I show my family Kemper's letter, everybody has something different to say. Will explodes with nasty names for him. Dad takes the letter and reads it over and over again, not saying anything, just reading. But it's Ma who finally tells us what it is we're going to do.

"Everyone kneel down right now and pray."

And we do, right there in our kitchen: Ma and Dad, Pete, Will, Frankie, and me.

Closing her eyes, Ma leads us. "Dear Lord, if it's in your plan, help us find a way to keep our home." She draws a deep breath. "Teach us to fight."

We all say amen and stand up. But then Ma surprises us all again.

"We are going to call a meeting," she says.

"Of who?" Pete asks.

"Of everyone in this valley who might be affected by what's in this letter," Ma says, holding it up. "All the neighbors still left. And anybody who wants to help."

"Even the Madliners?" I ask.

"*Everyone*, John Thomas," says Ma. "There's strength in numbers, and many minds are better than a few."

Ma holds that letter tight. Her face is like stone. My mother is going to war.

Dad goes to her, kisses her on the head.

Suddenly I feel better than I have felt in ages. Looking about the room, I see the fire's spread to each of us.

"When we having this meeting?" Will asks.

"Tonight," Ma says. "With as many as will come."

From my bedroom window, Frankie and me watch them come.

Sam is first. He arrives on foot, swinging the .22 over his shoulder. Butch runs to greet him as he lumbers up the lane, and Sam passes him something from the pocket of his overalls.

Next is a farm family from a few miles east of us, the Glattfelders. Most other families have sold out. Not them. Their boys are older than us, and one was drafted to Vietnam last autumn. Still in his work boots, Mr. Glattfelder has come straight from his fields.

Dad comes off the porch to greet both, taking their hands in his, looking them in the eyes, and thanking them for coming. He's still doing that when a long black Cadillac grumbles up our lane. The men watch as the shiny black automobile purrs its way up to our barn. For one awful moment, I think it's Kemper, that he's somehow found out about our meeting and has come to put a stop to it. But then an old wiry man rises from the sleek metal, dressed in a linen suit. Puffs of cottony white hair ring his head like clouds, and he carries a long cane with a handle of whittled deer bone. He is just about the exact opposite of Mr. Glattfelder.

"Well, I'll be." I whistle as below, my father greets the old man.

"Who's he?" Frankie asks.

"That's Mr. Halleck. That's the man Dad works for. What on earth is he doing here?"

Mr. Halleck is richer than God, or so Will always says. He's pleasant enough when we see him at his estate, usually only ever at Christmastime. He's never come to our house before. We don't hear what passes between him and Dad, but there's a certain look on my father's face when they turn for the house, something like a mix of pride and relief.

More cars. Ma's church-lady friends come bearing gifts—corn pudding from the looks of it, covered in tinfoil. And now Pastor Fenton. When he opens the passenger door, a pair of long legs, white as cream, slide out and Anna May rises into the summer evening.

"Ho-lee smokes," Frankie says, and now he whistles.

Her pretty eyes take in our house of stone, our old dusty barn, the pines ringing our hill, and I realize that she ain't ever seen Stairways before. She follows her father in and there's something about the way she moves, the way her dress sways around her willowy body, that makes me catch my breath. Don't know what it is, but I get to thinking just then that my brother Will is one of the luckiest boys I know.

Mr. Madliner comes last, and he comes alone. His scarecrow shape lowers itself out of a rust-colored truck and crosses the yard on thin legs that seem not to want to work together. I shudder. We have not told Ma or Dad about what happened with Caleb that night in the cave. I don't care to, neither. Just so long as I never have to see Caleb ever again.

When Mr. Madliner slips under the porch roof and out of our sight, I turn to Frankie.

"We'd better get down there. I don't want to miss one word of this."

Dad gathers everyone in the parlor and tells them we'll eat first and talk later. Seems to me the talking's the more important part, but then the tinfoil comes off those plates, and I smell the corn pudding, mashed potatoes, pork roast with herbs and seasonings, and fresh-baked blueberry pie, and I change my mind real quick.

Pastor Fenton asks the blessing, and this time the amen is loud on account of all the people packed in our parlor. They're piled on our couch and the kitchen chairs that Pete and Will have brought in, and along the hearth in front of the fireplace. Mr. Glattfelder and Mr. Madliner stand against the wall, holding their plates and resting their glasses on the windowsill. Will and Anna May sit on the floor by the screen door. Frankie and me perch ourselves on the stairs so we can see, and Pete joins us, a mountain of pork roast and mashed potatoes on his plate.

The sun is sinking low behind our hill when Dad sets his plate down and stands in front of the fireplace. A hush falls over everyone then.

Dad gets down to business. He tells everyone about Kemper's letter and the hearing. After the hearing, they'll decide whether to dam the creek and flood our valley. The hearing is scheduled for the first day of July.

"That's only a few days from now," says Mrs. Glattfelder.

"Why so soon?" asks Pastor Fenton.

From the rocker chair, Mr. Halleck clears his throat. "To give us as little time as possible to prepare for it, while still meeting their statutory obligation." He folds his bony hands over the deer-bone handle of his cane. "Standard procedure. Mr. Kemper does not want all of you to have time to organize against him."

Old Sam shifts on one of Ma's kitchen chairs, and he folds his arms over his stovepipe chest. "That feller come to my place one afternoon asking if I'd drink beer with him. Friendly-like. I'd never met him. 'I'll drink with anybody once,' I tell him. He was polite enough 'til he worked his way around to the subject of my land. He asked me if I'd sell it to him. When I said no, he got downright disagreeable and I told him"—Sam glances over at the ladies before going on—"well, never mind *what* I told him. We had *words*. Then Kemper spouts this business about taking my land from me. 'Pennies on the dollar' was what I'd get for it."

Around our parlor, heads nod. They've all heard the same speech.

Mr. Halleck speaks again. "Kemper knows every corner of the law, inside and out. He wrote it. He knows each of the local ordinances. He knows all the holes he can hide in."

That makes me afraid. All this time, I'd figured it was illegal what Kemper was doing. It was certainly wrong. But what if it was both wrong *and* legal? Did we still have to go along then?

"But aren't there other places they can build the reservoir?" one of Ma's friends asks.

"I suspect there are plenty," Mr. Halleck replies. "Why they insist on flooding you out, I have no idea."

Pastor Fenton clears his throat. "Look, we live in town, and this whole reservoir is being billed as more water for us—and lower utility bills, I might add. But I don't like bullies. People have a right to their land, their property. If I remember correctly, God made a whole commandment against stealing. But whether they believe in God or not, I think a good number of people in town will feel the same way. You might not have to fight this thing alone, just country folk against Kemper and his cronies, is what I mean to say."

Heads nod around the room. For the first time, I begin to feel a bit of hope.

Mr. Glattfelder shrugs. "But how are any of us supposed to fight somebody's got the law in his pocket?"

Mr. Halleck pulls a silver flask from his linen jacket, unscrews the cap, and takes a sip. "That is the whole question. When the hearing ends, the council will vote. Seven people sit on that council. You need four of them to vote against flooding. At this moment, Kemper has five who will vote for it."

Our parlor is silent as the old man takes another sip.

"You must persuade *two* of them to switch their votes."

There's a murmuring of voices then. From our place on the stairs, we hear snatches of phrases—"Then it's rigged; the whole thing's already decided"—"How we going to get two to switch if their minds are made up?"—"Must be money for them in it somehow."

The talk is cut off when Mr. Madliner raps his knuckles on the mantel and speaks directly to Mr. Halleck.

"You seem to know plenty about this business. And your house is on high enough ground. You won't lose so much as a flagstone if the county floods the rest of us out. Matter of fact, I expect you'd have lakeside property."

"Matter of fact, I probably would," Mr. Halleck agrees.

"Then my only question is this: Why are you here?" Mr. Madliner fixes his burning eyes on the old man in the rocker, and the whole room goes silent.

Mr. Halleck leans back.

"That's a fair question. I haven't bothered with politics since Truman beat Dewey in 1948. I don't have the stomach for it. But"—and here the old man lifts a bony finger and points to my father—"I admire *that* man. Very much so, as another matter of fact. And *he* asked me to come tonight."

All eyes fall upon my father, as Ma puts an arm around him.

But it ain't good enough for Mr. Madliner. "Easy to say. But you still stand to come out all right if we lose. And I'll tell you all something else," he goes on, looking around the room now. "Those council members mean to have our homes. There's some folk only answer to power. And this Kemper fella, he's that way. And unless we figure a way to get more power over him than he's got over us, we might as well all buy canoes."

The parlor is silent after Mr. Madliner's speech. And much as I hate to admit it, I believe he's right. Kemper will never stop. Not unless something more powerful than him *makes* him.

Ma answers him in an even voice: "You make a strong point, Arthur. If it comes down to power, then we'll get as many voters into that hearing as we can. This country is still a democracy, last I reckoned, and a push from good and honest people who won't back down is the best kind of power there is."

There's another murmur of voices in agreement with her. Around the room I see more heads nodding and even a few smiles. Dad grabs a pad of paper and a pencil. He passes them around the room and asks everyone to write down the names of friends and family they can ask to come to the council meeting.

"I think that's a wise suggestion," Mr. Halleck says when their talk has quieted down. "And may I make one more: our group should choose someone to speak for them at the hearing. It is a *hearing*, after all. Council members are supposed to listen to what the public has to say before they vote. I would like to nominate Gene Elliot." Mr. Halleck looks to Dad. "Of any of us, I think he has the best chance of getting them to listen."

"Hear, hear," says Mr. Glattfelder.

The others around the room all nod in agreement.

With the decision reached, we can feel the meeting drawing to a close. Someone asks Pastor Fenton to close with a prayer. When he finishes, people rise and begin carrying dishes to the sink or stepping out to smoke. Pete gets more pie. Old Sam slips a bit of dip into his cheek and makes for the porch.

Mrs. Glattfelder passes by us on her way to the door.

"You boys should be proud of your mother and father," she tells us. "It's as good a plan as can be hoped for. Let's hope we win."

"Yes ma'am," Pete tells her. "And we'll do a lot more than hope."

With all that's at stake, Pete is absolutely right. Losing would mean our home and everything I've ever known would be underwater. Stairways and the barn. Knee-Deep Meadow. The Sucker Hole. And that wrecked fighter jet too.

It's gotten hot and stuffy on our spiral staircase, and when I spy Will and Anna May going through the screen door, making toward the field, that seems a good idea to me. I go down the steps and follow them out onto the porch, which is now crowded too. At one end, Dad stands with Mr. Halleck and Sam. He and Mr. Halleck are smoking cigars; Sam is chewing. They stand with heads bowed, speak to each other in hushed voices.

Passing by, I can't help but overhear them.

"It's a good plan, Gene, but it won't be enough," Mr. Halleck says. "Kemper has money enough to buy votes to keep his people safe in the next election, and they know it. It doesn't matter how many people you put in that hearing room."

Sam spits over the rail. "Then that Arthur Madliner is right," he wheezes. "We need power. Where do we find it?"

Dad is silent, puffing blue smoke.

"The old proverb will serve us well now," Mr. Halleck says. "The enemy of my enemy is my friend—"

I don't hear what he says next, because now I'm off the porch and halfway across the yard, following Will and Anna May into the field.

Enemies or no, it's a perfect night for walking: grass is wet with dew, and the velvety dark above is pinpricked with the night's first stars. I'm about to run to catch up to Will and Anna May when a voice calls from behind me.

"Let them walk together, Jack." Frankie puts a hand on my shoulder.

"But it's crowded and hot back there," I tell him, whining now. "And I'm tired of political talk."

"Then we'll sit outside," he says. "And maybe Pete left us some pie."

Reluctantly, I follow my cousin back to where the light from Stairways falls in soft, yellow squares on the grass. Fireflies begin to wink at each other in the yard. The Glattfelders are leaving, waving goodbye. Mr. Madliner is climbing into his truck, and he doesn't bother. Good riddance.

Dad, Mr. Halleck, and old Sam are still on the porch, still talking. I overhear Mr. Halleck again:

"Who can say if they'll agree, but it's worth a try."

"Tomorrow then," Dad replies. "I think I know where we can find them."

Sam leaks brown tobacco juice over the rail in agreement.

Frankie and me don't pay any more attention to it. Instead, we go find a place in the yard and sit down in the sweet-smelling grass. Pete finds us there, and I see Frankie was right: he's brought us a slice of blueberry pie and three spoons.

"Last one." My brother drops down beside us and we take turns scooping up pie while the fireflies spread their glowing quilt across the meadow. It ain't long before Butch appears, his sniffer pulling him right for our plate of pie. We let him lick the plate when we're through, and lean back in the yard to watch the stars.

Frankie plucks a stalk of onion grass and sets it in his teeth.

Looking at him, barefoot with that stalk in his mouth, it strikes me.

"You know something, Frankie?"

"What's that?"

"Aunt Effie and Uncle Leone might not recognize their boy when he gets back home. He's looking mighty country right about now."

When all our guests but Pastor Fenton have left, we decide to play kick-the-can in the driveway. I get the old coffee can from the barn and we've gone two rounds when, from the field of bobbing fireflies, Will and Anna May walk out, holding hands.

"Mind if we join?" Will asks. He steps over the coffee can and stands with his knees wide, arms out.

"Does Anna May know how?" I ask.

"Just because I'm a townie doesn't mean I've never played kick-the-can before," she says.

"I'll give you fair warning," Will tells her. "We can play a little rough."

Fast as a whip, Anna May springs forward and kicks one of her long legs out from under her skirt. Before Will can even blink, that old coffee can clatters away across the drive.

The rest of us bust out laughing. Will's too surprised to be embarrassed. I run and grab the can again. We play a couple rounds, laughing, forgetting everything bad—the war, the riots, the fires, the floods. Eventually Pastor Fenton comes off the porch and calls his daughter; it's time for them to leave too.

Anna May kisses Will on the cheek, ignoring our ribbing, and dashes across the driveway.

We watch their red taillights fade through the trees. "Man," I say. "She's pretty good for a girl."

Will just sighs.

"John Thomas!"

Ma's voice. Turning, I see her framed in the doorway.

"You know you're not supposed to be playing outside! You're still sick! Get on in here right now!"

This time, it's Frankie who gets woken up by an idea.

He shakes me awake, whispering fiercely in my ear.

"Jack, I've got an idea!"

I'm half-awake and struggling to bring the other half around as he goes on. "I know how we can *still* make Pete famous and keep him from getting drafted."

That does it. I sit bolt upright, shooting a glance to where my brothers are both sawing logs in their bunk.

"The barn," I whisper.

We take the gutter to the porch roof. Roof to the yard. Up damp flagstones, two at a time. There Frankie finds the book of matches he's hidden over by the sewing table that doubles as his writing desk.

He lights the candle.

"We need to make Pete famous, right?"

"Right."

"And you figured finding that old fighter jet would do it, right?"

"Right again."

"I been thinking about it all night," Frankie says, "and this council vote is an even *bigger* story than that fighter jet."

"How so?"

"Because it affects *everybody*," Frankie tells me. "The people in town *and* the people who live outside it. Everybody has a reason to read the article."

"But how does Pete play in?"

Frankie smiles. "Easy. We'll get a quote from him at the council meeting. Then I'll put that quote in the story. And we'll have it!"

"Frankie, you're a genius! Now we just need to win that council vote."

"Mr. Halleck said all we had to do was persuade two council members to switch their votes," Frankie says. "And how hard can that be, *really*?"

Chapter 19

STORM CLOUDS

Early and dark in the barn. The wax spills down our little candle and runs in cooling currents across the top of Grandma Elliot's sewing table as Frankie types.

His fingers jab the keys, sending those little metal arms snapping out faster than I can see. They look like the antennae of some giant metal insect.

Outside, daylight is just beginning to paint its pale brushstrokes on the sky behind the pines. We been here all night.

"How's it coming?" I ask through a yawn.

He frowns and shakes his head, and I understand that means I'm not supposed to talk.

Frankie had the idea to begin writing the story *before* the council's vote and just leave space enough for whatever Pete will say and how close the final vote was.

I hope it ain't even close. I want us to knock Kemper right out of the ring.

I shift again on the upturned pail that's been my seat for the last few hours and go back to brooding. Pleased as I am with Frankie's idea, there's something about this whole council vote makes me nervous.

It's a good plan, Gene, but it won't be enough. Mr. Halleck's words to Dad and Sam last night on our porch. Mr. Halleck knows more about councils and votes than anybody else. If he's worried, that makes *me* worried.

"Ain't there something *I* can do?" I finally ask.

"Yes, there is," Frankie says. "And it's a very important thing. Something critical. And it'll be the hardest thing you've ever done, Jack."

"What is it?" I ask, sitting up.

"You can keep quiet and not say one single word until I get this finished."

That metal insect goes back to snapping its metal arms across the page.

I go back to being quiet.

It must be nearly five o'clock in the morning. Early yet. And so I am surprised to hear a car turn off Hopkins Road and come up our lane. Peering through the barn's cobwebby window, I see Sam's truck cough its way into our drive. Dad comes out of the house, climbs in. Sam backs down the drive, and within moments the two of them are gone, the sounds of Sam's tires eating gravel fading through the trees.

"Now, where do you think they're going?" I ask.

Frankie looks at me.

"Sorry. I forgot."

Frankie goes back to typing.

I go back to fretting.

All day long Ma is on the phone. She goes through each page of her address book and Christmas card list, calling friends and neighbors, telling each about the council vote. She keeps a pad of paper on her lap; she writes down the name of everyone who promises to come.

She barely looks up when Frankie and me come in from the barn.

"Orange juice in the fridge," she says, placing a hand over the receiver.

Frankie and me are both too tired to eat. We climb those spiral stairs for bed, and we're surprised to meet Pete and Will halfway. My brothers are bleary eyed, but I can smell the excitement on them.

"It's barely six o'clock in the morning. What is everybody awake for?" I blurt.

Pete don't answer me. "Get your shoes on and come with us."

"But, Pete, we're tired. Where we going and what for?"

"Town," Will answers as my brothers brush on by. As they round the corner below, he adds: "We're going shopping."

"Shopping?"

"Meet us out front in two minutes!" Pete calls.

I look at Frankie. Dark circles ring dark eyes.

"You look awful," I tell him, surprised to hear myself say it.

"You look worse."

We stand on the steps, both of us bone-tired and still trying to figure out what we should do.

"Jack!" Pete, from below.

"Well, Pete, what are we shopping *for*?" I call down the stairwell.

Pete's voice booms: "Beer!"

Beer?

I look at Frankie. He shrugs.

"Might as well, Jack," he says. "I'm too tired to sleep."

Four cases of beer. Ten pounds of ground beef.

That's what we bring back to Stairways that afternoon.

"And *Ma* said to buy all this?" I ask Pete as he swings one of the beer crates my way.

Pete ignores my question. "Take this up to the barn."

I stagger off with the box of beer clinking in my arms. Behind me, I hear Frankie puffing along with another crate.

"Don't make no sense," I say. "We've beer and beef enough for an army."

"That's the idea," Pete says.

It's long after dark when Dad and Sam come back. Sam's truck sputters off down the lane, honking once in farewell as he goes.

Dad stands in the drive, lifts one arm in a funny kind of way as a goodbye. He sways a little, then turns and comes for the porch in slow, measured steps. It ain't until he tousles my hair with one heavy hand and the evening breeze blows just right that I smell it on him: alcohol.

Dad and Sam been out drinking all day?

All of a sudden I'm scared.

Everybody knows somebody who got into a tight spot, somebody who turned to the bottle for relief. Lots of those same folks don't ever let go of it.

Dad goes to where Ma is sitting in the deepening twilight. He lowers himself down next to her, and I listen careful to hear what she'll say then.

For a while she don't say anything, and all there is to listen to is the cicadas humming in the trees behind our home. Then:

"Did you find them?" Ma asks in a tight voice.

My father nods and lets out a bushel of air. "Eventually. Some hole-in-the-wall joint three counties over."

He puts his arm around her. My parents sit together.

"Will they come?"

"Hard to tell. They might." Dad is quiet for a long time. "They might."

It's morning on the first day of July. The council vote is set for three o'clock.

Dad has us splitting pieces of firewood to keep us from getting too restless. He and Pete and Will trade out taking swings with the sledge. Frankie and me roll the logs into position and set the wedges for them. I'm kneeling beside one of those stumps and just about to set a new wedge when Mr. Halleck's black Cadillac eases up our drive. He don't even bother getting out.

Through his open window he calls to my father: "Got a call this morning, from a friend on the council. They will vote to flood."

"We'll testify anyway," Dad replies instantly.

Mr. Halleck nods, smiles. "Good. I'll be there."

Dad stands a minute alone after Mr. Halleck drives off, then he goes inside.

Us boys stand silent around the stump. The screen door slams, and suddenly hot tears spring into my eyes.

So it's over before we even have a chance to fight.

I don't understand.

"How can they make up their minds without listening to us?" The fire pours up out of my stomach all at once, burning hot and cold. I'm trembling.

Pete sets down the sledge. "John Thomas Elliot, you stop your crying this instant."

I don't ever remember Pete using my full name before.

"Didn't you hear Dad?" he asks.

"Yes, but—"

"But *nothing*. We're going down there and we're gonna fight anyway."

Pete looks at me hard.

"But, Pete, we're gonna *lose*," I cry.

205

"What difference does that make to whether we fight?" he asks. "Load up another wedge."

I pause. Sniffle a little.

Pete is still looking at me hard.

I do like he says and slide another wedge into place as he lifts that sledge again.

There's a heaviness in the air when Dad leaves for the council meeting. He's leaving early to make sure the council don't vote before it's supposed to, at three o'clock. He wears his one and only suit, gray, with his brown shoes and the tie Ma got him for Christmas a few years back. Our family gathers on our sinking porch to watch him go.

I'm wrapped up in my quilt again. I got that hot lead feeling in my stomach, but I know it ain't from any Lyme disease. Butch sits next to me and rests his chin on my lap.

Sometimes, when you know a good thing is over and done and won't ever come back, everything about it gets a whole lot sweeter. Each little leaf becomes something beautiful. You see the sunlight glowing through it, tracing out all those tiny veins inside. Each blade of grass is suddenly its own living thing, and not just one of a billion others that you stomp over on your way somewhere else. Suddenly it all appears in a way you've never seen it before, and it's so beautiful you wonder what in the world you were looking at in all the time that came before.

You notice it about people too. Looking around me, I see the lines around Ma's eyes and at the corners of her mouth appear deeper, and for the first time, I see the gray in her dark hair.

I see the scar on Will's chin where he busted it on the hearth one winter, years back. His face is the color of pale clay, like when he first learned about Bobby Kennedy's killing. Will was gone for days then. Where could he walk, if all our land got flooded?

Frankie cries silently. It don't matter it's not his house or that he's leaving come summer's end. Stairways has become his home, and he's losing it forever too.

The Ford rumbles to life. Dad looks once more at us, at Ma, and then puts the truck in gear and starts off down the lane. We watch him the whole way to Hopkins Road. An awful quiet falls over us then.

I wish like mad somebody would talk. Desperately I search for something to say, but I can't think of a thing.

Ma speaks in a soft, slow voice: "Pete, fire up the grill."

Going on in that same, even voice, she tells Will to get all that beef ready and to bring the glassware down from the cupboard. Frankie she asks to put a kettle on the stove for sweet tea.

"John Thomas, I'd like you to rest. On the porch if you like, or in bed, but I don't want you moving about."

None of us moves.

Suddenly Ma whirls about and charges across the porch for the screen door. Whipping it open, she shouts over her shoulder in a voice that is suddenly harsh and near to breaking. *"Boys, do not make me tell you twice."*

In the yard, my brothers stand about the charcoal grill's shimmering fire. Will holds the plate of beef patties, bloody in the day's heat. He has to wave his hand every so often over the plate to keep the flies away. Any other summer afternoon, it would be perfectly ordinary to see them like this. Not today.

None of it makes one lick of sense to me. Feels like somebody's taken the edges of the world in their hands and is tearing it right down the middle. Dad off to a meeting of liars who will flood our valley; Ma ordering us to prepare for a picnic.

Butch barks.

Turning from the grill's heat, I spy Sam Williamson coming up the lane. He parks, climbs out, and we see he's wearing a wrinkled blue shirt that's too small for him, with a faded brown tie. Blue suspenders hold a pair of pants high over his big belly. Never in my life have I seen Sam in anything but his long underwear, floppy hat, and mud-caked hunting boots.

"Figger better to be early." Sam stuffs another wad of chewing tobacco in his cheeks and goes to work on it.

Ma's glassware is set up on the picnic table. We watch from the yard as she pours Sam some iced tea. Sam leaks brown juice over the porch railing before accepting it.

"Pete, you got any idea just what is going on?" I ask.

He shakes his head. "I am at a loss, Jack."

"You see Sam wearing a tie?"

"Didn't think Sam even owned a tie."

It is not long after that more cars come up our lane. Four, five, six. Tires grumble over the stones, and clouds of white dust rise slowly out behind them. The cars park in a row in the field before our house. Butch trots down to investigate, but we stay in the yard, watching.

Among the people now walking toward our house are Anna May and her father, Pastor Fenton. A bunch of straw hats follow them, bobbing like ships on a sea. Ma's church friends.

The Glattfelders.

Hank Wistar, from the hardware store.

Ned Hudspeth from the barbershop.

And still more people. People I do not recognize. Strangers.

Anna May finds us at the grill. Another sundress. Bow in her hair. She takes Will's hand.

"Townies reporting for duty," she tells him, softly.

"All these people are coming to the hearing?" I ask her. "There's so many."

Burgers sizzle on the grill.

"I think that's the idea," Pete says as he flips another.

The people stand on the porch eating the burgers we've cooked and drinking the beer we bought a few days before. There are so many that some have moved into the yard, to clump in the shade of our tree. Butch wanders among them, sniffing for food. He gets lucky once or twice.

I do not remember ever seeing so many at our house all at one time. How many more could come, I don't know for sure.

Then we hear them. Rising above the talk from the people on the porch and Sam's raspy laughing and the clinking of Ma's glassware: a low rumble, like thunder beyond the hill.

Butch barks and bounds across the yard to where Ma is already walking down the lane, alone, toward the wall of shining metal that melts out of the trees and begins spilling up the road toward her.

Crash Callahan and his motorcycle riders have come.

We wrecked their bikes.

Sam fired his rifle at them.

Now, they've come for revenge. And right when we were least expecting it, and at just the worst time.

I realize I am running then, running after Ma, running *at* those riders, following my brothers. Frankie alongside me. All of us going down together. Last charge of the Elliot boys. We'll fight till there's no breath left in us, and who knows, we might take one or two with us.

Hard to see them now through all that dust, but their sound is everywhere around me. I see Butch ahead, a fuzzy shape in the swirling dust, but I can no longer hear him over the engines.

Lane's never seemed so long. I've been running for ages. All my life, it seems.

I'll kill Crash first.

Makes sense, taking out the leader. I know Pete and Will are thinking the same thing. They've pulled ahead of me, angling right for old Crash, who's out in front and who seems to be slowing himself down, coming to a stop.

The roar of motorbikes dies in a sudden avalanche of silence.

Ma stands like a statue. Tall. Proud. A cyclone of settling dust swirls around her.

Crash Callahan climbs off his glistening steel beast. He comes toward her, arms swinging easy at his sides. He wears a toothy grin along with his denim jacket and blue jeans. Long blond hair streams like fire off his scalp, held back from his sunburned face by a greasy red bandana.

"Why good afternoon, Mrs. Elliot," Crash says. "I do hope we ain't too late."

Chapter 20

The Worm Squishers

At two minutes past two in the afternoon, we leave Stairways—my family in front, riding with Sam; then Pastor Fenton and everyone from church and from town; and surrounding us all, like escorts for a convoy at sea, Crash Callahan's motorcycle men.

Twisting in my seat, I look behind us and find the line of cars stretches as far as I can see.

Will fiddles with the radio until he finds music. Bob Dylan, singing about his landlord.

Pete leans toward Ma in the front seat. "How'd you get Crash to come along?"

Ma looks out her window at one of the riders. "Crash and his men like to fish, hunt, ride, and drink. If the valley is flooded, they'll have no place to do any of those things." Ma pauses. "And your father promised they could do all of that on our land anytime they want. So long as we own it."

I can tell by her words that Ma ain't too pleased.

"*Dad* told them that?" Will asks. "When?"

"Three days ago," Sam says. "We tracked the Hoodlums down at a pool hall in Adams County."

Still watching the rider outside her window, Ma says, "I understand it was . . . tense at first."

"It was," Sam agrees.

"Sam, *you* went too?" I ask in disbelief. "But those riders hate you! And you hate them! They wrecked Myrtle's mailbox, and we ruined their motorbikes!"

Sam grunts. "Hate is a strong word, son. I don't much care for those young fellers. And I will never forget their offense to Myrtle's mailbox. They needed their asses kicked for that. But there's a value to them, as people, I guess."

I chew on that in silence.

Frankie: "But how'd you get them to hear you out?"

Sam shifts in his seat, glances uncomfortably at Ma, and chuckles. "You buy a man a few rounds, he ends up coming around."

Will sits back. "You got them drunk and then made a deal?"

Sam grunts. "Something like that."

And now I remember Mr. Halleck's words the other night.

The enemy of my enemy is my friend.

The council building sits right smack dab in the middle of town: a castle of dull red stone with fake battlements and a blocky tower that holds an enormous clock. There's not room enough in the parking lot, so we scatter to find what space we can along Main Street, then hurry our way up to the main doors.

Dad is somewhere inside, alone, waiting for us, keeping an eye out and making sure council doesn't vote before everybody can speak their piece.

Ma asks Crash to join us, and he signals his men to wait outside as we slip through a pair of glass doors and head down a hallway with walls the color of old vomit. Ma's high heels echo off the marble floors as we pass closed office doors with stenciled names like **SANITATION** and **FINANCE**. A giant corkboard tacked full with yellow notices and bulletins suddenly flutters at us as we pass, as if we've tripped some sort of secret alarm, and a pair of double doors opens at the end of the hall and a man in shirtsleeves steps out. His bushy black eyebrows go up at the sight of us boys and Ma, Pastor Fenton and Anna May, and all the church ladies in their floral dresses. Then he spies Crash and his bushy eyebrows climb even higher.

"Sorry, ma'am," he says to Ma. "There's no more room left in chambers. Full house, I'm afraid."

"We're glad to stand," Ma tells him and without stopping walks right on by, through the double doors and into the council hall. Anger clouds the man's face, and he seems about to say something when Pastor Fenton touches his arm and tells him in a firm but gentle voice that he's glad to stand too. "Be cool, man," Crash says, and he strides past.

The next thing I know our troop is inside a high-ceilinged room with a sea of metal folding chairs. There's no more than a dozen people sitting among them.

"But there are plenty of seats here!" I blurt.

"So it seems," Ma says tightly.

Dad sits in the very front row. Directly across from him is a long table. Seven men sit behind it, all in light-colored suits and patterned ties.

"You boys go up to the gallery," Ma says. "You'll see more from up there." Without waiting for any of us to answer, she walks down to where Dad sits in the first row. As the rest of our crew files in, the four of us boys and Anna May climb a set of creaking wooden stairs to the gallery overlooking the room.

We find Mr. Halleck sitting on a bench there, hands folded over the handle of his cane. He is dressed in a seersucker suit with a yellow bowtie. He looks distinguished. Elegant. He lifts a finger to his lips as we shuffle down beside him while below one of the council members taps the table with a tiny wooden hammer.

The nameplate in front of him reads, in blocky gold letters: **COUNCILMAN TRAVERS**.

"Council will come to order. Please stand for the pledge."

Metal chairs scrape over floorboards as everyone below turns to the flag hanging from a pole in the corner. We are almost through the pledge when Frankie elbows me in the ribs.

An eighth man has pulled up a seat at the table: Kemper.

"But he ain't on council!" I whisper.

Mr. Halleck bends to my ear. "He is their lead counsel."

I look at Will.

"He's their lawyer," he explains. "It's all rigged."

That anger hits me again. A cold, cold wave. Down below, everyone finishes the pledge and takes their seats again. Kemper settles himself just behind Travers's shoulder, at ear level.

Travers is talking now, reading a list of names of people who will be allowed to speak. He points to a podium in the middle aisle of the folding chairs. Anybody wanting to talk has to do it from there.

"Council will now hear testimony from those wishing to speak on the topic of Proposition 22, 'Requisitioning Appropriate Water Resources for the Municipality of New Shiloh and Surrounding Regions.'"

"What's all that mean?" I ask.

Mr. Halleck sighs. "It's the proposal to take your land and flood your home. Now hush!" He leans forward.

A pack of three men in suits moves to the front of the room. One goes to the podium while the others set up an easel with a map of the town and the valley. I recognize Apple Creek right away. A big blue oval is drawn over it: the reservoir.

Our house is inside it.

The man at the podium says New Shiloh is growing fast. He reads off a series of numbers about population estimates. Then he recites some more numbers about how many gallons of water all those people will need.

I can't help myself. "Who's that?"

Mr. Halleck grimaces. "He's a representative from a chemical company. They want the reservoir built to provide water for their factory. He has some projections about population growth and water shortages that he's trying to scare the council with." Mr. Halleck pulls the silver flask from his jacket and takes a sip. "It's working."

I can't follow the man at the podium, but the council members don't seem to have any trouble. A few take notes. One man is nodding.

At last Councilman Travers taps his tiny hammer again, and the chemical company men take down their map.

Just then Kemper leans forward, whispers in Travers's ear.

"You men can leave that up," Travers says. "It will be a helpful reference for us."

The map goes back up.

Will snorts.

Next up is a thin, wiry man in a flannel suit and thick glasses. He's some sort of representative from a group of businessmen, and he also wants the reservoir. After him comes a big, beefy man with a red face and red hands. He owns a construction company. He wants it too.

Slowly, I realize: all of the people who want the reservoir are getting to talk first.

I look at Frankie and see he's figured it out too.

It goes like that for half an hour: a whole parade of people who are for the reservoir walking up to the podium and telling council how good a thing it will be if they flood us out.

Then Kemper stands up.

"Council will now hear from its legal counsel," Travers says.

Kemper looks even smaller behind the podium. His tie is a tiny knot under his monstrous Adam's apple.

"It's true I am legal counsel for the council," he begins in a surprisingly strong voice. "But I would like to speak today in a purely personal capacity, as a citizen of the county."

Mr. Halleck says "Hmm," and leans ever so slightly forward.

Kemper looks out over his audience.

"We have heard from some excellent witnesses. All reliable, trustworthy men. Pillars of our community. What they say gives us the cold, hard facts of the matter: our town is growing. We need water not only for its families, but also for the industries and businesses that provide them with good jobs and good salaries. We can give them this water, by building a reservoir right where you see it on that map. Now, I understand this will mean a terrible inconvenience to a very small percentage of our neighbors. And some might mistakenly believe they're being pressured to leave land their families have owned for generations. Let me assure you: nothing could be further from the truth."

The people below are silent—spellbound, it seems, by Kemper's words. I ain't ever heard him talk like this before. His squeaky voice is powerful behind that podium.

A terrible pit forms in my stomach as Kemper draws a breath and continues.

"This is America. We are not about to force people from their homes . . . But this is 1968, and we are about progress. Times change. Needs change. Attachments to old things, when they no longer serve the greatest good for the greatest number, *must* be severed. To refuse to let go of these attachments might at first seem an overstrong dose of sentimentality or nostalgia. Let me tell you, it is far worse. It is *selfishness*. Disguised and hidden, but selfishness nevertheless."

My jaw drops.

Next to me Will starts forward off his bench, catches himself.

"This selfishness is subtle," Kemper goes on. "It says 'Let my neighbors fend for themselves; I care only about me and mine.' But that is not who we are. Such thinking runs contrary to everything we believe in as a society. It is frankly un-American."

I'm boiling inside. Kemper is leaning forward over his podium, like a deranged pastor filled with the fervor of his own words.

"To those who think this way, I say this: You can still choose to do right by your neighbors. You can even profit from it. You will be generously compensated. So let go. Don't stand in the way of progress. Don't stand in the way of kindness. Do the right thing."

Kemper looks out over the room, stands up straight, and finishes:

"If those people want to ignore the rights and needs of their neighbors, that's their business. But it is *not* the business of this council," he thunders on. "We cannot make them *see* the right thing. But we can make them *do* it, whether they wish to or not. Council has that power. Council should use that power. I urge council to support the measure. Thank you."

Kemper returns to his seat, smiles as several people in the front clap. A few even cheer. A cold salamander feeling runs down my spine as I see several men *at the table* clapping. When they finally stop, Travers looks down at his list.

"Council will now hear from Mr. Gene Elliot."

I automatically come forward at the sound of my father's name. Down below us, Dad rises from his chair and walks stiffly to the podium. He looks oddly different in his suit and tie: out of place, not like Kemper or the chemical company men. But then he puts both hands on the podium and stands up tall, and I feel a certain change fall over everyone in the room. The people in the seats go still.

My father ain't even spoken yet, but everyone is paying attention.

Dad begins by thanking council for holding the meeting. Travers smiles tightly. Kemper's black eyes seem shiny and dark at the same time.

Next Dad looks to the chemical company men. "I appreciate you gentlemen bringing your topographical map. I have lived my whole life along the creek, aside from a few years in Korea. During the war."

The men narrow their eyes at him.

Next to me, Mr. Halleck says quietly, "That was good."

"How so?"

"Your father has just reminded everyone of his valor during the war."

"What's that got to do with any of this?"

The old man turns his white head, looks down at me. "Nothing. Except this is a battle between your father and Kemper, and Kemper called him selfish. In life and politics, you fight selfishness with self*less*ness."

At the podium Dad speaks again to the chemical men. "Yes, I have lived my whole life along the creek, so I know this area well, and your map is as accurate as any as you can find. It also shows a naturally occurring geographic depression, approximately seven miles northwest of the proposed reservoir site. This depression is essentially a big bowl in the earth, wider and longer than the proposed reservoir. And your map shows no homes in it."

Dad pauses. Council stays quiet.

I know then that Dad isn't saying anything they don't know.

Dad goes on, "I make no objection to those who have spoken before about the rate of growth in our town. Our country is growing; our *town* is growing, and we will need the water. And a bigger reservoir would better serve our businesses and our families."

Dad looks at the audience. He turns to the council members. Now Dad levels his blue eyes at Kemper.

"So why not build it in this other location?"

Dad puts his hands in his pockets.

"Well, it's true there are no houses in that other location. At least not yet. But that land is privately owned by a company which has on its board several people who are sitting in this room today. And if the council builds the reservoir where it is currently planning, that other location will become very valuable. It will be beside a beautiful lake. I expect you would see many houses built there then."

Behind their long table, the council members sit still as stone.

Kemper stares hard at Dad.

"It's not a question of personal virtue," says Dad, drawing to a close. "It's a question of principle. Do people have a right to keep what they have worked and paid for? Should government become a partner in profit to help some people make money by taking things from others? I say no. And so I ask the council to vote against this proposition. Thank you."

Dad returns to his seat next to Ma. Our people in the back of the room clap and cheer. I clap till my hands sting. But Mr. Halleck stays very still.

At their table, the council members whisper to each other.

"What's happening?" I ask.

"Your father's rattled them," Mr. Halleck says. "He's told the whole world that some people will make a lot of money from this reservoir if it's built. It was a stellar performance. But it won't be enough."

He returns the silver flask to his jacket and begins to tap the floor with his cane.

Mr. Travers reaches for his hammer and raps it against the table several times. The sound is suddenly very frightening.

"At this time, if there are no other persons wishing to testify, the chair would look favorably on a motion to close the hearing and move into voting procedure," he says.

An electric silence fills the chamber. This is it. Dad's words were powerful, but I see Kemper sitting down there next to Travers—*right there*. Green as I am to politics, I know we don't have a chance.

That's when Ma raises her hand.

"I'd like to speak on behalf of a group of concerned citizens."

"And who might those be?" Travers asks her.

"The New Shiloh Nature Society," Ma replies.

Travers's eyebrows go up. "I'm afraid I'm not familiar with any such organization."

God's honest truth, neither am I. And one look to both my brothers tells me they ain't either.

"It has been recently formed," Ma tells him. "But if you check your registry of local civic groups, you'll find all the necessary paperwork is in order."

Travers frowns. "I'll take your word for that. Please proceed."

Ma doesn't go up to the podium; she speaks from the floor. "The members of the society register their strong opposition to the proposed reservoir, as its construction would result in a significant loss of habitat for several of our region's rarest birds."

Travers blinks. "Rare birds? Which ones in particular?"

"The great egret and the yellow-crowned night-heron, among others."

Travers seems stunned. A few of the council members chuckle.

"You are here on behalf of rare bird species?"

Ma's green eyes hold steady. "Yes, I am."

Travers sits back in his seat. "Duly noted, Mrs. Elliot; thank you for your testimony."

But Ma stays standing. "Councilman Rogers," she says, and I see she's speaking directly to one of the men at the end. "Your wife serves as recorder for the society. She would like me to ask you to vote no on today's proposition."

More chuckles now, from the audience. Ma smiles at him and sits. Councilman Rogers turns beet red.

Travers smacks the table with his hammer again. "Thank you, Mrs. Elliot. Are there any *other* persons wishing to speak? Perhaps someone who *isn't* a member of the Elliot family?"

The chamber falls silent.

"Then, in that case, I motion to—"

"Yeah, hold up."

The voice comes from the back of the room. Crash Callahan comes down the center aisle. "I'll talk," he says.

There's more murmuring from the people on the folding metal chairs as Crash struts up to the podium.

Kemper rises in his place at the table then. "Councilman Travers, this is inappropriate. This is a hearing for a serious matter regarding the future health and economic vitality of the town. It is *not* a circus."

Crash scowls. "You like circuses, little man? Here comes a lion." He growls at him. So help me God, Crash Callahan growls at Kemper in front of all those people.

The room is utterly silent.

Slowly, very slowly, Kemper sits down.

"Please state your name for the record," says Mr. Travers coldly.

"Crash."

"Your last name too, please."

"Callahan."

"Thank you, Mr. Callahan. And what would you like to say to us this afternoon?" Travers's voice ain't so pleasant anymore.

Crash clears his throat and leans over the podium. "Listen. We don't want you fellas flooding the valley. We like it just fine how it is."

Everyone in the chamber stares. Crash sees he's got himself an audience. He stands up a little straighter and takes hold of the lapels on his blue denim jacket. He goes on, tapping the air with his chin as he speaks.

"We take our recreation out that way, and it's a fine place. And there's some families live there. It'd be a crying shame if they lost their homes. Downright criminal to do that when you don't have to. And so we ask that you boys drop this idea. Build your pretty little lake someplace else."

Silence.

Travers blinks. "Mr. Callahan, you say 'we.' Might I ask, whom do you represent here today?"

That does it. Crash's eyebrows go up. He's stunned. Insulted.

He stomps over to the tall windows. He seizes the bottom rail. He yanks the window open. Then, whirling to face the council members, he jabs a finger to the courtyard.

"My associates, councilman. All *those* guys!"

From outside the chamber comes a deafening roar of motorbikes. A chorus of whoops and hollers pours through the open window and echoes around in the chamber. Everybody in the seats jumps to their feet. They rush to the windows and look to where Crash's bikers are gunning their engines. And beyond the riders, formed up in ranks on the lawn, is our crowd—neighbors, townsfolk, and friends. They've got a banner: **SAVE THE GREAT EGRET**.

Suddenly, one of those riders takes off. He rides a ring around the courthouse. Next thing we know, they're *all* doing it, burning rubber, riding rings around the building, howling like wolves.

Crash himself stamps his foot and smacks his palms against his thighs, wild with delight. To Kemper he shouts, "Told you, little man, this here's the circus, and I'm the lion!"

Pressed against the window, those seven council members see it all. One of them lets out a low whistle. His face is the color of ash.

"Lawrence," he says to Travers. "My little Nancy's wedding is next weekend. I want to be able to walk her down the aisle. Emphasis on '*walk*.' I'm switching my vote."

Kemper rushes over. "Damn it, Henry!" he tells the man. "There's no more than a hundred voters out there. I'll deliver three times that in one corner of your district this November!" He thumps the windowsill with the flat of his hand.

But the councilman shakes his head. "November is five months away, Mr. Kemper. We won't last five minutes with that crowd if we vote to flood these people out."

Councilman Travers nods his head quickly. "I motion to table the proposition! Is there a second?"

It's hard to tell just how many of them second the motion: they all shout it together.

"All in favor?" Travers asks quickly.

All of us in the gallery join in: "Aye!"

Crash gives a wild whoop of his own then and runs over to the table. He lifts that tiny wooden hammer and smashes it down so hard the head comes off. Then he dashes down the center aisle and flings those doors open wide.

Everybody's moving now—Kemper, the council members, the chemical company people. In all the hustle, there's only two people who aren't watching the show outside: Ma and Dad.

Travers walks slowly over to them. "You've won, Gene," he tells Dad. "Care to call off your huns?"

Dad looks away from him. He puts a cigar in his teeth and lights a match.

In the gallery, we're celebrating. Will kisses Anna May. Pete gives an ear-splitting whistle. Mr. Halleck lifts his flask. We make it down from the gallery just in time to meet Ma and Dad at the bottom of the stairs.

"We did it!" I shout, tears of joy running down both cheeks now. Our family's stopped Kemper. We saved our home.

Mr. Halleck shakes Dad's hand. He looks at Ma and lifts his cane to the windows. Outside, the riders are still swirling about the building.

"Just listen to all those good and honest people." The old man laughs.

Chapter 21

THE FOURTH OF JULY

Apple Creek glitters like a jewel thirty feet below me, tossing back pieces of the evening sky. Frankie, Pete, and Will tread water in the deep hole, looking up, watching, waiting.

From the top of the railroad piling I take a moment and freeze them in my mind. I'll remember this forever.

I jump.

The creek's perfume storms through my nostrils as I fall, the ageless scent of silt and sand rushing into my lungs. I open my mouth and let it fill me completely as I stretch my arms out wide as I can reach and just fall.

Toweling off in our room back at Stairways. Our home of stone that has stood for two hundred years and which is still standing, safe and sound thanks to us. There's bits of shiny mica on the tops of my feet and between my toes from that brown-sugar creek sand that never really comes off.

Frankie is finishing up on the telephone downstairs, talking with Aunt Effie and Uncle Leone. When he comes into our room, he's wearing a smile a mile wide and tells me Uncle Leone is home from the hospital now. Walking stiff, but walking.

"Doctors wanted him to use a cane, but he refused. That's my old man," Frankie says, smiling.

He goes over to his mattress and the pile of typewritten pages on the floor next to it. He wrote up the rest of that story as soon as we got back from the council meeting. Dropping onto his mattress, he scoops them up.

"You know something, Jack," Frankie says, thumbing through them. "Once we publish this, your whole *family* will be famous."

"Think so?"

"I sure do." Frankie thumbs the pages. "This story's got everything: heroes, villains, a great challenge, and, most importantly, a happy ending."

A happy ending. I think on that. Ma and Dad sure were clever to convince Crash and his riders to show up for us. And their plan certainly saved Stairways and a good many other homes in our valley. But would my plan be enough to save Pete?

"You really think it'll be enough to make Pete famous?" I ask Frankie.

Frankie nods. "I really do."

He hands me the pages. I read a few lines and I realize: I'm holding a treasure. In these pages, in these splotchy, typewritten words, is a chance at saving my brother.

"We'll deliver these to the newspaper office first thing tomorrow," I say.

Then, another idea: "Wonder if we could get a picture of Crash and his riders to submit with it?"

He looks up. "That'd be great. But good luck finding them. Your dad and Sam said they hunted through every bar in the county to find them."

"Won't be that hard," I answer. "They're fishing down under Hopkins Bridge right now."

There's just one problem when we get into town next day: the newspaper building is closed. The big glass door is locked. A sign in the window reads: **CLOSED FOR THE FOURTH**.

"But it's not the Fourth yet!" I exclaim. "Why on earth would you close before the Fourth?"

I feel hot on my face and my bare arms. Like the sun has suddenly jumped down right next to me.

"Take it easy, Jack," says Frankie. He shifts the story, wrapped up in a brown paper bag, under his arm. "We'll figure something out."

"Take it easy?" I cry. "But we're too late! We've missed our only shot!"

"Maybe not," Frankie tells me. "Maybe we can deliver these first thing after the Fourth. It's only a few days after Pete turns eighteen. That should still be plenty of time."

My heart is beating faster. My breaths come in short gasps. Inside, I am fighting a wave of doom. I've been living on borrowed hope ever since our failed expedition, but now I feel like a noose is starting to tighten around my throat.

"Come on, Jack," Frankie says. "We'll go down to Ernie's and grab ourselves some ice cream. You're all right. Pete too."

Wordlessly I follow my cousin down the street.

At the end of the next block we pass a street cleaner hanging red, white, and blue streamers off the lights. It's the Fourth of July tomorrow. New Shiloh will have its big parade.

But me and Frankie are too late.

The Fourth of July. Pete's eighteenth birthday. Sun comes up just like any other day and burns a bright hole through the pines next to Stairways. Mist rises off Apple Creek and burns into perfect blue sky.

Ma's made a big breakfast: waffles on the iron, maple syrup, whipped cream, fresh blueberries, strawberries, and raspberries. Pitchers of orange juice and cold buttermilk. I ask her extra nice and she puts chocolate chips in the waffles for Frankie and me.

Pete and Dad ain't in the kitchen when we sit down. Then I hear the truck in the drive and a minute later they stride through the screen door, and I wonder where they been so early in the day. They seem different; they wear solemn, proud looks on their faces. Ma turns back to the iron as they pull up chairs, but I catch sight of her face before she does. There's the barest trace of sadness to it, like the shadow from a cloud that's being chased across the sky.

Pete pretends like he don't know what day it is. But then there's Ma ready with his waffle, everything piled high, and a single lit candle peeking out of that whipped cream. He acts surprised when we bust out singing.

"Pete, you got to make a wish before you blow out that candle," I tell him. "Make it something real good."

I know what I'd wish for: for us all to be safe and together here. Always.

Pete puts on a face like he's thinking real hard, then he lets loose with a breath that blows flecks of whipped cream off his plate and across the table. Ma makes a face. Dad laughs.

That afternoon we pack into the Ford and Dad drives us into town for the parade. New Shiloh's Fourth of July parade is the town's grandest occasion. It runs from the Lutheran church all the way down Main Street to the train tracks far side of town.

People are already lining the sidewalk in folding lawn chairs when we park behind Ernie's ice cream parlor. Out front they've got a table and a giant silver can of root beer on tap. We pull up a patch of sidewalk right alongside it and a boy in a white paper hat fills us paper cups of dark, foamy soda for five cents.

I can see the blazing red metal of the fire trucks assembling down at the church. They always go first in the parade, with the New Shiloh High School marching band coming after in their brown and gold and white uniforms. Then it's a whole mess of floats from all different kinds of organizations: the Lions Club, the Knights of Columbus, and the New Shiloh Historical Association. Last to come will be the veterans. They are all ages, from a whole bunch of different wars. The oldest is a man who fought in the Spanish-American War. He walks every year despite being ninety years old and having not one tooth left in his head.

Will leaves to hunt for Anna May and her family somewhere along Main Street. Dad and Pete start for Hudspeth's Barbershop. I spy them going and figure on getting Frankie and me some gumballs.

"Cherry, right?" I ask him.

"Right," he says.

I leave him and Ma and needle my way through the crowd after them.

It's red, white, and blue banners and flags everywhere I look: stitched into people's clothes, on their hats, in the tiny American flags they hold and wave. There's a man in a kilt playing a bagpipe at the corner, though why he's doing that on the Fourth of July I don't know.

The sidewalk fills up. The parade will start soon. I dodge out of the way of a group of kids who come running by, ice cream cones dripping in their hands. One of them crashes into a woman holding a red-and-white-striped paper bag of popcorn. That corn goes flying every which way. The kid loses his ice cream cone and starts crying as the pigeons scuttle across the pavement for the spilled corn.

Down Main Street, one of those fire engines gives a blast on its horn. A cheer goes up from the crowd. The parade is starting. I dash across the street and through that barbershop door that's tied open by a string and into the cool dark. Right away I smell aftershave and newsprint, but it's a moment before my sight comes back.

The barbershop is packed with men. Men smoking; men laughing. I don't see Dad and Pete just yet. Gumball machine's in the back, but I don't have any change so I wander between the forest of creased trouser legs and big bellies and make my way toward the counter, looking for them.

Suddenly, I hear Dad's voice. "Can I have everyone's attention, please?"

Everybody's talk dies down. I don't see him just yet, but then a man in front of me steps aside and a hole opens up in the crowd. Through it I see Dad and Pete standing at the counter, Mr. Hudspeth leaning over his cash register behind them. Outside the shop, the first fire truck is rolling by, but nobody pays it any mind. All eyes are on my father and Pete.

"There's something I'd like you all to know," Dad says, putting a hand on Pete's shoulder. "But I'm going to let my son be the one to tell you."

I smile. Dad's letting Pete break the news to all his friends that we beat nasty old Kemper at the council meeting. That's just like my father. I stand on my tiptoes so I can see them better as behind me the fire truck gives a honk on its horn.

Dad looks at Pete. "Go ahead," he says, softly. "Tell them."

Outside, the crowd cheers for the fire engines, but it's quiet inside that barbershop. Overhead, the ceiling fan hums, that metal cord clinking as it does its little dance.

Pete stands up straight and tall. He looks at the men and says:

"I signed up for the Marines this morning. Soon, I'll ship out for Parris Island."

My heart stops.

The fire engine gives a shattering blast of its horn.

"Gene's boy enlisted!" someone cries. A cheer goes up.

Pete grins. When the men keep cheering, he waves. Dad's hand on his shoulder tightens, and suddenly all the men move to Pete. They fall upon him, shaking his hand, clapping him on the back, tousling his hair.

I can't move. I can't breathe. I just stare.

Pete keeps right on smiling and shaking their hands and thanking each one of them, and now all the men are turning to Dad and they do the same to him, only they say, "Congratulations, Gene!" and "That's three generations now!" and "Chip off the old block!"

Outside on the street, the fire trucks have rolled past. The band starts up. I hear it like I'm underwater. All I can do is stare at my brother.

Another hole opens up in that crowd, and through it, my brother sees me. For an instant, his grin slips. He calls out to me, lifts his hand to wave me over.

Next thing I know I'm running. But not to Pete. To the door and the blazing day beyond it. I burst from the shop and nearly crash into Will and Anna May. The street is packed with people, people cheering, waving, laughing. The band marches past us in perfect step.

"There you are!" Will says. "Where you—hey!"

I rush past them, into the crowd, into the bumping bodies and the heat and the noise.

There's no need for Uncle Sam to draft Pete now. He's signed up.

My brother is going to Vietnam.

I turn and run down the alley between the barbershop and the shoe-re-pair store, past dirty red bricks and crumpled balls of wax paper with mustard smears. Under a rickety fire escape I surrender to my sobbing and look back the way I've come. At the alley's far end the parade streams on, topped with rippling flags on long poles, speckled with reflections of bright sun on brass instruments. The drums are beating. Kids in uniform march in step.

A shape appears in front of that slice of blazing color, the shape of a boy coming down the alley: Will. He trots to where I've stopped under the fire escape.

"Jack, where you going?" he asks. "Come on back here. You're missing the parade."

"I don't want to see any stupid parade!" I shout as hot tears run down my cheeks.

"Don't be a fool. You love the Fourth of July parade."

"Not anymore I don't!"

He stops. "What's wrong?" He looks at me. "Is it about Pete? About him . . . getting drafted?"

"No!" I shout. "It's not about him getting drafted. It's about him *signing up!*"

Will goes still. "What?"

"He signed up for the Marines this morning! He's leaving us, Will! He signed up and he's leaving us. He *wants* to go." Fresh sobs rack my chest. Snot bubbles out my nose. "After all Frankie and me done to keep him here. After all we done to keep him *safe*. He goes and signs up!"

Will stares at the bricks like he can't hardly believe it. Behind him those drums beat and keep on beating.

"He signed up . . . ," Will says quietly to himself. "He signed up . . ."

Hot lava rises in my stomach. "If he wants to go, then fine! I don't care what happens to him anymore!"

That's not true, but I'm so mad at Pete for joining up I can't help myself. My whole body is trembling.

Will looks down the alley at the parade going by us. It's all the soldiers from wars past streaming along now. An old and glorious line of men in uniform walking slow and somber, faces set like rock as all the people cheer and cheer. Will watches them a long time, and when he turns back to me he looks so sad I think he's about to cry too.

He kneels down in front of me. Puts his hands on my shoulders.

"Hey, Jack," he says, real gentle and slow. "Do you know anybody, and I mean *anybody*, who can run faster than our brother Pete?"

His question don't make no sense. Time like this and he's asking me about Pete's running. But I think for a minute, and then I shake my head.

In a voice that's barely a whisper he asks, "You know anybody who can swim faster than him?"

I shake my head again.

Tears brim in Will's eyes. "In the whole world, is there any boy tougher or stronger or smarter than our brother Pete?"

I sniff and shake my head.

Will nods. "That's right. There ain't. And so you don't have to worry about Pete going to Vietnam and getting killed. He'll be just fine. And he's gonna come back home just fine too."

One of his tears breaks free. Now we're both crying there in the alley between the barbershop and the shoe-repair store.

Then Will does something that surprises me more than anything he's ever done.

He hugs me.

It's late evening when Dad hauls the crate of fireworks out from the garage. Sun's dying in the west, shooting fingers of fire into a deepening purple sky. In that failing light, my father carries the crate into the meadow where he and Pete line up the rockets.

Our family's gathered to watch them do it. It's just like every Fourth of July far back as I can remember, only we got Frankie and Anna May with us this year. Frankie and me sit on the porch steps, eating bowls of ice cream. Anna May lies next to Will in the yard. They're talking quiet and peaceful until Butch wanders over and licks her face.

This Fourth is different in another way too: it will be the last time we're all together. Maybe for years, maybe forever.

Frankie puts an arm around my shoulder, almost like he's reading my mind.

"It'll be all right, Jack. He'll be all right."

Frankie cried too, when I told him. Pete ain't even his brother, but he broke down bawling just the same. Don't know what it is about sharing a person's pain, but it makes it just a little easier to carry. We sit with our arms around each other on the porch. Me and my cousin. Me and my best friend.

Pete finally told the family at dinner earlier, but there wasn't a person at the table didn't already know. Dad brought out the bottle of whiskey from the cabinet next to the fridge and poured glasses. He gave Pete a toast and told us how proud he was of him. Like he's not afraid at all of him getting killed or blown up.

And that's the thing. I'm proud too. Prouder than I can bear. My brother is doing one of the most selfless things you can ever do. And I am so, so frightened.

"I know it's one of the most special things you can do," I say, and I feel my lower lip start dancing up and down. "And I still just *wish* he wasn't going."

The tears come again, and I don't even try to hide them. Frankie gives my arm a squeeze. We sit that way a while and watch the fireflies start their show across Knee-Deep Meadow.

In the yard, Will is telling Anna May a story. It's about the night a few winters back when Dad arranged some railroad flares in a giant circle in the snow. He woke us boys up and told us aliens had landed.

"And you believed him?" Anna May laughs.

"You'd have believed him too if you'd seen a red circle glowing in the snow," Will tells her.

"What happened next?" Anna May asks.

Will laughs. "Dad told us, 'Stay here while I go and see what they want.' So we did and he went out and smoked a cigar in the field and let us get more and more scared wondering why he wasn't coming back. When he finally came in, he told us the aliens wanted us to do our homework and clean the dishes after dinner every night. That's when we knew he was faking."

"That all true?" Frankie asks.

I sniff and nod. "You bet."

In the yard there's a sound like a giant snake hissing. Next thing we know, one of those rockets is whizzing skyward, a trail of orange sparks spitting out behind it. It climbs a hundred feet.

Pop!

White smoke hangs in the air, blows out over the trees.

Anna May claps her hands.

"That's just the start, Anna May!" I call out. "Just wait until—"

A sudden shape racing across the yard makes me stop. It's Butch, running lickety-split for the lane, scared out of his mind from the rocket's burst. We forgot to tie him up. That dog is terrified of loud noises. He just takes off running for miles and miles. Next thing we know, my dog is gone into the night.

I am up and about to chase him when Ma comes through the screen door. "Sit down, John Thomas. Don't you forget you're still sick. If Butch doesn't like the loud noises, he's better off running than being chained up having to listen to them. He'll be back."

She's right. I just don't like him to be scared is all.

Ma sits down beside Frankie and me. "Relax and enjoy the show. Look, your father and brother are lighting another one."

In the field, there's another hiss as Pete and Dad set off a new rocket. Then another and another. There's pops and bangs and flashes of red and green sparks. One leaves a white-hot splotch on the sky that burns its fuzzy shape on the backs of our eyeballs so we're seeing it long after it's gone. Next comes a high-pitched whistler that makes us cover our ears.

Dad and Pete keep firing off rockets, and after a time I get used to the explosions. The breeze blows the smell of burnt fuses and cordite back our way while above, wisps of smoke stretch pale and thin across the moon. I almost forget about Pete's joining the Marines this morning. I almost forget that he's going to a place where the rockets don't just shoot up and explode harmlessly into pretty pictures. But then it all comes back to me in the dark and I stop my oohing and aahing.

Ma knows. Ma understands. She puts her arm around me and draws me in close. She rocks me gently as those rockets take off.

"This has been a hard summer for you, John Thomas," she says. "But you are holding up. I'm proud of you. And I love you."

She squeezes me tight.

We watch the fireworks for what seems like hours as the dew falls and that white smoke becomes part of the mist creeping up the creek. At last Dad and Pete's crate is empty and they come back, smelling like smoke.

Dad brings the pickup around to drive Anna May back to her house in town. She and Will are just about to climb up when she lifts a finger and points.

"What's that?"

Across the valley, a light twinkles at us. A flickering light.

Then Ma says in a low voice, "My God, Gene, you've started a fire."

Chapter 22

Back to Madliner Place

It's a tiny little light. Noiseless. Gentle. Like the flame from a candle.

Pete hops up on the truck fender to see better. "Can't be us. Our rockets can't reach that far." He squints. "That looks like it's clear across the valley. That looks like . . ." His voice trails off. "Like it's at the Madliner place."

A hush falls over us.

Then Will says suddenly, "It ain't us. It's *him*. Caleb's lit a fire. He's a firebug! What'd I tell you?"

Ma tells him to hush, but Dad moves for the house. "I'll call Arthur," he says. "Could be he's just burning rubbish."

Dad goes inside to make the call while we wait and watch that far flickering light.

The sudden awful feeling in my stomach tells me something ain't right at all. Something about that far light has got me spooked.

"Who burns rubbish on the Fourth of July?" Will is asking. "Nobody, that's who. That's one of Caleb's fires for sure."

"But why'd anybody light a fire on purpose?" Anna May asks.

"Because he's a firebug. He *likes* fire. He likes watching things burn."

Anna May tells Will that what he's saying is hearsay. Will tells her it ain't, and the two of them go back and forth about what hearsay is and what it isn't.

But me, I don't take my eyes off that little light on the hill. It holds me hypnotized. And that awful feeling in my stomach gets worse and worse. And then it hits me: a fire at Madliner House could easily spread to the trees. Or the meadow. And somewhere in those trees or that meadow, running scared, is my dog.

"Butch!" I say suddenly. "Butch's out there!"

Anna May and Will stop their arguing. Everyone looks at me.

"He got scared from all those fireworks and took off running. If there's a forest fire, he'll be out in it. We've got to find him!"

Ma pushes out her lower lip. "John Thomas, there is *not* going to be a forest fire. And our family is *not* going looking for Butch." She turns to Will and starts in on him about how his fire talk has got me upset.

Right then and there I decide. Maybe my family isn't going looking for Butch. But *I* am.

Dad comes out of the house. His face is grim.

"No answer. I called the fire department. Chief Coop's sending a truck." Dad walks toward where our Ford is parked in the drive. "I'm going to have a look."

Pete follows him. "Not alone you're not."

"Now wait a minute, Gene," says Ma, sounding alarmed for the first time. "Arthur could have been outside. He might not have heard the phone."

Dad turns back to her. They start arguing. Will joins in. It's my chance. I simply turn and walk away. That's something good about being the youngest: you get overlooked occasionally. I aim for the barn, but then I circle right back around to the truck and come up with it between me and my family. Silent as a shadow and half as quick, I'm up into the bed. I lie down flat as a board on those rivets and wait for what I know will happen: Pete and Dad will drive over to check on Madliner

House. And they'll be taking me along for the ride. And while we're there, I'll look for Butch.

I'm in that truck bed a full minute before I hear the gravel crunch on the other side of the fender.

Frankie's voice comes in a whisper. "You can't sneak off easy as that, Jack."

"Fooled everybody else," I whisper back.

"Yeah, well, not me. Come on down from there."

"Nothing doing, Frankie. Butch's out there and I'm going to find him."

From the direction of our porch I hear Dad telling Ma to keep near the phone. Their discussion is over. He and Pete start this way.

"Get back, Frankie, or they'll see!" I whisper urgently.

"You shouldn't be up there, Jack. Let your dad and Pete go and check on the Madliners. If Butch's there, they'll bring him back."

What he says makes sense. But it's too late now. Dad and Pete are no more than a stone's throw away.

"See you in a bit, Frankie."

He goes quiet as Dad and Pete climb into the cab.

The Ford's engine roars to life and I feel the bed tremble under me. Soon we're rolling, and I chance a glance over the lip of the truck as we turn out of our drive. Twin headlight beams slice through the dark. But beyond them that little light across the valley burns fierce. Could be just my imagination, but that light seems bigger than it did a few minutes ago.

Dad turns onto Hopkins Road and gives the engine some gas, and now the three of us are racing through a night that is warm and getting warmer and not so dark as it used to be.

We're just past Sam's trailer on Hopkins Road when I smell an oily smoke on warm wind. When Dad turns us onto the dirt drive that leads up to Madliner House, that smell gets stronger.

I brace myself against the truck side and keep close to the cab so he and Pete can't see me in the rearview. It should be dark enough, but there's an orange glow in the sky now, an eerie second twilight that lets me see twisted tree trunks rushing by along either side. We hit a big old hole and I lose my grip and slide down to the back of the pickup. I'm out in the open now, and all Pete or Dad would need to do is glance in the mirror and they'd see me splayed out plain as day. But they don't.

The truck shudders again and again over potholes as we climb their hill to its bare top. Mr. Madliner sure never kept up this drive. *Tough on visitors,* I think, before wondering if maybe that ain't the whole point.

We're getting near the top of the hill now, and there's other smells among the smoke—roof tar and plaster and rubber. Orange cinders float above me, searing into the dark and leaving trails like comets. Those sparks are especially dangerous: riding clouds of black smoke, they stay hot and travel far on high winds to start fresh fires in places you don't expect.

Dad hits the brake and I slide again in the truck bed. That orange glow in the sky is much brighter now, and I hear a snapping sound over the truck's engine, like a flag on its pole in a strong wind.

The Ford comes to a stop. Truck doors open and slam. I wait a good ten seconds before craning my neck to peer through the windshield. What I see makes me gasp.

Madliner House is on fire.

Sheets of red and orange flame ripple behind the wavy glass of the second-floor windows. Smoke curls out from under the eaves and rolls in black clouds into orangey night. The first-floor windows are dark: the fire is only eating the second floor now, but the front door is ajar and a stream of smoke blows from it too. Dad and Pete follow it inside.

I suck in a breath of smoky air then, for I imagine that roof collapsing down on them, trapping my father and my brother in an avalanche of fiery timbers. But it doesn't. The roof holds, and from inside I hear them shouting for Mr. and Mrs. Madliner and Caleb.

Next thing I know I am down from the truck and running for the house too. All thoughts of finding Butch are gone as I realize now how stupid I am. My dog has more sense than to be anywhere near here. I don't.

I'm a stone's throw from the house and feeling the fire's fierce heat on my face and on my bare arms when, away to my left, a movement catches my eye. As if by instinct I turn toward it, away from the house. Rounding the corner, I come to the crown of the hill and the empty space where that old oak tree once towered. The whole of the valley lies before me. Stairways twinkles in the distance, on the far side of Knee-Deep Meadow.

But the yard is empty. There's no one and nothing, just that old oak stump sitting short and fat in the flickering firelight, and—

I stop.

There's someone there. Someone sitting with their back against that stump, so low I almost didn't see them in the twitching shadows.

It's Mr. Madliner.

I run to him. Drawing closer, I see he's got his long scarecrow legs splayed out, and his bony hands at the end of his long arms rest in the dirt, fingers curled like he's pulling weeds. His head leans back against that stump like he's just sat down to rest and watch his house burn.

"Mr. Madliner!"

He don't answer me but just stares at his house, which is beginning to pop and creak and hiss. The roof is going. I shout to him again, but still he don't answer. I know when some people get awful scared they just go rigid so they can't talk or think or hardly move, and I wonder if that's what's happened to him.

And then I see it in his forehead, above his right eye: a small, dark hole.

The eyes are open, and in the white places I see twin reflections of the burning house behind me. But that's the only light left in Arthur Madliner's eyes. He's dead.

My mouth goes dry, electricity surges down my spine, and I hear a new sound in the night: my own voice—screaming. A plank drops somewhere in the house behind me. There's a fresh hiss of sparks. Hot smoke blows on the back of my neck. But now I'm the one so scared he can't move. I am rooted to that spot in the yard, like the dead tree stump and the dead man propped against it.

Mr. Madliner is dead. Shot through the head.

Scared as I am, I know he didn't die here. Someone *dragged* him here and set him up to watch the burning of the house. The marks in the dirt made by the heels of his boots are clear as day in angry firelight. And there was that movement that caught my eye before—the shape that first drew me around this side of the house.

Shadows writhe across the yard. They are joined by one more. A tall, broad shadow that appears beside mine in the fire's hellish light. The hand on my shoulder turns me around, and now I am staring straight into the eyes of my father. His face is dark with soot. His clothes are singed. Smoke curls out of his hair.

The anger at seeing me lasts only an instant. In its place comes a deep and terrible sadness. My father's eyes move to Mr. Madliner, then quickly to the yard, and the trees rimming the hill. They sweep the dark trunks, then the fringes of the meadow grasses below us.

"Did you see Caleb?"

He has to shout it over the fire, now a wild, roaring animal. But I can't answer. I cannot speak.

"Jack, where is Caleb?"

I shake my head. "Dad, he's dead," I finally manage and I point.

Without another word, Dad lifts me into his arms and turns for the truck. I catch a last glimpse of Mr. Madliner sitting against that stump. Staring his dead man's stare at the burning house. That's when my mind pieces it together. Caleb!

We come around the corner and I see now that the roof has caught fire. The first-floor windows are glowing bright. Smoke pours through cracks in the bone-white plaster. The whole place is being eaten alive by fire.

I want it to burn. Burn straight to the ground.

Through the truck windshield I see Pete is already in the cab, his clothes also charred. His face changes too when he sees me. A storm of anger at my sneaking along.

Dad carries me closer to the truck. But when Pete leans over and opens the door, I see there's someone else there with him, wrapped in a dirty blanket. Pete has one arm around that someone, holding them tight.

And now I know why Dad asked me where Caleb was. Because in Pete's arms, unconscious and covered in blood, is Elmira Madliner.

Mr. Madliner is dead. Mrs. Madliner is unconscious. But Caleb is nowhere in sight.

Dad slides me into the cab and slams the door.

Next thing I know, we are speeding down the lane, with the cinders from Madliner House chasing us as we go.

We meet the fire trucks on Hopkins Road. Three of them, splashing red light along the pavement. They do not blare their sirens. There is no one on the road to warn.

Through his open window Dad tells them: Arthur Madliner has been shot dead. Caleb's missing. Madliner House is beyond saving. With the wind, there's a strong chance the fire will spread to the trees.

As if to give weight to his words, that smoky breeze blows soft and warm through the open window.

I shiver.

The fire engines leave us in swirling red dust. Just this morning those firefighters were parading down Main Street, waving to the people. Now, they'll battle the flames of Madliner House, fight to keep the fire inside its cage.

"Will it spread?" Pete asks as we take off down Hopkins Road again.

Dad does not answer, and that's all the answer we need.

In Pete's arms, Mrs. Madliner stirs and moans. It's an awful sound. Dad buries the gas pedal. The Ford eats up the road now.

The lights are on at Sam's trailer. The old man is in the road. Long underwear and hunting boots and floppy hat. Dad brakes again.

"You'll need all hands on deck when it reaches the meadow, Gene," Sam says. He climbs into the bed, spits over the side, and slaps the glass to tell Dad to drive again.

Sam's words are frightening. He believes it's already certain the fire will spread to Knee-Deep Meadow. And from there it's an easy march to Apple Creek, and Stairways just on the other side . . . A few sparks on the wind might be all that is needed to start fresh fire on *our* side of the creek.

Sam's words must have frightened Dad too, because the truck engine makes its own roar now. We race across Hopkins Bridge, the metal beneath us rattling an eerie wail. Dad barely touches the brakes as we turn onto our lane. Next thing I know we come screeching to a halt in our driveway.

Ma rushes off the porch.

"Gene! Gene! Jack is gone!"

"No, he ain't." Dad jumps down and moves for Pete's door.

When Ma sees me her face goes dark with fury. She storms over the stones and is about to let loose when Dad opens the other door. Pete steps out, cradling Mrs. Madliner in his arms.

"My God, Elmira!" Ma cries. "Bring her inside, Pete!"

They move toward the house, Ma shouting for Will to call Doc Mayfield.

I stand shaking in the drive until Sam comes off the pickup. He looks to the east, where the sky is a dull red. Like the dawn is coming too soon. An orange mist seems to be rising at Knee-Deep Meadow's far edge. The wind blows and it smells like charcoal.

Sam sniffs the night. "This one will be bad. Worse than forty-seven." He means the fire of 1947. I'd only ever heard stories about it. A wall of fire a mile wide that burned for two days.

Sam turns to me, leans over, and drops both his rough hands on my shoulders.

"Son, where do you fellas keep the buckets?"

I am sitting in our living room and wrapped up in Grandma Elliot's old quilt again when Doc Mayfield arrives. He's wearing slippers and carrying his black bag. He sees Mrs. Madliner lying on the couch—a pale, wasted skeleton of a woman, covered in dried blood—and he gasps.

"Saints above, why, it's Elmira Madliner," he exclaims.

I have not seen Mrs. Madliner since that night at the Ticking Tomb. We thought she was a witch come to kill us for disturbing her dead husband's rest. Now she lies still and helpless, eyes closed, her lips tracing words I can't hear. Elmira Madliner is flesh and blood sure enough, but she's like Hiltch's witch in one way now. Her husband is dead too.

Doc Mayfield takes her pulse. Then he tells Ma he has to check her for other injuries and asks her to help him remove some of her clothes. Ma puts me out onto the porch then, out into the warm night.

Will and Anna May are there. Pete leans against the railing, arms folded, his face turned to the meadow. Frankie paces the yard. When

I come out they all rush to me, wanting to know what happened. Everyone but Frankie.

I tell them as best I can and make it the whole way through without crying.

"But where is Caleb?" Will asks when I finish. His voice is cold.

I shake my head. "I never saw him."

Will and Pete look at each other. Both of them put the pieces together. Mr. Madliner dead. Caleb missing. Madliner House burning.

"My God," Will whispers. "Caleb Madliner has killed his own father!"

Pete is silent for a long moment. He seems about to speak when suddenly we hear sirens in the night. The fire trucks are giving warning as they race along Hopkins Road. They are racing toward us.

Frankie hears their howling with an odd look on his face. He'd hopped a train and traveled hundreds of miles to get away from his burning city. The fires found him anyway.

"If the fire spreads to the meadow, it will be partly our fault," he says.

Will's head snaps up. "What are you talking about?" he demands.

Frankie goes on in a quiet voice. "It's the brush at the bottom of Madliner Hill that's fueling the fire now. *We* tossed those branches there, after we cut that oak down."

My brothers look at him.

I realize then that Frankie is right. It's an awful thing to realize you've made fuel for the fire that's about to burn your house down. All that kindling needed was for somebody to light it, and I suppose that murderin' Caleb was happy to oblige.

Will draws Anna May close as the fire trucks come up our lane, spinning lights stabbing into the smoky dark. But we don't need fire trucks to tell us what's coming. Bits of what seems to be burnt paper float like snow across our yard.

Chief Coop meets Dad in the drive. We hear him loud and clear.

"Fire's burning this-a-way, Gene," he says. "We aim to dig a trench on the other side of Apple Creek and slow it down before it reaches the water. That will give you all *two* lines of defense instead of one."

"We'll be right there," Dad tells him.

"Appreciated," Chief Coop says and turns back to his trucks. He whistles and waves his arms.

The firefighters come out of their metal boxes. Their bulky, helmeted shapes tramp down our hill and disappear into black trees. We hear them splashing through the shallow part of Apple Creek. A minute later, we see them rise again onto the far bank and march in a thin line into Knee-Deep Meadow's orange haze.

Sam comes around the barn. He's got every last bucket and pail we own in his arms. He dumps them into the grass.

"Pick yer favorite."

I fall in next to Frankie as we follow the firefighters down to the creek. We are a ragtag army: my father and brothers, Anna May and old Sam, Frankie and me. For a time, nobody talks and all we hear is the shovels and buckets clinking in the dark.

"I'm sorry," I say to Frankie as we enter the trees. "I should have listened to you."

"You made it back safe. That's what counts," he replies. "It's just . . . there's some things you can't ever unsee."

I know what he means. Long as I live, I'll never be able to forget Mr. Madliner sitting against that oak stump and that bullet hole in his head. It will stay with me forever.

"You knew there was something awful there, didn't you?" I ask.

"There wasn't going to be anything good. That's for darn sure."

The path drops under us and I feel cold creek air on my face. The hairs on my arms and the back of my neck stand up. We are coming to the creek, and I think to myself that this is our shield against the fire. Apple Creek is our armor. A wall of water.

Apple Creek won't stop a bullet.

The thought shoots out of the mist. Strikes me square in the chest. If Caleb killed his father, then somewhere out there in the dark is a boy with a gun. A gun and a twisted mind. He might be anywhere by now. Tracking along some distant highway to a faraway place or waiting for us in the reeds at the bottom of the path.

The gentle sound of rolling water reaches my ears. Apple Creek is just ahead. Dad and Sam murmur to each other about the direction of the wind. Sam says it's against us and likely to remain so.

Dirt turns to sand under our feet. Dad and Sam lead us into the shallows where the water is just a few feet deep. The creek is no wider than a stone's throw here. Anna May hikes up her skirt for the crossing.

My thoughts are chattering to themselves inside my head: Did Caleb Madliner really kill his own father? If he didn't, that left just one other person who might have . . . and she was lying on the couch back at Stairways.

We come out of Apple Creek into Knee-Deep Meadow and a terrible quiet.

There is no singing of crickets in the long grass. No bullfrog lullaby or symphony of cicadas. But faint on the warm wind there comes the gasping breath of fire, the snickering of flames in the thickets.

A blanket of orange fog rolls, ghostlike, toward us. The firefighters spread out in a long line and, at a signal from Chief Coop, they bend and begin to dig, their spades biting into the earth, opening the gash in the meadow that will become for us our trench and first line of defense.

Behind us is Apple Creek. Behind that is Stairways.

Chapter 23

The Battle of Apple Creek

Never thought I'd go to hell. This night, hell comes to me.

Knee-Deep Meadow is on fire.

The honeysuckle is on fire.

The trees along Hopkins Road are on fire, burning like torches.

The butterfly weed burns, spewing sparks and choking black smoke. And beneath all that smoke, stealing across parched earth and dry grass, is a wall of hideous yellow flames that marches toward us, roaring like a wild animal, whipped by the eastern wind that blows and blows and won't stop blowing.

The firefighters dig their ditch from Hopkins Road in the south to the field's far end in the north, anchoring it at a bend of Apple Creek. The first fingers of fire rush against it, slip along its edges, devouring the high grass, furiously seeking some way across. From behind us in Apple Creek, the *thump-thump* of a pump starts, and now that hose is giving answer to those awful flames, spraying cold water into that shimmering wall and soaking the grasses before it. Clouds of steam leap into the air. There is a great hissing sound, like some enormous snake is writhing in the burning butterfly weed.

The men run back and forth before that crackling wall of red flames, their hunched shapes dragging lines of hose, swinging shovels, flinging dirt. My father and my brothers work with them, stabbing the earth in silent fury, their skin slick with sweat as they hurl earth in their desperate struggle to smother the onrushing fire.

Sam throws bucket after bucket of black creek water, passed up by Frankie, Anna May, and me. He tosses them faster than we can fill them, pitching the empty pails down in fury and shouting for more.

All my life I have heard how dangerous fire can be. It can move in ways you don't expect. Sneak up on you. Burst upon you. Trap you. Fire can travel underground, burning through tree roots you did not even know were there until the tree behind you cracks into whistling flame. Fire can jump. It can travel *through the air*, eating whatever dust or bits of leaves might float there. I remember all these things as I pass the leaky pails.

Like all living things, fire must eat to stay alive. If we can hold it up long enough, it will burn up everything there is to burn. It will starve itself out. But first we've got to *hold* it. And if our trench fails, Apple Creek will be our last line of defense.

Chief Coop runs up to Dad.

"Fall back! It's too hot here!"

And we do. With our shovels and our buckets we retreat across Apple Creek and, shaking and coughing, watch the fire pounce upon our thin, jagged line of trench. Our little platoon has fought bravely. Now we see if the trench can hold.

For a moment it seems it will. Then a patch of grass suddenly bursts into flames on *our side* of it. Then another, and another. We've lost. The fire has jumped our ditch.

Chief Coop shouts for us to spread out, to watch for fresh flames on our side of the creek.

We do. And that's how I find myself walking upstream next to Pete. He's quit his shirt in that heat, left it somewhere on the opposite bank. His face is flushed and his cheeks are black from ash. He smells like smoke.

"Still with me, Jack?" he asks in a ragged voice.

"Still with you." I'll stay with him forever.

"Good boy! We'll lick this thing yet. Keep your eyes open!" Pete tells me as we thread along the bank, between tree trunks. The fire is almost upon Apple Creek now. Black water reflects its shivering flames. There's a chattering sound from the fire now. Like rain. Funny. Fire that sounds like rain.

And barking.

I stop.

The barking comes again and my heart leaps into my mouth.

"Butch!" I scream.

Pete turns and seizes my arm. "Where?"

I point across the creek. But the far bank is bare. Nothing but a few black trees before a withering sheet of flame. We strain our ears against the crackling and snapping of the fire, but the barking does not come again.

"I *heard* him, Pete! I swear I did! He's over there!" I start to sob. My dog is over there in that hell, trapped, surrounded on some island of unburned earth, alone and scared and wondering why we ain't come to save him. Frantic, I sweep that far bank again and beg God to let me see my dog come running out of it all.

But I don't.

I see someone else.

A wiry shape runs before that wall of fire, stumbles, crashes into the brush, rises, staggers on.

Caleb Madliner.

Caleb comes running for the creek, bent low, his hands holding his shirt up over his nose and mouth, his body shaking with coughs. And running right behind him, barking like mad, chasing him away from the fire, is Butch.

Pete and I rush to the edge of our bank. Across Apple Creek, Caleb crashes through the trees and comes to the edge on the other side. He don't see us.

"Caleb!" I cry out. "Caleb, jump!"

He looks up, sees us, and stops.

"Caleb, jump and swim!" I shout to him.

But Caleb doesn't jump. He stands like a statue, framed against that fiery wall, staring at us. His mouth hangs open in a mix of surprise and fear. His ash-darkened face is streaked with tears.

Beside him on the bank, Butch barks, confused as to why he don't jump. My dog bounds in closer and bites the hem of his shirt and tries to drag him to the edge. But Caleb jerks away and his shirt tears free in Butch's teeth. That boy never takes his eyes off us.

Through the smoke that drifts across the creek, I look into Caleb's eyes and I see something I have never seen there before: shame. That horrible fire that tormented him for so long is gone. It has burned its way out. It burns our valley now, but it has gone from him.

And suddenly I know he won't jump, no matter how much I shout. Caleb Madliner will choose to stay on his bank and burn. He will stay because he doesn't believe he deserves to live.

"Caleb, you've got to jump!" I shout again. "There's a way to fix it—all of this!"

Behind him, fire roars furiously. A new wave of black smoke billows across the bank. Fingers of it curl around his shaking body. The fire *wants* him.

Then, to my horror, Caleb Madliner takes a step backward.

Panic seizes me. "Caleb, no!" I shout. "No! No! No! Jump! Jump right now and swim! You can make it!"

Caleb gives no answer. He shakes his head and takes another step backward.

"Pete, he ain't jumping," I tell my brother. "He's not going to do it!"

Next to me, Pete watches in stunned silence.

"Pete!" I suddenly cry. "Pete, you got to go get him!"

Butch barks again.

I scream.

Without a word, Pete dives into Apple Creek.

Pete knifes through black water and the rippling reflections of the fire burning on the far bank, his arms and legs slicing those flames in rapid, powerful strokes.

Caleb stares in amazement. He's still staring when Pete springs from the creek, the water already curling off his body in waves of steam, and crawls hand over hand up the muddy bank until he rises before Caleb. Caleb stands mesmerized. Weeping.

Pete grabs him by the shoulders and shouts over the fire's roar. "Come on, Caleb! If you stay here, you'll die!"

Caleb shakes his head. "Go back, Pete! Go back!" He tries to twist away, but Pete holds him tight. He can't break loose. Pete is too strong.

"Let go of me, Peter Elliot!" Caleb cries.

And then, in a sudden rapid movement, Caleb hits him low and hard in the stomach.

Pete sinks to his knees. He bends double, his mouth wide as he gasps for air, a look of surprise spreading across his face. And that's when Caleb kicks him in the stomach.

"Pete!" I scream.

Caleb turns toward the fire. He don't get far. Pete grabs hold of his ankle and with a single wrenching motion pulls him to the sand and rolls over on top of him. Now it's a fight.

Their shapes collide: Pete grasping for a hold, desperate to drag Caleb to water as he slams his fists over and over again against Pete's head, neck, and shoulders. Hot ash falls around them as they grapple, kicking and cursing. Black smoke sweeps over the bank once more, hungry for them *both*.

"Hit him!" I scream to Pete. But he can't hear me. Whether because of the fire's crackling or Caleb's crazed shouting, Pete cannot hear me. I am about to scream again when a fresh blast of black smoke strangles my words in my throat.

And now my nightmare has become real. My brother faces death across the river, and I am helpless on my side. Only it ain't some jungle in Vietnam, half a world away. It's here at home. It's Apple Creek.

There is only one thing left to do.

I jump too.

Apple Creek swallows me whole. Water fills my mouth and nose, and my clothes cling to my arms and legs like lead. I fight their dragging weight and the current that pulls me downstream as I kick and claw and pound the water for that far, burning bank. I pray for speed, for strength as I cut my own way through the fire's glimmering reflection. I am splashing too much to see, but with the smoke and the sparks there's nothing to see anyhow and so I just swim: stroke, breath, stroke, breath.

I smack into that muddy wall so hard, stars explode across my sight. My teeth feel loose in my head. But I'm across.

I lay hold of the bank with both hands to pull myself up. Mud squelches through my knuckles and I slide back into blood-warm water. Above I hear them fighting still, cussing, screaming. Frantically, I try again. This time my fingers close on dry roots.

I pull. The roots hold.

I pull harder.

The roots hold still.

I climb. Left hand, right knee. Right hand, left knee. The air is thick with smoke, and it burns the back of my mouth and my throat as I climb. Suddenly I feel sand under my fingers—hot sand. I'm up. I roll onto the baking bank and feel the hot breath of fire on my face.

My eyes water instantly so that I can hardly see. Somewhere in front of me, Pete and Caleb fight in that swirling smoke.

And then they burst onto the sand before me, locked in each other's arms, coughing, cursing, kicking, spitting. Pete's face is a bloody mess, his eyes swelled up, lip busted. Caleb strikes him again and again. Butch appears, teeth bared, tiny little flashes of white in that smoke, barking, snapping. Pete rolls toward me, to the edge of the bank, and that's when I throw myself upon Caleb and wrap my arms around his neck and latch on tight. He comes off the sand, desperate to throw me. But he can't.

Pete falls back, gasping, and I have got Caleb Madliner now, got him tight, my elbow locked around his throat. He is helpless against me, the boy who tried to feed my fingers to the snapping turtle, the boy who lit this fire, who killed his father, who fought my brother.

Caleb goes very still as I lean forward and whisper in his ear:

"You're the sorriest boy I ever met, Caleb Madliner, but I ain't letting you die tonight!"

I step backward into empty air.

Chapter 24

End Times

I lose him soon as we hit water. Was gonna let go anyway, but he kicks me, gets me good in the ribs, and I yell even though I'm underwater. I swallow half of Apple Creek before I break the surface. When I do it's nothing but smoke in the air, and I cough a fit and it's forever before I can suck in a breath.

Caleb is nowhere in sight and a piece of me wonders if he's hiding below, waiting to pull me under and drown me. I tread water and wait for his hands to close on my ankles. They never do. Caleb is gone.

Lots of thoughts go through my mind, but now they're about Pete and Butch and whether they're safe. Smoke pours over the bank. Pieces of falling ash sizzle in the water around me. I am just about to climb those roots again to go up and look for them when both my brother and my dog come sailing over the ledge. Pete misses me by a foot. He comes up shouting my name and whipping about in the foamy water.

"I'm here!"

Pete grabs hold of me and begins swimming for the far shore, carrying us away from that burning bank with his measured, powerful strokes. Butch is right behind us, his big head and pointy ears bobbing along in our wake.

I try telling Pete that I've lost Caleb. But that smoke gets its way again with my words; they die in another coughing fit.

Soon I feel soft mud bottom under my feet, but Pete won't let go until we've crawled onto cool sand. Butch shakes himself, barking and whining. He won't let us stay here. Too much smoke.

The far bank disappears under a writhing wall of yellow fire. I throw a wild look up and down the creek. But the water is empty too.

"I don't see him," I pant to Pete. "Couldn't hold him . . . couldn't pull him across . . ."

"He could only come by choice," Pete says.

He rises to his feet and pulls me up too. Then, with Butch, we run back up the path.

At the top of the trail our family and the firefighters are watching for fresh fires on our side of Apple Creek. Everybody fans out and searches the length of the creek for Caleb. We never find him.

Twice tiny flames spring up along the edge of our lane. Little pockets of dried leaves that burst into licking flame only to be doused at once with a stomp of a boot or the splash of a bucket. Anna May stamps one of the fires out. Her skirt catches and Sam has to clap his hands against the fabric to put her out.

We fight the fire all night, my family and me and the men from the fire department. Apple Creek holds it, a wall of hellish light burning bright behind black trees of the far bank.

It is an hour before dawn when the wind picks up again and carries the cinders across the creek to the roof of our house. There, in the shingles above the attic, where the snakes sleep and the screech owls nest, a small fire starts. Just a few quivering flames at first. Then it spreads. Suddenly Stairways is on fire.

Dad races inside and next we know he and Ma and Doc Mayfield come out carrying Mrs. Madliner between them in Grandma Elliot's old quilt.

The firemen work fast. Ladders and a pump. Cold creek water arcs through the night. Our stone house is strong. But the roof above the porch catches and now it's burning; our home is burning. Black smoke pours from the windows. There's a sound of groaning timbers; the bones of our old house are giving way. The men fight on. Another pump, more water. The porch collapses, its black skeleton crumpling in on itself, and I know that we've lost our house.

A bleak and gray light has started in the east, but by the time the dawn arrives, the fire has eaten our house. Early morning sun breaks over a fire-blackened stone shell. After more than two hundred years, Stairways is no more.

Knee-Deep Meadow is charred to a crisp, pockets of smoldering embers still spitting smoke that rises in thin columns high into a hazy morning sky.

The fire is out. But we've lost our home.

Chapter 25

The Game Preserve

Mr. Halleck's house is enormous. It's so big each of us boys could have our own bedroom if we wanted it. All four of us decide to stay in one room. It's got a tall window that faces west. Ma and Dad take a room just across the hall.

Mr. Halleck has offered to let us stay here long as we need. Dad begins calling for apartments in town the very first day after the fire.

Two days after the fire, a police cruiser draws up to the metal gate in the stone wall that surrounds Mr. Halleck's house and grounds. Dad lets them in and directs them up the lane to the house.

We meet them in the dining room. Ma and Dad and me.

Detective Ingleside is short, with a high and tight haircut. Like a Marine. He wears a gray suit and a black tie and surveys the room through heavy-lidded eyes. If he's impressed, he don't show it. The uniformed police officer with him is very impressed. He keeps looking out the window at the view of the valley. At one point he whistles.

Townie.

Detective Ingleside asks me about the night of the fire, about finding Mr. Madliner.

"Son, you say you found him by the side of the house?"

"Yes sir, but I was looking for my dog."

"Did you see anyone else there?"

"No sir. Well, a shape, maybe. But it was gone quick."

He jots something down in his book. The officer with him folds his arms.

Ma asks them if they'd like a cup of coffee. The officer says yes. Detective Ingleside says no.

"But you and your brother saw the boy Caleb later that evening, is that correct?"

"Yes sir."

"Across the creek?"

I nod.

"What was he doing?"

"Running."

"Running where?"

"I don't know. My dog was with him. He was trying to shepherd him away from that fire. Butch is like that. He's always looking after people."

Detective Ingleside don't seem to pay any attention to my talk about Butch. He goes back to asking questions about Caleb. "Your brother swam across the creek to try to get Caleb to come back with him. Caleb resisted. They began to fight. You swam over to help your brother. And you pulled Caleb into the creek with you?"

I nod again.

"But you never saw him after that?"

I shake my head.

Detective Ingleside looks at Dad. He leans in and folds his hands over the corner of the table and looks at me with gray eyes.

"And you're sure you didn't see him after that?" he asks. "Maybe swimming downstream in the creek? Maybe crawling out on your bank *with you* and then running off?"

I shake my head. "No sir."

He looks at Dad again.

"Jack doesn't lie, Detective," says Dad.

He looks back at me.

"Son, this is important. We have strong reason to believe that boy Caleb killed his father. *Murdered* him, you understand? Now, we know Caleb had it rough from his old man. We know he took a lot of wallops from him, and more than he ought. But that's no excuse for killing. Now, Caleb may be a friend of yours, but that doesn't make it okay to lie—"

"Caleb Madliner ain't no friend of mine!" I explode. "And I'm *not* lying! I pulled him off that bank and he disappeared into the creek, and that's a fact! And what makes you so sure Mrs. Madliner didn't kill her husband, anyway?"

Ma comes in with the coffee then. Hearing my words, she starts and spills some down her front.

Ingleside looks at me and frowns.

"Mrs. Madliner is an invalid. She's wheelchair bound, partly because of her time with Mr. Madliner. We believe he hit her too. At any rate, the woman can't walk. It's highly unlikely she—"

But now it's my turn to cut him off. "She can too walk! I saw her do it! All us boys did. Midnight at the Ticking Tomb, we saw her. Right after Frankie laid down over Hiltch's grave to summon his widow witch. She came and we thought she *was* the witch. She cried over a grave and then she walked off, same as you or me!"

My father sits utterly still, watching me with a face as smooth as water.

But Ingleside sits back in his chair. Beside him the officer takes the coffee cup from Ma and sips it. Ingleside looks at him, and he looks back.

Ma says to the policemen, "I think he's a little worked up now."

"I am *not* worked up!" I insist. "These people don't believe me, but I'm telling the truth!"

Detective Ingleside puts his notebook away. "If we can talk to the other son now, Mr. Elliot."

"Of course," Dad tells him, though his eyes are still on me.

Ma reaches for me. "Come on, John Thomas."

"Tell them to go and ask Mrs. Madliner!" I cry. "Go find her! Bring her back from the hospital and ask her! She can walk. I'm telling you, she can walk!"

Detective Ingleside smiles thinly and dips his close-shaven head. "I'm sure she can, son."

That night we eat pizza for dinner in the dining room, surrounded by tall, dark cabinets filled with pale porcelain plates. The table is long and could sit nearly three times as many people as we've got.

"Found two places in town to look at," Dad says over his crust. "Your mother and I will drive in and take a look tomorrow morning."

Will puts his fork down. Pete chews slowly. I got no appetite. My slice of pizza grows cold on my plate, little pools of oil drying into shiny pieces on the cheese, like wax from a candle.

"How long will we have to stay there?" Pete asks.

"What do you care?" I ask. "You're leaving in a few days anyhow."

Ma sets down her fork. "John Thomas, you apologize to your brother at once. *At once.*"

I frown. I look at Pete. "I'm sorry."

He looks down. "It's fine, Jack."

Dad finds me after dinner, in the hall upstairs.

"Jack."

"I already told Pete I was sorry," I tell him. "I know he feels like he has to go. For you. For Grandpa Elliot too. To make you both proud."

Dad is a silent, dark shape in the hallway. "I want to ask you about Elmira Madliner."

That stops me.

"You said you saw her walking."

"At the cemetery. Walking just as plain as you or me. And looking at graves."

I cannot see my father's face in the dark, but I feel the change come over it. A sense of pity. There in old Mr. Halleck's house, I get the feeling that Dad has guessed all along that she could walk.

"Why was she there, Dad?" I ask him. "What was she doing?"

"Not all those graves are old ones, son," Dad says. "I expect she was saying goodbye to someone. Again." Dad pauses. A piece of silence grows in the inky dark. Then: "Plenty of people knew Arthur Madliner was a hard man to live with. No one had any idea he was so cruel."

Standing across from him now, I feel it too: pity for poor Elmira Madliner. Whoever's grave it was she was visiting that night, I will never know. And I do not care to find out.

"What will happen to her?"

"She's out from it now," Dad answers after a moment. "And Caleb's on the run." Dad is silent a minute more. "He is . . . on the run, isn't he, son?"

"God's honest truth, Dad. I don't know where he is now."

He says nothing more, and neither do I.

There is one piece of good news that night. It comes in the *Evening News*. Frankie brings it in to where us boys are gathered in Mr. Halleck's study. Pete and me sit at the table playing checkers. Will lounges in a leather armchair with one of those fat, dusty books from the shelf open on his lap. Frankie drops the newspaper on the table beside me. In bold lettering I read the headline he wrote: *Local Family Thwarts County Plan for Reservoir; Local Biker Gang Lends a Hand.*

"They ran our story!"

Pete looks at the story over Frankie's shoulder. "Not bad."

"Yeah, and listen to this!" I read it out loud: "'The unusual coalition between local families and the notorious hell-raising biker gang was orchestrated by Mr. and Mrs. Elliot and their sons, Peter, William, and John Thomas!' That's us!"

"Sure is." Pete jumps my piece and lands one of his on my back row. "King me," he says.

"You're famous, Pete!"

"Hardly," Will snorts.

I look at Frankie. We finally did it. We got Pete into the papers. But it's too late. It doesn't matter now. Pete's already signed up. He leaves for training at Parris Island in three days.

Next night, Pastor Fenton and Anna May have us over for dinner at their house in town. It's new and shaped like an L, with a sitting room that looks onto a little yard and another house across the street that looks just like it. I could whip a baseball from their front door to the other and then some.

We sit on couches all covered in crinkly plastic and eat cheese and crackers while Anna May serves iced tea in tall glasses from a tray. The crackers are dry as sawdust but the cheese is all right, and I'm reaching for my third piece when Anna May asks me to help her with dinner.

"I need a sous-chef," she says as we make for the kitchen. She throws Will a sly wink.

"I don't know how to make soup," I answer, "but I'll try."

Frankie must be having trouble with the crackers too, because he coughs at that and reaches for his iced tea.

In the kitchen, Anna May puts me to work slicing a loaf of bread while she checks a roast in the oven.

"Your family's been through a lot of change," she says.

I nod. "And more coming." Pete's leaving in a few days. Frankie's going back to his city not long after.

Anna May straightens up from the oven and fixes her pretty blue eyes on me. "I hear you know a thing or two about fishing, Jack."

That puzzles me. "I guess so."

"I was hoping maybe you might show me how . . . maybe after Pete leaves. I've never been, not really, where you go out early and are gone the whole day and everything. What do you think?"

The idea of Anna May with a fishing pole is a hard one to figure, but I shrug.

"Okay."

She comes over next to me and starts laying the pieces of sliced bread into a bowl. I can smell her perfume along with the rosemary from the roast. "Will tells me fishing is peaceful, and I don't know about you, but I'd like some peace for a change."

I help her with the slices. "It can get boring sometimes, if you don't catch anything. But as long as you know before you go, you can have a pretty good time."

"I'm just fine with boring. But I won't do worms. That'll have to be you."

That gets me to chuckling, because now I know if she ever catches anything, I'm the one who'll have to take it off the hook for her. Oh well.

We finish with the bread, and a timer over the oven dings and she goes back for the roast. She has me dribble some broth over it and then carry it carefully to the dining room with a pair of oven mitts. We get the plates and knives and forks out, and I line them up the right way the first time. Anna May notices it and says how nice it looks and how there's maybe two boys in town who would know how to set up a table how I did.

I know what she's been doing, asking me to help with dinner and to go fishing, and I don't mind. When you're losing a brother, you don't turn your nose up at the chance of getting a sister.

We sit down to dinner and say grace. Over the roast, Pastor Fenton tells us the church is raising money to help rebuild Stairways. He says how much, and Ma sets down her fork and starts to cry.

I don't believe there's a boy on earth can see his mother cry and not do the same.

Mr. Halleck has two television sets in his house. The one in the upstairs den is in color. The night after dinner with Pastor Fenton and Anna May, my family gathers around it for the evening news.

"Preparing for the summer, the federal government has designed a system of priority airlift for troops to areas of civil disorder. The Pentagon and the air traffic control network will cooperate in using reserved altitude assignments for troop airlifts . . .

"There is strong belief in some quarters of Democratic political leadership that President Johnson will accept a draft to run for a second time in his own right as the party's nominee for president . . .

"Despite the rising hopes of peace talks, a fresh contingent of US soldiers arrived in Vietnam yesterday to the Mekong Delta region . . ." [1]

I don't stay to hear the rest of it. Color or no, I don't want to watch television any more tonight.

I leave and take the big staircase down to the first floor and from there head out the back door.

---

1   "The Week." *National Review.* July 16, 1968.

I am going to see Butch.

We've got him set up in an empty kennel behind Mr. Halleck's house. It's far bigger than the shed he used to have at Stairways. He's stretched out in the dirt when I come up, but his tail starts to beat the earth and I know he's happy to see me. I sit down next to him, rub his big head, and scratch behind one of his pointy ears.

It's a rose-colored twilight above us. Low clouds of blue and black lie along the horizon. High up in the atmosphere a jet traces a slow line behind them.

"It's different here, isn't it, boy?" I ask him.

He yawns.

Wish I could go down to Apple Creek. Hunt through the mud for salamanders. Skim some stones.

The back door opens and I look up. Pete.

Hands in his pockets, head bowed, he strolls casually over to where me and Butch sit. He sits down too.

"I read that article in the paper," Pete says. He talks funny from the swollen lip. His right eye is still bruised and dark from where Caleb hit him.

I pluck grass.

"That was a great story Frankie wrote."

"M-hmm."

Pete looks down. In the sky, that jet is slipping behind the first long black cloud.

"You been worried all summer about me leaving, haven't you?"

Pete's words surprise me. I nod and pluck more grass.

"I'm grateful, but you don't have to worry, Jack," he says. He reaches over and steals a piece of grass from my pile. "I'm going to be just fine. And so are you."

I sigh. "But what if you're *not* fine, Pete? What if something happens?"

He looks at me.

"So what if it does? Would that make me love you any less? Would *you* love *me* any less?" He shakes his head; a wave of feathery blond hair drops down over his eyes. "Impossible."

Tears well up in my eyes. It seems to me I done more crying this summer than any other.

"I just wanted to keep you safe," I say through my tears.

"You've always been a fixer, Jack. But sometimes you have to let things go. Let them be. Maybe they get broken. Maybe they don't. But you don't have to worry, because nothing stays broken forever. Nothing's permanently lost. Knee-Deep Meadow's burned up. It will grow back. Stairways is burned down. Dad and Ma will rebuild it. You wait and see."

"But Pete, a person is different. Once you're killed, you're killed."

Pete shakes his head.

"People are the least killable things there are. They have a piece of forever in them. And nothing can take that away. But"—and here my brother leans over and touches his shaggy head to mine—"I don't think you need to worry about that. Because I'll be coming back."

I look at him.

"Do you promise?" I ask.

"I won't promise something I can't. I love you too much to lie to you, Jack. But I'll tell you I believe in my bones I'll be coming back."

There's flinty purpose in his green eyes. He means it. He *really* means it.

A few days later, we have a last supper for Pete in Mr. Halleck's dining room. Ma prepares a real feast: sirloin steak, roasted potatoes, sweet corn, fresh salad, and applesauce. Mr. Halleck joins us. So do Anna May and old Sam Williamson. Pete sits at the head of the table, hair brushed, dressed in a button-down shirt which he's got tucked in like it's Sunday and he's going to church.

After a dessert of ice cream and peach cobbler, Mr. Halleck pours everyone a glass of sweet-tasting wine from a dark green bottle and we move into the living room to listen to Anna May play on the piano. She asks me to sit next to her on the bench and sing along, and for a preacher's daughter, she sure knows some fun ones.

Will, Ma, and old Sam stand around us and sing as she plays "Roll Out the Barrel" and "The Maid of Amsterdam." When she switches over to "Whiskey in the Jar," Mr. Halleck sings too, and after we sing that final verse about that poor old robber getting turned in to the police by his lover, he laughs as if he ain't done it in years.

By this time the wine has got me feeling fuzzy and warm and sleepy, so I climb up next to Dad on the couch and listen to him tell Mr. Halleck about the new house in town he and Ma looked at. It's brand new, part of a development that's sprung up just beyond the railroad tracks. Square fence. Square yard. Young, short trees.

Mr. Halleck pours Dad some more of that sweet wine and listens. The old man looks thoughtful.

"Once you're settled, let's talk about Stairways," he says. "The house may be gone, but such things can be rebuilt. You've still got the land. That's the most important thing."

Dad sips his wine, but then he rests his big-knuckled hand on me and gives me a pat.

"Not quite the most important."

At the piano, Anna May plays a final song of the evening, and it's one of Dad's favorites: "Danny Boy." All about a father watching his boy go off to war:

> But come ye back when summer's in the meadow,
> or when the valley's hushed and white with snow.
> 'Tis I'll be here in sunshine or in shadow
> Oh Danny boy, oh Danny boy, I love you so.

I don't think there's a dry eye in the room when Anna May finishes it and the final notes softly fade. Ma dabs at her eyes with the hem of her skirt. Will weeps openly, crosses the room to Pete, and gives him a hug. Pete looks embarrassed, but he don't push Will away. Next thing I know, I'm up and across the room and hugging them both.

"I'm proud of you, Pete," I tell him.

"I love you, Jack," he tells me.

Next morning, early, Dad drives Pete into town to the bus station. Before he goes, Pete gives Ma a kiss on the forehead and Butch a last scratch behind the ears. To Will, Frankie, and me, he just waves from the passenger seat and grins a final grin.

I watch them go until the Ford disappears through the metal gate at the end of the long drive, until there's nothing but a cloud of gray dust hanging on the air over the road.

A couple days later, hot sunlight splashes down all around us. We stand in the middle of that concrete slab in the field of simmering butterfly weed and wait for Frankie's train. Clouds are stacking up in the west behind us. Another storm.

Will waits in the truck in the lot. Since Pete left, he's been the one to drive us around. He's said his goodbyes and is giving me and Frankie a last few minutes together.

We spend them in quiet. It has been the most eventful summer of my life. From floods to fires, from Mr. Madliner's murder to Caleb's disappearance to Pete's leaving for the Marines, I have never known a faster-changing time. And through all of it, our cousin Frankie was my best friend and constant companion. I know there's something special in that. He was there with my brothers for our last summer together; he's one of us last summer boys. And I want to tell him. I just don't have the words.

But then Frankie sets down his suitcase. "There's something I've been meaning to ask you, Jack."

I'm grateful for that. "Shoot. Better make it quick though. I can see your train coming."

He turns to where a streak of sunlight flashes against silvery metal on the horizon. Suddenly, more than anything, I don't want him to go.

Frankie turns back to me. "It's about the night of the fire."

I flinch. Across the field, the train sounds its horn. "What about it?"

"Pete said you *asked* him to go get Caleb that night."

I blink in the hot sun. "Yes."

"Why? You spent all summer long doing little else but think of ways to keep Pete from danger. Yet you asked him to do something very dangerous. You asked him to risk his life. And for Caleb Madliner, of all people."

I'm still. "You saying it was wrong to do that?"

Frankie shakes his head. "No. Not at all. I was just wondering why you did it."

Below us the rails begin to rattle. The train lets loose another blast on its horn.

"Tell you the truth, I don't know," I begin. "No, wait, that ain't it. I *do* know. But it might not make any sense."

He looks at me. Waiting. But that train is thundering closer now. I don't have time to think. So I do what I do best. Talk:

"It's something Ma told me back beginning of the summer. It had to do with people who felt their life wasn't worth anything. Like they had no value. Ma said when a human being feels trampled under, they'll do anything to show they matter. If it's lighting fires, they light fires. I figured Caleb was one of those people."

Frankie watches me close. His train is coming into sight now. Getting louder. I make it quick now.

"But I think *everybody* matters. Whether they think so or not. Whether I like them or not. Heck, they matter even if they've hurt somebody else, even if they've hurt *me*. People . . . just matter. I believed Caleb Madliner mattered. And I didn't want him to die."

I'm done. It's just as well. The train's brakes squeal out in protest as it approaches our platform. With a last blast on its horn, that hulking metal creature groans up to the station.

Frankie keeps his eyes on me. At last, a slow smile spreads across his face.

"John Thomas Elliot," he says at last, "you are the toughest, kindest, wisest boy I have ever known." He laughs. "I'm glad we're cousins. And friends."

I grin. "Yeah, yeah. You're not so bad yourself. But if you don't get moving, you'll miss that train."

I give him a hug. Then he lifts his mud-brown suitcase and turns for the train.

"Come visit me in the city sometime."

"I'd like that a lot, Frankie."

He laughs again and steps onto the train. "No, you wouldn't. But you'll come anyway."

When Frankie's train disappears over the rim of the world and the field is empty once more, I make my way back down to the lot where the parked cars bake in late afternoon sun. Butch cocks his head and gives a puzzled look from the bed of the pickup. He's wondering where Frankie went.

"He's gone back to his city, Butch," I tell him. "Won't see him again for a while, I guess."

I climb up next to Will in the cab, who sits fiddling with the radio. The music comes in scratchy here. The reception's no good. I'm quiet for a bit as he twists the dial.

"Well, he's off," I tell him.

"Yeah," Will says distractedly. "Going to miss him?"

I nod.

"Just give me a second here," Will says. "Gotta find the right music for it."

"For what?" I ask.

Just then Bob Dylan's voice comes through the speakers. Will puts the truck in gear. Then he reaches down in the seat next to him, pulls out a piece of paper, and hands it to me.

It's folded in squares and stained dark in several places. I open it up. It's Dad's map.

I look at him.

"What do you say we go find us that fighter jet?"

He twists the key in the ignition, and the truck engine roars to life again.

ACKNOWLEDGMENTS

I would like to thank Annette Kirk and the Russell Kirk Center for Cultural Renewal in Mecosta, Michigan: they hosted me for a summer and made available the center's private library as a haven to complete *Last Summer Boys*. When it comes to writing, I am convinced there is no better or more hauntingly reflective environment in America.

The University of Pennsylvania provided a fellowship that made possible my stay in Michigan that summer.

My agent, Dean Krystek, is as warm as he is devoted to the authors and stories he serves. A Vietnam veteran, he understood the story in a way more deeply than I ever could. This book would not have been possible without his passion and expertise.

I am beyond grateful to editor Alicia Clancy and the peerless Lake Union Publishing team. They made my first encounter with the publishing industry little short of a dream. I felt part of the process at every step.

Lastly, I owe the deepest debt of gratitude to my family: my parents, for instilling a love of storytelling; my siblings, for being the most honest critics; and my wife, for her endless patience and encouragement. I love you all so very much.

ABOUT THE AUTHOR

Bill Rivers grew up along the creeks of the Brandywine Valley in Delaware and Pennsylvania. A graduate of the University of Delaware, he earned an MPA from the University of Pennsylvania as a Truman Scholar, one of sixty national awards given annually for a career in public service. Bill worked in the US Senate before serving as speech-writer for US Secretary of Defense Jim Mattis, developing classified and unclassified messages on national security and traveling throughout Asia, Europe, the Middle East, and the Americas. He and his family live outside Washington, DC, where he still keeps a piece of a crashed fighter jet they found in the hills of southeastern Pennsylvania.